ming

Tabish Khair's previous novel, *The Bus Stopped*, was short-listed for the Encore Award in the UK. A poet, novelist and critic, his awards include the All India Poetry Prize. Born in India in 1966 and mostly educated there, Khair now lives in Denmark. *Filming* is his third novel, and the second to be published internationally by Picador.

Also by Tabish Khair and published by Picador

The Bus Stopped

TABISH KHAIR

Filming

A Love Story

PICADOR

First published 2007 by Picador

First published in paperback 2008 by Picador
an imprint of Pan Macmillan Ltd
Pan Macmillan, 20 New Wharf Road, London N1 9RR
Basingstoke and Oxford
Associated companies throughout the world
www.panmacmillan.com

ISBN 978-0-330-41923-9

Copyright © Tabish Khair 2007

9 8 7 6 5 4 3 2 1

A CIP catalogue record for this book is available
from the British Library.

Typeset by Intype London Ltd
Printed and bound in India by
Gopsons Papers Ltd., Noida

This book is in memory of
***Saadat Hasan Manto**,*

and it is dedicated to
Khushwant Singh:

for both travelled the routes of barbed wire
between India and Pakistan
and survived
with their humanity and art intact.

Acknowledgements

are due to the Hong Kong Baptist University, for the precious and rare gift of time to write, to Aarhus University for a mostly manageable daily routine, and to my family for their varied responses to films: my father, who could whistle most film tunes from the 1950s and 1960s, my mother's bemused toleration of various kinds of cinema, my brother's enthusiastic discovery of art cinema in school, my sister's delight in good entertaining films, and Trine's ability to hum all those Raj Kapoor love songs that she did not understand and I seldom remembered. Acknowledgements are also due to all those directors, actors, technicians, extras of Indian – especially Bombay – films who made the 'pictures' I grew up watching: films that were often dismissed by Anglophone Indians for being fragmentary, plagiarist, a mishmash of serious and light, classical and popular, Western and Indian elements, for their exaggerated histrionics and many sub-plots, for depending on 'formulas' and songs, for catering to the pop religiosity of the masses, for falling back again and again on some version

of the love story. But my list of acknowledgements –
like the annals of the Bombay film – is unending, for
there were many uncles and aunts, cousins and friends
with whom I saw films. And there were many other
secret invisible companions – books – that made it easier
for me to see, feel and write: these can only be acknowledged in the derivation or adaptation of a word, phrase,
notion or fact in the pages that follow. My thanks to
Anuradha Roy and Nasreen Munni Kabir for their
useful comments and to Pankaj Mishra, Line Henriksen,
Lotta Strandberg, Aamer Hussein, Shruti Debi, and,
when I needed it most, Annette Lindegaard and my
editor Sam Humphreys for their belief in this novel and
its writer. Finally, how can I even begin to acknowledge
my debt to *Saadat Hasan Manto and his bald angels of
Bombay?*

"The eight (rhetorical and aesthetic) Sentiments recognised in drama and dramatic representation are as follows: Rasa Erotic, Rasa Comic, Rasa Pathetic, Rasa Furious, Rasa Heroic, Rasa Terrible, Rasa Odious and Rasa Marvellous." – Bharatamuni

"If the quantity of shadow increases because of the extension of the object's limits in such a manner that sight is lost in it, this shadow is called darkness, like the situation at night. Then the name of shadow vanishes, just as the ability to perceive its limits also vanishes."
– Ahmad al-Biruni

"Of the thing now gone silent, named Past, which was once Present, and loud enough, how much do we know? Our 'Letter of Introductions' comes to us in the saddest state; falsified, blotted out, torn, lost, and but a shred of it in existence; this too so difficult to read, or spell." – Thomas Carlyle

"It would seem a paradox that the cinema is said to be, in one sense, the most real of all media, but that it is also an enormously effective medium for the unreal, the fantastic and the dream-like."
– Alexander Mackendrick

Dé di hamain azaadi bina khadag bina dhaal
Sabarmati ké sant tu né kar diya kamaal
– Song from the film *Jagriti*

"Hé Ram!"
– *Mahatma Gandhi's last words*

STARRING

Saadat Hasan Manto

as

Himself

and

M. K. Gandhi

as

The Sant of Sabarmati

FEATURING

Harihar .... a bioscope-wallah

Durga .... the prostitute who ran away with Harihar

Ashok .... Harihar and Durga's son

Chotte Thakur .... the younger son of Raja Sahib, a Zamindar

Bade Thakur .... the older son of Raja Sahib

Badi Maalkini .... Bade Thakur's wife, also called Badi Ma

Hari Babu .... the Director

Rajkunwar .... Producer and Studio-owner

Bhuvaneshwari .... Hari Babu's wife

Saleem Lahori .... silent-film star

Maulvi Sahab .... Lahori's father, a Muslim scholar

Gulabo .... Lahori's mother, a Hindu prostitute

Satish Mama .... Lahori's uncle, a mill-worker

1947 .... Independence/Partition into India and Pakistan

Avik Sen .... one of Lahori's friends, a Hindu

Bala(subramanium) .... one of Lahori's friends, a Hindu

Ashiq Painter .... one of Lahori's friends, a Muslim

Doctor Surender Singh .... one of Lahori's friends, a Sikh

Nitin Kumar .... a 'talkies' film star, a Hindu

'Joshilla' .... Batin's co-writer, Lahori's friend, a Muslim

Seth Dharamchand .... businessman, financier

ALSO INTRODUCING

Rizwan Hussain 'Batin' .... scriptwriter,
Urdu short-story writer, immigrant

Mrs Hussain .... Batin's wife

AND

A HOST OF MINOR ACTORS!!!

Reel 1

Rasa Terrible

Under the green leaves green grey wood of this tree
I who never slept under a tree sleep dream wrapped in
quilt dream or do I am I dreaming again of horses as I
always do of a horse a thoroughbred horse am I dreaming or am I sleeping if I am awake why do I see him the
Sant of Sabarmati no horse this time I see myself lying
here on a charpoy under the green wood green tree a
young man with the dented pair of US Army binoculars
which I feel for in my sleep here I feel it next to me this
thing that cost me a week's salary under the green wood
tree am I dreaming if I am who is this like me like me
he starts spitting when he talks of the famous sage the
famous Sant of Sabarmati saliva bursts from his mouth
like shrapnel splattering the villagers clustered around
him he speaks as if he knows the Sant personally and in
a way he feels he does I do he does so much has the
Sant walked through the dreams of this land the land of
his dreams but actually this young man speaking shrilly

3

now like I will speak when I wake if I am sleeping now if under the green wood tree like him I will speak obscenities exploding from his mouth I have never he has never has never seen the Sant he has never gone to any of the Sant's halting increasingly slurred speeches heard him say shay shay shh shh the sound that escapes most often from his mouth the Shage the Shant of Shabarmati shay shh shh I hate him I even threw away newspaper pictures of the old man the old sage and the only picture I can recall is from almost a year ago when most of India was burning in that grimy black-and-white photo the famous Sant was just a tired old man tired old man frail and half-naked he leant heavily on his wooden staff he was standing in the middle of rubble smouldering furniture blackened bricks metal plates that had melted in the heat fluttering scraps of charred paper warped plastic the group of young men and woman who accompany him everywhere and the police party that he had been provided with recently for protection rather than detention now crowded the open doorway of the blackened house there was no door to keep them out I see it now in sleep or awake am I dreaming of it again there was no door to keep anyone out the fire had eaten all demarcation away reduced everything to the bone of soot and death even in the mute photo it was it was obvious that the young men and women wanted him to come away they pleaded with him they gesticulated the

paunchy police officer in the backdrop looks worried he
says I hear him say under the green wood tree I hear
him say not safe not safe this area is not safe saar but in
the photo in the picture in my dream under the green
wood the green tree the Sant had refused to budge from
the place he had refused to hear them he had shut them
out by chanting a mantra or that is what they thought
he was doing this stubborn old man until one of them
only one of them in the beginning paid attention and
heard him repeating no not a Sanskrit phrase not even a
Hindi verse the Sant was repeating a single word which
I hear now in sleep awake just one English word over
and over and over again terrible terrible terrible ... I
curse the Sant to the fascinated and slightly scandalized
villagers outside this remote studio where I am doing
what what am I doing here outside my dream in my self
I curse the Sant to the villagers I am not dreaming for I
can think can one think in dreams I can think I know
that what fills me with such bitterness that saliva
explodes from my mouth when I think of the frail old
Sant is this is this I see again the newspaper item I see
myself read it under the green I see I read that the Sant
had been visiting a section of the city previously inhab-
ited by the minority community call them mullah I
shout call them mullah I scream I shiver am I dreaming
I thrash in sleep under the green wood the green tree
I am the young man who thinks who dreams of the

burned-out house the warped plastic the charred bricks but always my thoughts are interrupted my dreams broken by the old man's broken chant of terrible terrible terrible ... the old man who lisps who cannot say ss who says shhh as if he was asking for silence to pray to meditate to weep to say terrible terrible terrible the Shant of Shabarmati shays terrible terrible terrible I cry I weep I laugh

He awakes to find himself on the charpoy that has been lent to him by one of the villagers, sleeping under the peepul tree just outside the compound of the studio, wrapped in his brown quilt because it is a winter day. The sun is still out: he mostly sleeps during daytime now. He is a city person. He has trouble sleeping outside. He has trouble sleeping during daytime. But he has to do it. He has a duty to perform. He gropes around for his dented pair of US Army binoculars. They are still there.

The Magic Lantern

Once upon a time, or, in reality, exactly nine days after Holi in 1929, a bullock cart could be seen trundling up the narrow dirt track leading to the village of Anjangarh. A six- or seven-year-old child was running after the cart. He would sometimes be lost in the white dust churned up by the huge wooden wheels and the hooves of the two bullocks. Then he would emerge again, running up to the cart and hanging on to it, swinging from the back timber before jumping down and skipping into one of the adjoining fields or pausing to examine the spare trees or bushes by the sides of the track. If he ventured too far into the bristling, newly harvested fields, a woman's voice would call him back. The voice was heavy, almost like a man's, and it sounded slightly hoarse, as if the speaker had been shouting for a long time.

The late noon sun had curtailed all shade; the cart was crawling on its own shadow. The day was still, the slight breeze occasionally filling with the warmth of the coming summer. Once in a while, the wind would pick up and a gust would caress the boy's face as if there was an invisible giant breathing down his threadbare collar. The boy was startled once by what he had taken to be earth clumps in a field suddenly lifting up with a flutter of wings, a flock of yellowish-brown sandgrouse lifting like dry yellowish-brown earth to the sky. The dust on the track was as dry, but finer, lighter. The boy's bare legs were almost white with dust up to the knees.

The cart was bigger than those used in the district, the back a lumpy mass covered with tightly tied tarpaulin. It was not heading for the village of Anjangarh, but for a large open space before a somewhat decrepit-looking mansion, walls white and stained with rain and fungi, to the south of the village. Built like a haveli around a courtyard and rising to three storeys of sullen shuttered windows on one side, it appeared to be a practical and smaller version of a fort, and had probably given the village its name: Anjangarh.

The boy had already scrambled to the door of the mansion – gate might be a more appropriate description – before the cart came to a lumbering halt outside in an open field, demarcated irregularly with broken and sagging stretches of barbed wire, an oddity in the villages and always, the boy knew, a sign of links to urbanity or the regime. The boy shook the brass rings attached to the door and banged on it with a stick he had picked up, calling, 'Khul Simsim, khul Simsim!'

This magical invocation of 'Open Sesame' did not

seem to please the woman in the cart. She stopped making soothing sounds to the bullocks and shouted at the boy. Stop that, Ashok, stop that this moment, she shouted in Hindustani. When the boy did not heed her, she jumped out of the cart and dragged him back by the scruff of his neck. I will tell Pitaji, I will tell Pitaji, the boy whimpered.

You will sit here, she replied, lifting him up and dumping him into the cart. And be quiet, she added, don't wake up Pitaji. He is ill. He needs to sleep.

There was some mumbling and movement from inside the tented section of the cart.

I'm feeling better; you go and speak to them. I will keep him here, a man's voice sounded from inside the cart.

It would be good if they allow us to set up in the field, the woman replied as she walked briskly towards the gates of the mansion. She was a young woman, not older than twenty-one or twenty-two, with a pretty, slightly freckled face and shoulder-length dark brown hair. She was dressed in a light green sari with flowery patterns in darker green and golden edges of brocade-type work. The material of the sari, and the way she wore it, indicated that she was not from the village – or from any village in the region.

She walked with a slight, almost imperceptible limp.

★

Had it been some other time of the year, the cart would have been trailed by a gang of village children by now. But this was after the harvest, so, with very little work for them to do, the children had been sent to the village school: this was one of the few weeks of the year when the old headmaster and the younger science teacher, who comprised the entire staff of the school, got to see more than half the boys – and even a few girls – whom they were supposed to be educating.

And yet the cart had not been unobserved. Some of the villagers had even guessed what strange animal lay tied down under the thick brown tarpaulin, its legs sticking up here and there, even if they could not read the two small boards hanging on the sides.

Bioscope, Bioscope-wallah, a young man outside one of the huts shouted and, tucking in the loose end of his dhoti, he sprinted towards the maidan, twisting through the straggly strands of barbed wire. His cry was taken up, and a couple of minutes later – when the gate of the haweli opened in response to the woman's entreaties of 'huzoor, faryaad hai; huzoor, faryaad hai', the cart was already attracting open-mouthed spectators like a succulent jalebi collects flies.

'Have I mentioned that Seth Dharamchand had two main sources of income: investing in films in the black – the interest rates were exorbitant during the war and official funding even

less likely after independence – and manufacturing barbed wire in the white? He owned a mill and later went into the construction business too, but it was really wire and films that provided him with his initial fortune.

It was a good time to be manufacturing barbed wire. In the 1930s and 40s, barbed wire started being used widely by the authorities: its usefulness had been established by two world wars and a series of concentration camps, set up for the Boers by the British, for the Cubans by the Spanish, for the Filipinos by the Americans, for the Jews by the Germans, and then finally by almost all modern nations for the peoples of other nations. If I remember correctly, young man, Seth Dharamchand had an unofficial monopoly on all government contracts, before and after Independence. But I haven't told you about the Seth yet, have I? I am sorry, I forgot: we are still almost two decades from Independence.'

The Munshi who came out of the gate, accompanied by a couple of moustachioed, bare-chested youths, was old and racked by coughs. He looked so brittle that every bout of coughing seemed about to crumble his body to bits and pieces, leaving in his place not bone and skin but other odds and ends, paper slips, pencil nub, withered green cardamoms, eye-piece, caste thread. It was only when he looked at her through a monocle that dangled from a kurtah collar that the woman glimpsed the underlying steely perseverance of the old man: this was someone who had buried many enemies, and was prepared to bury more. She addressed him as if he was the owner of the mansion. The conceit pleased the old man, though he gave her a sharp glance as if to say he was not taken in by it.

He interrogated her roughly, less about the 'bio-scope' and more about the fact that she – and not her husband – had come to the door with the request to set up their show in the maidan.

My husband is very ill, otherwise he would have come to pay his respects. He is lying in the cart, she replied, pointing behind her.

Her gesture, or the need to shoo away a couple of village urchins intent on uncovering the mystery under the tarpaulin, brought Harihar, followed by their son, Ashok, out of the cart at exactly that moment. Even from a distance, the Munshi could detect signs of ill-ness on Harihar's haggard, unshaven face, could see the difficulty with which he moved. Harihar, in his turn, mimed an elaborate, somewhat theatrical greeting in the Munshi's direction, folding his hands in a namaste as well as bowing low like some feudal courtier. Ashok, copying his father, namaste'ed much more stiffly and then, overcome with shyness, climbed back into the cart.

And the two of you are enough to run this, this

contraption? You do not need helpers-whelpers? You do not have servants?

The Munshi was a man who equated respectability with servants. The more servants one had, the more respectable one was. Look at all the raja sahibs, look at the English officers: would any of them ever keep less than a dozen servants in their retinue?

Once again, the woman came up with rehearsed answers, even wiping tearless eyes with her aanchal. She told him their three servants had run away with some of their money and the other cart on the way to the village. (It was not altogether a lie. The last man they had hired to drive the bullock and go about the villages advertising their show – see the greatest show on earth, see the wonder of science, see, see, see the gods descend on earth – had run away with one entire night's ticket collection three days ago: he had not been paid for a week. And the only permanent worker they had, old Mehto from Calcutta, had disappeared earlier that morning with the cycle he used to announce the shows. They were used to his disappearances, which happened about once a month, and knew that he would lie under the palm fronds of a low toddy joint, drunk and drinking, for a night or two, before miraculously finding his way back to them.)

The Munshi looked unconvinced. I will have to ask

the Thakur sahib. Only huzoor can decide, he said, in response to her request to be allowed to set up a 'bioscope' in the maidan. Wait here. And then, as an afterthought: What's your name, woman?

Durga, hazoor.

The two burly men pulled the gate shut behind the tiny Munshi. Durga stood there, dwarfed by the enormity of the gates. She looked back, and the bullock cart appeared so small in the open field, Harihar and the villagers inconsequential before the sullen, stolid might of this three-storeyed haweli, its shuttered windows, its dank, lime-washed walls, its immense brass-studded gate. At times like these – especially lately, with Harihar ill more often than not – she would begin to doubt the dreams they had once shared.

Those were other days. That was another place.

And yet she knew that Harihar only had to put up the tent and arrange the few folding chairs and benches, their legs poking like dead sticks into the tarpaulin cover right now, and set up the single projector, and, and suddenly – like light streaming on to a white screen in the dark – hope would flow back into her. She would be flooded with something elusive and tangible that she felt was shared by the spectators who paid as little as three anna for a show – or sometimes even paid with a quantity of wheat or rice.

★

She had not been convinced when Harihar, who was at least fifteen years her senior and a widower with one married daughter in Borali, a village near Ranchi, had first told her about the future of the bioscope. Growing up in Calcutta, she was familiar with films. Some of the women she had known had recently appeared in films in insubstantial roles. But even her mother – who would sit on a stool, legs bared to the knees, layers of fat leaking out of a crumpled but expensive sari, mouth filled with paan, and bargain her three daughters' prices with every new customer – considered it immoral to work in films. Her mother had been convinced that seeing films made one blind, and exposure to the camera lens impaired the health of women, turning them into ailing, barren, flat-chested, narrow-hipped hags. To be told by someone like Harihar – an older man from a Brahmin caste and that too one with a college degree – to be told that 'the bioscope is the world, the bioscope is the future of the world' was to be provided with a perspective on something ordinary and scorned. Like realizing one day that the khaat you slept on was actually a flying chariot that could whoosh you away to distant cities and palaces.

Harihar had come to her the usual way: through her mother. She had no idea what he had paid for one night with her. But having entered the small and dark, one-window, gecko-infested room – with a couple of wilted garlands of bela flowers strewn on an old harmonium on the plank-bed – and closed the cracked wooden door to the sounds of revelry elsewhere in the house, Harihar had stood looking unhappy. When he had finally spoken, he had said: But I had no idea, I had no idea. You are younger than my daughter.

It was a strange relationship to recall in a room reeking of body fluids in spite of the cheap attar and the wilted flowers. Durga – though she had another, a Muslim, name then – had been nonplussed but had recovered soon and, getting off the bed to caress him, had lisped in what she thought was her most enticing voice, But I am not your daughter, Sethji.

(Her mother had taught her to address all Muslim men as 'nawab sahib' and all Hindu men as 'Sethji'. When in doubt, she would use 'huzoor'.)

She did not know it, but her lisping attempt at adult passion always revealed her for the young girl she was and, in almost all cases, brought the man to her not because he considered her a grown woman but because he realized exactly how young she was. However, Harihar had disengaged himself after a moment and flopped down in the old armchair that stood in one corner. They had not had sex that night. Instead, he spent half the night telling Durga about the death of his wife five years ago and how, after he had arranged his only daughter's marriage two years ago, he had quit his job as a postal clerk. He did not have any other responsibilities – his parents were dead – but he had a dream. Piling together all his savings and selling what he could, he had bought the best projector he could afford and leased Phalke's stupendous success from many years ago, *Lanka Dahan*. He could not afford to lease anything more recent, but had showed that film in villages around Calcutta, even travelling as far as Borali, where his daughter had settled with her husband. This was the passion he had guarded like an infant through all his years of marriage. He made it sound as if money was his goal, he told Durga stories about travelling bioscope-wallahs who had earned enough money to buy theatres or even produce films and it was only later that she came to notice and understand the gleam that came into his eyes when he discussed films or mentioned producing films: Harihar had a dream so dear, so irrational and so private that he did not dare put it into words. He could not explain the fascination that films held for him, and so he spoke of the money that could be made.

Later that night, he joined her in bed, sitting, legs pulled up, in one corner, while she lay diagonally across the charpoy and fiddled with the cotton of his kurtah, listening as he told her about his plans of buying a bullock cart – it would reduce the expense of hiring one all the time and he had, by now, learnt to drive a cart. I could get a cart and a new film, and travel right across the Presidency – from Calcutta to Patna – showing films all the way.

It was curious the way he used words and expressions like 'Presidency'.

She had listened to him with a faint smile, an eyebrow raised almost imperceptibly at times, until he straightened himself, lay down beside her and fell asleep almost instantaneously. It was the first time any man had revealed his innermost dreams to her. It was the first time any man had fallen asleep beside her or permitted her to sleep soundly through the bought hours without the stickiness of his sex oozing down her thighs and jolting her awake with nightmares of drowning in a tub of molasses.

Molasses occur in many of Rizwan Hussain 'Batin's' stories. They do not occur, as one might expect, simply in the mode of nostalgia: their significance varies, ranging from the salvage of some memory of childhood or first love to the stickiness of congealing blood. And I had used that word – gur – in my letter to him, arguing that a meeting with him would be like the taste of gur in these lands of refined sugar.

That I had decided to interview Batin was largely incidental. I had finished most of my PhD research and everything indicated that Batin, though a character, was undoubtedly a minor character in the colourful drama of

1940s talkies. There is actually, I believe, not a single surviving photo of Batin with any recognizable film dignitary and when, in 1973, he went back to India for a visit, he did not call on any film personage. The only industry person with whom he appears to have had some contact after leaving for Pakistan was his co-writer, Sheikh Taleb Deen 'Joshilla', who died in 1971 or 1972 and who was always remarkably reticent on the topic of Batin in his interviews. I recalled reading in an unpublished Bombay University PhD thesis on Joshilla that the only time Joshilla had been pressed by an interviewer to recall his collaboration with Batin, he had replied with a chuckle that Batin would have been a great actor if he had not been such a good writer.

No, Batin was by no means the hero of the drama of 1940s talkies, not even the hero's best friend or father; he had at best a walk-on role, a brief cameo to play in it. I do not deny that I admired Batin as a writer, having read him in Urdu, but that admiration had very little to do with my academic interests and there was hardly anything to indicate that Batin had been anything other than a scriptwriter of the second order. True, he had co-written the script of at least three golden-jubilee hits – the first starring Devika Rani in 1939, the second with Ashok Kumar in 1944 and the third marking a pinnacle in the 'Lover Boy' career of Nitin Kumar in 1945 – but there was very little else of interest. (The last film co-scripted by him – Aakhri Raat – *had been a minor hit too, but by then he was already in Pakistan.) Even in Bombay, no one really recalled him as a scriptwriter. What finally made me decide to interview Batin was hardly of professional significance: Batin was not only alive but also accessible. And perhaps, as I was to realize later, there was also the pull of resentment, the irksome bewilderment of a Muslim from a family that had not left India for another Muslim who* had left *for Pakistan after Independence.*

After moving to Karachi in 1948, Batin tried to make a career as a writer in films and radio in Pakistan – he failed abysmally, and managed to survive by publishing short stories in Urdu magazines and papers. Then in 1954, after two court summons for obscenity in his stories, he emigrated to Copenhagen, though how and why remain unanswered. Soon afterwards, he published his second collection of short stories, brought out in Delhi and Lahore, which were noticed in critical circles and resulted in the republication, a few years later, of his out-of-print first collection, Bandish, *which is still considered his best work. He was to publish only one more book after that, though he contributed a number of semi-autobiographical essays about Bombay to various Urdu magazines. Most of what we know about his life in Bombay comes from these essays.*

Later, I reasoned that Batin's lack of international significance might have had to do with his emigration to

Denmark – London might have made him visible but Copenhagen was removed from all established routes of Urdu, Commonwealth or postcolonial narratibility. That and, of course, the fact he did not publish anything after 1973, when his third and last collection of stories came out in India and Pakistan: it was also the only time he went back to India for a visit.

Three collections of stories of which the first was published by such a small Delhi house that not a single copy of the original edition has survived, and the third published after a gap of three decades: these are not exactly the ingredients of literary celebrity, whatever they might become posthumously.

So one frosty wintry day in November 1988, I wrote Batin a letter in warm flowery Urdu, and asked a friend of mine (who had a doctorate in nineteenth-century Deccani Urdu poetry and drove a taxi in Berlin) to correct it. I did not have Batin's address, but I knew he lived in a place called Frederiksberg in or near Copenhagen and I assumed there could not be too many Batins or Rizwan Hussains around, and that the Danish post was probably not as overburdened and underpaid as the post back home in India.

I had almost forgotten about the letter when, in early January, I received a postcard from Batin. It was of the sort that you can pick up free in cafes, advertising Tuborg beer, and on it, writing in slightly old-fashioned English, he gave his exact address and phone number and invited me to fix up an appointment for some weekend. I still had a few days before semester began, so I rang the number. The phone was answered by a woman who said Hello but, in the usual subcontinental manner, did not identify herself (although I could tell from her husky voice that she was probably old). I asked for Batin. It's for you, she shouted in Urdu to someone else. Who, came the response. Your good name please, she asked me in English, but with such a heavy accent that I switched immediately to Urdu. I identified myself and my purpose, and asked for an appointment. Some student who wants to speak to you about films in the 1940s, from Berlin, she shouted again in Urdu. Ask him to come next weekend, the male voice replied. Are you sure? Yes, yes, ask him to come one evening next weekend. (There was obviously no consideration of enquiring whether or not this suited me. Batin, I reasoned, still thought of 'students' in the Indo-Pakistani way: as people with flexible schedules, who could in general be made to run errands.)

As I had little to do the next few days, I told her I would be there around six on Saturday evening. Assuming – with what later stood revealed as the sneaking prejudice of the convent-educated Indian – that they ate late like all Pakistanis (and from the talk on the phone they did seem to be very Pakistani), this would give me two hours for my interview. I doubted I would need more.

★

Not here, said the old Munshi on his return, huzoor does not want cheap, two-cowrie nautanki outside the haweli. There is a field on the other side of the village, beside the pond. It is not being used and has just been cleared of crops. You can set up your bioscope-vioscope there.

But, mai-baap, Durga begged, we want to offer the entertainment to huzoor and his family. We have come all the way from Dhoda and Gaya for Raja Thakur sahib and cultured people like your highness, not for uncouth dehati peasants.

Durga did not say this too loudly. She did not want the villagers, crowding around the bullock cart, to hear. It was they who paid for the show. But they could not give her permission to set up the show or bestow on it the respectability that it still lacked in the villages, not to mention the safety of the haweli's proximity: to be allowed to show the bioscope outside the haweli of the local landlord is to be extended the protection of the status quo; it keeps you from getting into trouble with the conservative elements and it is a warning to thieves, Harihar always told her. Harihar had a way of making ordinary statements sound like lines from a book.

The Munshi was not to be budged, however. There, beside the pond or nowhere in this village, woman, he barked, and began a fit of coughing, limbs shaking like the doors and windows of a decrepit house during a storm.

Durga did something that no one – not the Munshi, not the villagers crowding around the cart, not even Harihar – had anticipated. She squatted in the dust and clutched the Munshi's legs, wailing about her helplessness and her husband's illness, beating her left hand against her breast and head when she could.

Such a performance would not have been unusual for a low-caste village woman. But this was a woman who was dressed in town clothes, an expensive brocaded sari, and whose language did not sound rustic. The spectacle drew most of the villagers away from the cart. Even Harihar came running, gasping, as the Munshi was trying to extricate his legs from the woman's clasp. Had she been a low-caste village woman, he would have kicked her away or asked his henchmen to remove her with a few blows from their well-oiled lathis. But a woman like this – pretty, well spoken and well dressed – how did one deal with such an uncharacteristic display from a woman like that?

Suddenly the crowd that had collected around the woman and the Munshi parted to cries of 'Jagah do, jagah do, Chotte Thakur aa rahe hain! Jagah do, jagah do, Chotte Thakur aa rahe hain!' A young man walked into view. The crowd fell back around him, not even brushing against his clothes; the process resembled a hot knife running through butter. The man, who had appeared from the direction of the fields, was wearing a long richly embroidered silk kurtah over pyjamas that were tucked into English riding boots and was carrying a sleek black and silver whip. He led a horse by the reins.

What have you been up to now, Munshiji? The Munshi was still trying to squirm his way out of the woman's grasp, but every time he managed to disentangle one leg, the woman clutched the other leg.

Nothing, huzoor, nothing, the Munshi stuttered. I will drive these people away. I did not know you were out for a ride. Here, Pyaaru, Ramavtar, Kallanwa, are you all dead? Come here, come clear a way for huzoor, send these, these people away . . . The Munshi's frame shook with coughing even as three or four henchmen, wielding lathis, moved up to carry out his orders.

No, stop it, ordered the young man. Take my horse in and bring this woman and her people to me.

But, huzoor – the Munshi controlled his coughing with visible effort – but Bade Thakur sahib might not want these people to set up their tents here.

Why not? Is the maidan being used for some fair or puja these days?

No, huzoor, but . . .

I will speak to bhaiyya-sahib. Here, woman, get up, stop making a scene, what's your name?

Durga, huzoor, her name is Durga. The Munshi provided this answer, and was ignored.

Durga, tell your people they can set up the bioscope here. But not too close to the haweli.

Durga, now joined by Harihar, started offering elaborate thanks even as the Munshi collapsed once more into coughs of impotent rage.

Enough, enough, said the young man, keep the rhetoric for your shows. He started walking into the haweli. Then he stopped and turned around.

What is it you will be showing? he asked Durga and Harihar.

Star Film's *Krishna Arjuna Yuddha*, huzoor. We also have Baburao's *Sairandhri*.

The Baburao film I have already seen, but not *Krishna Arjuna Yuddha*. Put it on for us tomorrow evening. We will inaugurate your show. Make sure you have some music too.

Having said that the young man tossed his whip to one of the henchmen and entered the haweli.

He enters the cool, damp corridor of the haweli with the old music pounding in his head. It had been their title song, their curtain song, written by a Bengali poet who sang, like so many other poets of the time, of revolution and liberty and solidarity and Home Rule, all somehow palpable and within reach. The poet's name has slipped from his mind, but the tune has remained, although he has not heard it for years now. But the moment he saw the woman and realized what the cart contained, the tune returned to him, with a sudden lucidity that startled him and made him think, for a fleeting second, that someone had put on one of his gramophone records upstairs. Except this was a tune that was never captured on the gramophone records he collects and has started listening to again, after about two years of silence.

He is surprised by the clarity of the tune that comes back to his mind across the years, the ease of accuracy with which he can recall it, a gramophone playing in his head, a forgotten voice (and desire) returning from the past. Even the Bangla refrain, though he has forgotten much of his Bangla in recent years: We lift the curtain from your sight / And show what's wrong and what is right. (The refrain alone had made the authorities keep track of their performances, though they had specialized in Bangla adaptations of Shakespeare, sometimes merging two plays into one, and the occasional *Shakuntala*.)

He climbs the narrow high stairs leading to his section of the haweli, and the music keeps step with him in his head. He waits for it to stop. He thinks of the time when he had actually heard this melody in the flesh, as it were, waiting behind a curtain or in the wings of some impromptu stage for the melody to finish. He was eighteen, had not even finished his BA at Hindu College. And he knows why the melody had disappeared from his memory, to come back only now, only today: his father's shadow had fallen on the tune, obscuring it. Now, again, he waits for the sight of his father's face, heavy-jowled, large-eyed, brush-moustached, glowing with anger, almost floating in the murk of the tent, he waits for his father's face to appear in the audience, as it had that last evening, and stop the music. He waits for the pounding of remembered music to change into the throb of his back, flayed with birch sticks and leather whips at the slightest excuse for weeks after that.

He was familiar with his father's palm and birch sticks, but the whips were new. He had only seen them used on servants, and that – perhaps more than the pain – left a mark on his soul. To be whipped like a common servant! He had been hit many times as a child, always for the same failure: weakness, or effeminacy – are you a boy or a girl, you . . . you . . . his father would splutter. He had been slapped and caned, but never whipped until then, until after he was discovered, a young man of eighteen, performing on stage in Calcutta.

And how it had come about that first time in the haweli, his first whipping – after he had been slapped by his father in the dressing room and taken away from Hindu College and Calcutta – this is what he has never been able to forget or forgive. How it had happened in the haweli because he had walked into the kitchen and tried to show his mother how to make a rehu curry and his father's spies had told his father, how it had happened here in this haweli: he had looked at his mother and been surprised to see her face drawn into a mask of unseeing. Had she agreed with his father? Had she been too afraid? Why had she not intervened, not done anything except send a maid to apply balm to his back later? Would she have stood there, like a statue, letting his father whip him to death? Two or three of the older female servants had started weeping and shouting, no more Raja Sahib, have mercy, he is your son, your own blood.

And then a memory from even earlier; he must have been five or six, when he had, unseen by anyone, stolen into his mother's dressing room and emerged with lipstick on, and rouge on his cheeks, talcum all over his face, clips in his hair, a grinning hybrid of a girl and a clown. He had come out expecting to be congratulated, for he had achieved something and he felt he was someone. But his father's face had blazed. His mother had made a half-hearted effort to defend him: just a child, he is just a child. And his father had only slapped him once, hard enough to send him reeling into the bedclothes, but still only a single slap, not that flaying of the skin with a riding whip.

And so back again his mind moves, swinging on the

the long thin thread of hurt, to that later memory. The kitchen. The rehu curry. His mother standing there, face frozen, unmoving, the frying pan still in one hand, watching her son, a grown man, being abused and whipped by her husband.

The husband included her family in his abuse, alluding to their liberal values, in particular cursing the 'Bombaywalli mausi', an aunt now dead always religious, whose only fault was that she had once come to Anjangarh and taken the family – the children and the mother, for Raja Sahib had refused her invitation – to stay with her for a summer in her mansion, which was actually tens of miles from Bombay, between the townlets of Khopoli and Rajmachi. She had never been forgiven for that act of unsanctioned initiative; the relative proximity of her house to Bombay had been used again and again to implicate her in lewdness and amorality. But though his mother had revered the older woman, she did not utter a word. Not a word to defend the dead aunt or to protect her living son. His mother stood still and mute. She who had once been known for her accomplishments and wit: she came from a liberated landlord family in Bengal and had been taught to read and write, sing and, it was rumoured, dance.

She had stood there, incapable of speech or gesture.

And what had driven his father into such a rage in Calcutta, such a rage that he had slapped his son publicly with his chappals – was it the fact that he was part of, as he put it, a 'nautanki', or that he had been playing a woman?

'How did I first suspect something like this about him? Well, we all did, we all did. You could see it in his face – the effort of not dreaming, of not being what he was in his stifled imagination. He lived at an angle to his fantasies and inclinations, perpetually tilted. Yes, I guess all of us saw it on his face – though some gave it a less charitable interpretation. But that was another place, another time. I am getting ahead of my story again, young man. Give me a second. A second.'

Music might have been what brought Harihar back to Durga after that first night, though she was called something else in those days. He had woken late, around ten in the morning. Durga had already been up for a few hours, cooking breakfast and then washing the dishes with her sisters and two 'cousins' who were by no means related to her. It was her mother's policy to let patrons sleep as long as they wished. The longer they sleep, the oftener they return, she would say. Durga realized that Harihar was awake when she heard the sounds of harmonium, played very badly, drifting out of the room. She wiped her hands on a rag and went to him.

Harihar was sitting on the cushioned plank under

the single window. He had opened the window and pulled out the old harmonium. In the daylight, Durga could see he had the nondescript look of the proverbial clerk, a man average in every way, unremarkable down to his small trimmed moustache and his choice of dhoti, kurtah and sandals, so much without remarkable features that it was impossible to tell his age.

Shall I fold a paan for you? Durga asked him.

No. Sit down here. Can you play this thing?

Durga could have told him that all the women in the house – and most houses like it – could play and sing a bit. Her mother, undoubtedly the coarsest and most mercenary person in the house, was the best singer of them all. People still came to listen to her if she let it be known that she would be singing. In her younger days, before she moved to this suburb of Calcutta and set up on her own, she claimed, she had been patronized by the aristocracy in Lucknow.

Durga did not have a voice capable of as much variation as her mother's, but she had been rigorously trained, and not only in music but also in other skills such as playing indoor games or telling fortunes, each skill an intricate net in which to snare patrons. Most patrons expected women like her to be able to sing, she could have told Harihar. Instead, in reply, Durga arranged her sari's folds and sat down beside him. She pulled the harmonium to her and played a few notes.

Sing, he then said, sing the lines. He was staring at her, fascinated, as if seeing her for the first time.

She sang a composition by Umar Khusro. When she finished, he was silent for a moment. Then he got up and headed for the door. At the door he turned and looked at her. I might come back, he said.

It is their first night outside the Anjangarh haweli. They have used part of the tent canvas to form an extra side to the section on the cart; they did not have the time – understaffed as they are – to pitch the tent itself. Old Mehto is still missing.

The brisk night wind probes the canvas. Its sides flap and fill and fall. It looks as if there is a gigantic unseen animal outside trying to get in, or perhaps it is trying to escape.

Durga's eyes are as mobile as the canvas. They are closed. But they do not rest. Something pulses behind those shut eyelids, something trembles and hesitates and flickers. The eyeballs are ricocheting from dream to dream. But one dream comes back again and again. There is a house, there is a tree, there is a shadow from the bars of a window falling on a wall in a room of the house. The tree casts shadows on the wall too, shadows that are as restless as the animal wind struggling with the canvas of the tent. There is a girl sleeping in the room, afraid of the shadows on the wall. In her sleep,

Durga wants to wake the girl up and reassure her. But someone else does so. Someone in the dream. Someone creeps into the girl's bed and holds her. A woman. A woman, like her. But it is not she, not Durga. It is someone she has never seen. For a moment she is surprised, even in her dream: it is a sense of being surprised, like light sensed through a blindfold. (When she wakes up at dawn she will remember only this feeling of surprise, as one remembers a taste.) She is startled. And then she feels oddly reassured. It is all right. The girl is safe. Durga sighs in her sleep and slips deeper into it, as if it were a familiar quilt.

Next to her Harihar sleeps, eyes at rest. He hardly ever dreams at night. Ashok sleeps diagonally, curled up an inch or two from their heads, one of his hands resting on Harihar's shoulder.

'Dreams, my young scholar, are not just a happening in your head.'

This is the first sentence in the notes I took that evening, though it could not have been the first sentence Batin spoke. Surely, a lot of other things must have been said, a lot of hesitant and inconsequential things – for my memory of the first few minutes of the meeting is of awkwardness – before such a magisterial statement could be uttered. (And my original notes were by no means as flowing and complete as they became; they were desperate scribbles in longhand, abbreviated words, slashed phrases, dashes and dots where I had trusted memory to insert the missing words if I ever had occasion to want to fill in the blanks.)

The initial awkwardness was only partly due to the fact that I had miscalculated: they did not keep Indo-Pak time. When I rang the downstairs bell to Batin's fourth-floor flat, it was almost 6:15 in the evening. But when I entered the flat, the first thing that struck me was the smell of onions frying in garam masala. I could also see the small kitchen table laid with three plates. At least as far as dinner was concerned, Batin and his wife obeyed a Danish clock.

It later struck me that they even ate the European way – in the kitchen.

The flat was rather cramped and in a decidedly unfashionable part of suburban Frederiksberg. I had been let in by an elderly woman, thin and alert, with a finely wrinkled face and delicate features, wearing a cotton printed shalwar-kameez. I took her to be Mrs Hussain. She might have been in her seventies, or perhaps even her eighties, but she gave an impression of youthfulness, accentuated perhaps by the nose stud that she sported. He is waiting for you, she broke in before I had finished introducing myself. This way, she added, ushering me through an L-shaped corridor, hung with small Mughal miniatures and two fake-antique papyrus paintings, into *a large sitting room. The room was unremarkable, pots of tough-leaved plants and papery flowers, a vase containing somewhat wilted pink roses, a fashionable wooden book-rack, a cushy sofa and two rattan armchairs of colonial vintage. There was no one in the room.*

I took one of the armchairs and helped myself from a pile of magazines and papers – in Danish, Urdu and English – from the table in front of me. This ivory-studded table was the only piece of furniture in the room that had definitely come all the way from India or Pakistan, probably India. Later when I thought of it, the flat differed from other immigrants' flats that I had been to only in the fact that it was singularly devoid of any symbols from living religions: no photo of Mecca and Medina, no inscription from the Quran, not even the usual Ganesh carving or Krishna painting, no Sacred Heart calendar. Whatever there existed of religion belonged to dead ones: Mohenjodaro statuettes on a shelf and fake papyrus paintings.

I had been sitting there for about ten minutes – alone, as Mrs Hussain had gone to the kitchen – when I heard a door open behind me. I had not noticed the door. Putting down the magazines I'd been browsing through, I turned around, just as Rizwan Hussain 'Batin' appeared from a room that was lined with shelves and cluttered with books. He closed the door carefully before registering my presence.

Batin was a tall man, at least six feet, and he must

*have been taller when young. He had a gaunt face,
accentuated by his wide shoulders and long, rather thin
arms. A faint sweetish odour had accompanied him into
the room, and I could not make up my mind whether to
attribute it to some ancient perfume or to extreme age. His
hands were heavily veined, as if flesh had fallen away
from them with age leaving the underlying network of
blood vessels exposed. Much of the rest of him had the
same look: of something that, though still big and broad,
had shrunk in size over the years. It was only his stomach
– a regular pot belly stretched his shirt visibly – that
seemed to belong to another person.*

*His wife had spoken to me in Urdu, but Batin
addressed me in crisp English of the sort that my grandfather, an Indian officer in the British police force, used to
speak. (It reminded me of the English of Nehru or Jinnah
in oratorical mode, though never of the English of any
post-Independence politician.)*

*I could see that Batin's gaunt fingers trembled slightly,
and he tried to hide this by keeping his hands busy,
holding glasses, fiddling with albums and magazines for
the first few hours of our interview. It was only late in the
night that he forgot about his trembling fingers, rapt in
the stories he was telling me, and perhaps a little drunk.
It is from later in the night that I would retain the image
of his glass of whisky, quivering visibly in his grip, like
a shrunken circumscribed sea.*

Well, young man, I hope you did not have difficulty finding the place, he said, or some such remark.

Without really listening to my reply, he crossed the room and threw open the curtains. There, he said, let there be light, not that it makes much of a difference. Through the glass partition, I could see a small balcony on that side of the flat, the metal railings gleaming slightly in the icy cold. Beyond the railings, a few roofs, mostly corrugated, and an expanse of sky that would have been quite impressive on a sunny day. But it was dark outside and a cold and biting wind was blowing. There was the constant sound of vehicles, the grumbling and occasional coughing of engines, and I could imagine the dull homecoming of parents from dutiful weekend outings with children or godless mortgaged Protestants returning from their offices as religiously on a Saturday as their ancestors would have returned from church on Sundays.

Having slept in the cart that night, they got up at the break of dawn – as they usually did when 'touring' (another of Harihar's words) – and as soon as Durga had made them some roti and sabzi on their transportable stove, started pitching the tent and arranging the chairs. They hired a villager for a couple of hours to help: it was hard work, and harder for Harihar, now that he was ill.

A flock of greenish haariyals descended on the maidan and were assiduously – but ineffectively – stalked by Ashok with his small sling. Some villagers were out in the fields, relieving themselves. Smoke curling out of huts had wrapped the entire village in the thin gauze of mist. The haweli was still and secretive, its walls sweating with dew, its shuttered windows like eyes closed to the world outside, some sparrows on its lower ledges. If the servants were up inside, they were taking care not to make any sound.

Durga hammered in the last safety pegs and hurried to help Harihar with the heavy benches. A month ago he would have carried them alone, but now he could not even drag them a few metres without getting out of breath. When she reached him, he had pulled a bench out of the cart and was sitting on it.

I can carry it, she said.

We will do it together, he replied, but kept sitting. He was breathing heavily and trying to smother the coughs that had twice made him retch. Durga knew that his forehead would be hot with fever.

He looked out beyond the maidan, in the direction of the village and the fields, the hills in the distance, the toddy trees with crows fluttering like rumours in their elephant-ear leaves, squabbling and drunk on the dregs of the toddy collecting in earthen gourds which hung like strange fruit. The toddy-tapper would be around any moment to climb up the smooth, slightly ridged trunks of the trees, pulling himself up by means of a band tied around his ankles, to collect his gourds. Or he might leave them there all day so that they would ferment in the sun. Durga had seen him climb last evening, his thin, muscular body bare but for a loincloth, and had forced herself not to think of how a man like that might make love. Men like that had never come to her mother's place. Men like Harihar had – though Harihar had later told her that his initial visit was the first such occasion for him. Still, the men Durga had known had been like Harihar, middle class and middle aged, mostly urban. No toddy-tappers, no Chotte Thakurs. The former probably went to cheap whores and the latter to rich mistresses and courtesans.

It is beautiful, isn't it?

Harihar broke into her thoughts. She nodded.

He shuddered and stood. Picking up one end of the bench they had been sitting on, he said: Not much longer now.

What? she asked.

He was silent.

What? she repeated, sharply this time.

You won't have to help me like this much longer, he said.

She chose not to reply. Lately, he had started making such ambivalent remarks – statements that could allude either to death or to getting better. They were fine-barbed statements. Durga realized they referred, indirectly, to the difference that had surfaced between them after their first year or so together. The first couple of years had been an optimistic time for Harihar. He had improved his show considerably by convincing Durga to sing before the films and during the intervals, and that had brought him a step closer to his dream. But then he had realized Durga had a dream too – and hers had little in common with his. It had come to him as a shock: this sudden divergence in what he had thought was a shared hope, the lurking violence of diverging desires between two people yoked together by choice or circumstances.

Durga wanted a house, a family, home; she wanted to be settled. After the birth of Ashok, she had gradually become almost obsessive in her desire for a home for her son and it was this – not Harihar's cinema – that kept her matching his exertions now: she was dreaming of the time they would have enough to stop, put down roots. But this desire pulled against Harihar's dream and he resented this. He resented the fact she was not simply a part of his vision of life and the future but had her own ambitions. This caused him to make these statements that posed him as a burden, a hindrance Durga was yearning to be rid of, even though Durga lacked the single-mindedness with which Harihar stalked the morning glow of his dreams from horizon to horizon.

Ashok came running, shouting, See see what I have caught. He displayed a large green grasshopper held tight in a pinch.

See, see, see, the greatest show on earth! See the best film ever made; see *Sairandhri*! See the film that made Baburao famous! See, see Bheema battle with Keechak! See the gods and heroes! See the past, see the future! See, see, see the greatest show on earth!

Having run out of money and so unable to see her regularly, Harihar had brought his bioscope into Durga's neighbourhood, even though he knew his dated films would attract fewer spectators in the city and, moreover, he had no permit to exhibit in that district. He had known her for three months by then and they considered each other lovers. Durga took other customers, but Harihar knew that without asking. He still spent much more time talking about films or listening to her sing than making love, and she thought she loved him for that. She had never felt any physical desire for Harihar, or any man. But it was only after she had been to his show that she knew that she would go away with him one day.

She had seen other films. She had even seen *Raja Harishchandra* (which he was recycling then), and in a theatre too, when the film came to Calcutta for the second time. But she saw all four of the shows he put on in the three days that he set up his tent in the public park behind the alley. And she discovered another world altogether. It was as if she saw not only *Raja Harishchandra*, but all films ever and the world behind the films through Harihar's eyes. Or perhaps it would be more accurate to say she heard it in Harihar's voice, for while the eyes were hers, the voice was Harihar's: he would fill in the silent pictures with more than what other subtitle readers did. He could change voices and convey passion; he would even use metal plates and shoes to create background noises. Suddenly, the film was not just an ancient story or something made by someone else. It was a palpable presence that joined one to the past and the future, and to those hundreds of viewers in the present. It was a living, changing thing, like the days and nights of men and women, and different each time it was shown. You could live it, you could breathe it, you could travel with it, sleep with it: more than one could do with lovers or husbands or wives.

By the last show she was infected. Or that is what she thought.

Later that night, lying with his head in her lap after she had playfully read his shadow for him and seen all in it that would please him, Harihar said, Think of what I could do if I had the money to hire musicians and singers. Then he added, Think of what you could do. Think of the money we could make, the places we could visit.

She had looked into the glass jar in which she had read Harihar's shadow and she had seen nothing there, no trace of movement, no sign of fame, nothing. (But then she never did see anything. She had learnt to 'read' shadows from Madame, a companion of her mother who ran a brothel further down the street and claimed to be half-Polish, although she could have been any-thing. Tall and angular, fair and brown-haired, she could have been Afghan, Punjabi, or half-English. But she claimed to be half-Polish, perhaps because she had a reputation as a seer, and who had ever heard of an English, a Punjabi or an Afghan seer? Madame would fill a glass jar with water and stand it in the shadow of a man. Then she would let wax from a burning candle drip into the water and read the man's fortune from the shapes the wax took as it solidified, from the shadows it cast. An old Polish custom, she claimed, and it had become known in the neighbourhood as shadow-reading. It was this Durga's mother had forced her to learn – inflicting similar lessons on her other 'daughters', the reading of cards, tea leaves, palms etc., all for the sake of 'biznuss'.)

So that night, Durga went through the motions, reading not what she saw, which was nothing but wax and shade, but what she knew Harihar wanted to hear. And Harihar, by no means a believer, was pleased; he spoke of the musicians he would hire, the places they would visit.

They were running out of kerosene, but they lit all four lanterns in honour of Chotte Thakur. Harihar even brought out his prized Aladdin lamp. Or Aladdin-model-6-style-150-made-in-America floor lamp, as he used to put it, the entire description sounding like one long aristocratic name. That is how it had been described by the old Englishwoman who had sold the second-hand lamp to him. It had been standing surrounded by various other lamps, big and small, in her reclusive antique shop at 36 Chowringhee Lane and she had told him repeatedly that it would have fetched a 'goodly sum back home'. But she was letting it go for a pittance. This was after all Calcutta. It wasn't back home. She had been in India long enough to pick up Anglo-Indian memsahib mannerisms but she had never lost sight of 'home'. Such tenacity of vision fascinated Harihar. He had visited his parents' village in Bihar once and he did not think of it as home. He doubted whether he thought of Calcutta as home in spite of being fluent in Bangla.

He had bought the lamp mainly because of its name – Aladdin, the discoverer of magic, the projector of wonderment, the man who had his wishes fulfilled – than for its long and elegant shape or its lost status in the Englishwoman's world of lamps. He used it only on special occasions. This evening he cleaned it carefully, filled it with kerosene, and stood it next to the screen. Next to it, he placed, as he always did on such occasions, a low stool and on the stool a clock that kept unreliable time, and four sticks of agarbatti stuck in a lump of clay. In the gathering gloom, the Aladdin lamp burned more brightly than any of the other lanterns, its thin white stem and the golden enamelled decorations at its base and the top of the stem scratched and peeled, the original silk shade replaced by coarse cotton.

One night in her mother's kotha, Harihar had talked about his marriage and the job he had quit. He did not mention either his job or marriage again after that. And even that evening, he had not used too many words. Years later, Durga would still recall the few sentences he had spoken. She was not able to recall the first time they had made love, but she could recall almost all the words he had spoken that night and the expression on his face – an ordinary face, lit up by something bigger than him at that moment.

The strange thing about being a sorting clerk in the post office, Harihar had said in his precise, measured way, his voice only a shade over a whisper, is that places become either more real to you or less so. Destinations pass through your fingers. All those letters bearing strange stamps and addresses. But you yourself stay where you are, perched on a stool in front of your cabinet of wooden compartments. Most of the people I worked with, Harihar said, could not care a jot for the places those letters came from. But at times I would lie awake half the night trying to imagine somewhere far away – Rangoon or Cape Town, London or Peking – trying to conjure it up from handwriting, a stain, a stamp, the whiff of a scent. I was married, I had been married at the age of nineteen, and I was conscious of my duties: I could not pack my bags and leave, but I could dream. I could dream. I had not been allowed to see a film by my parents, who had brought their rural Bihari values to Calcutta, and so I think I was twenty-five: I saw my first film purely by accident. We were invited to the postmaster's house for some occasion and the postmaster was an amateur photographer; he had also recently purchased a projector and some really old reels, from ten years back or more, I think he showed us something called 'Railway Train in Full Motion', I felt as if I had been run over by a train. It was a shock. Here was something that could bring the world to me and my parents were talking about it being decent or indecent, real or unreal, good or bad magic. I loved my parents; they had sacrificed so much to give me the education they never had. But this time I decided to ignore their wishes. I started sneaking into theatres. I bought books and magazines about films and cameras; I read about the Lumière Brothers and how their cinematograph had arrived in India within six months of being exhibited in Paris. I read about Edison and Skladanowski and Pathé and Professor Anderson. Later, I became aware of Save Dada and Phalke and other Indians who were actually making films. I was told of Abdulally Esoofally, who started with one touring bioscope in 1901 – he took it all over the Raj, from the forests of Burma to the mountains of Afghanistan – and became a millionaire and theatre owner in less than two decades! It was a revelation. It was a secret I could not even share with my wife. But when the moment offered itself – after my wife's death and my daughter's marriage – there was no doubt in my mind. I wanted to be out of that stool in the post office. I couldn't wait to be part of that world outside, and I knew I would make more money showing films than sorting letters. I still believe so. Films are the future, not letters. Films are the world. The bioscope, meri jaan, moving pictures, not the fixed alphabet.

Harihar had not made much money. Every time Durga and Harihar returned to Calcutta to lease a new film, he hoped this would be the one that would make his fortune. This film is a super hit, he would tell Durga. It will attract viewers like flies. You will get your house after this tour, he would add as an afterthought.

Her years with him had fallen into a pattern. Each year consisted of two periods: the longest was the seven-to-eight-month period they actually toured the hinterland and the shortest was the period they spent in Calcutta, when Harihar leased the picture or, if he had made money on the last tour, two pictures. He disappeared for days, with people who scavenged around the edges of the film industry, brittle-boned, blade-eyed, sharp-voiced people, hovering like crows around a pile of garbage, making a living from whatever had been discarded as old or useless. He also disappeared into offices like that of the Electrical Inspector for the Presidency, where he applied for and received, usually after bribing some babu, the licences he required. But he also required other permits, and this sometimes took him out, usually alone, to the district magistrates' offices along his planned annual route. Harihar's route was more or less the same: he worked the districts to the north-west of Calcutta, moving in a zigzag line from Alipore to Raniganj, though this time they had ventured even further, showing in Parasnath and Giridih, skirting Kodarma and hoping to turn around at Nalanda, a place Durga had never been to before.

Harihar never made enough money to rent the latest

films. He would rent films that were no longer showing in the cities and would make some profit, but never enough to rent a more recent film next time, or hire the regular staff he needed to set up equipment and visit the villages announcing the show. (Old Mehto was the only 'regular staff', as Harihar liked to call him, they had ever had. They usually hired people by the day or the week – and these were often rustics who could not be trusted with the equipment and whose announcements some-how made the show look tacky and ancient, while Old Mehto, whenever he was trusted to go too far with the cycle and the dented tin funnel that they used for a megaphone, was liable to disappear into a toddy joint for a couple of days or more.)

With age and illness Harihar had been getting des-perate. Durga could see it in his haggard, unshaven face. On each recent trip, he had ventured farther and farther from Calcutta, though never as far as this. This time they had gone beyond Gaya, and Durga was frightened by the fixed look on Harihar's face whenever she sug-gested turning around. She knew it would take months to get back. They could, of course, sell the bullocks and the cart and take a train from Gaya: it might even make sense as bullocks and carts were cheaper in and around Calcutta than in these parts. But there was something in Harihar that refused to countenance this suggestion.

He had achieved a miracle in Calcutta last time: he had convinced Motilal, the distributor, to let him have a film that was almost new, promising to pay him a thousand rupees extra on return. He had returned with a packet of Sandesh. We have made it, he had cried out on seeing Durga and Ashok, this time we have made it. Or as he had phrased it in Hindustani: Our lives are made!

But their lives had not changed. They had not made it. And Durga could see the fear in Harihar's eyes.

And yet, when some local nobility – even someone like the Thakurs who were obviously nothing more than rich landlords – booked a show, Harihar would perk up. Durga would begin hoping too; their petty disagreements would disappear, almost. Harihar would go through the schedule with her and Ashok, who had started contributing to the effects lately. He would light the lanterns and his Aladdin lamp. He would take out the old cushions and lay them on the folding chairs, covering a couple of them with two sheets of rough silk. He would spread a reed mat under the chairs. He would even hang up his old banner – a roll of silk cloth announcing the show, Best Bioscope, the two B's reworked to resemble a tripod camera, in maroon and yellow and gold.

Having arranged everything, he would stand outside

the tent – bought second-hand from a circus, where it was only a side tent, and not able to contain more than eighty people at a crouch – and look upon his creation.

Durga had begun to understand the shadow of sadness that flickered over his face at times like these. He was thinking of the person he thought of more and more with time: the Abdulally who had turned a touring cinema into golden theatres, Abdulally whose tents could seat more than a thousand people, Abdulally who would hire local bands to play music during the shows, Abdulally who traversed the length and breadth of Asia and was not limited to Bengal and Bihar. Harihar would stand looking at the tent, yellow lamplight pouring out of the torn slits and holes, and then, abruptly, walk back inside.

This evening, Durga joined him. He was surprised. He looked at her and made one of his increasingly rare statements of affection. She would remember his words later, years later, and in another place.

But I have you, he said.

And Ashok, he added.

'She recalled that statement to Saleem Lahori much later, when time had burdened it with so many meanings she could no longer believe in its innocence. By then innocence had become unbelievable all around us. It had been shaken from us as the wind shakes raindrops out of trees. But to be fair to Harihar, *young man, I think he meant it then in a way very different from what it became.'*

Durga had never found Harihar physically attractive. To her he was almost an old man, though it was difficult to tell his age, and he reminded her too much of her other customers: lower middle class, about forty years old, at times slightly unkempt, and with the ability to withdraw behind a screen of his making, only this screen was not social or intellectual in Harihar's case, nor did it have to do with the financial relationship established between them. There was an element of genuine loneliness around him, it enveloped him like a shawl: something that told you that he would not, could not tell you everything. It was the loneliness of someone who knew he would be laughed at if he spoke the truth, or of someone whose deepest aspirations had leeched him of the capacity to share in other people's realities. He could not always speak of other things, was expressive only in the realm of dreams, of films. And he was lonely because we are always alone in dreams.

And yet she had fallen in love with his words. Or the difference of his words. Or so she thought.

For instance, when she had told him that she was pregnant, he had asked her, What name should we choose? She had been sleeping with other men, any man who paid the amount her mother was then demanding, and he had known that. But he had assumed a kind of fatherhood, and in spite of the differences of age, class and faith between them.

Harihar's response had confused Durga. For the first time, she had wept in his – or any man's – presence. And, with his intermittent, surprising ability to say the right words, he had dried her tears. Let's call him Ashok, he had said, Ashok – the one without sorrows.

She had smiled and replied, The greatest of India's kings.

The coming king of Indian films, Harihar had shouted joyously.

Are you ready, Ashok? Chotte Thakur will be here any moment.

Yes, pitaji.

Have you counted them?

Yes.

Count them again. Count them aloud. Tell me what they are for.

Two coconuts and a wooden board for footsteps and the sounds of animals, two brass plates for the clash of swords, one conch shell.

Good. The harmonium, Durga?

Durga, seated on a covered charpoy to one side of the screen, played a few notes in reply.

Good, good, said Harihar. He picked up a bottle

filled with rose water, a large lemonade flask fitted with a winding metal spout, and went to stand at the tent entrance. They could not collect ticket money – or ticket grain, as Harihar used to call it at times – this evening. But they were sure that Chotte Thakur would arrange for money to be given to them. That was how it happened in all the places.

It was almost dark outside. Small bats were flitting in the sky, sometimes highlighted against the redness of the western horizon. There was still the occasional tinkle of cattle returning to the village, but it was becoming more and more infrequent, the village was again shrouded in smoke from cooking fires. Some poorer villagers had come to watch: they were standing at a distance, leaning on their wooden staffs around the edge of the maidan, near the barbed wire, well aware that they could not view the show along with the Thakurs.

The Munshi, accompanied by a henchman, was the first to arrive. The clock registered a quarter to six, but it could well have been an hour more or less: it was an eccentric clock and they had not met anyone with a watch for a few days now.

The Munshi walked into the tent and, not expecting the smoke from the cowdung-cake boarsi they'd lit to keep the mosquitoes out, began to cough. Harihar had sprayed the air liberally with rose water too and the smouldering agarbatties were contributing a different but heady fragrance as well. The Munshi, no longer racked by coughs, raised his finger at the folding chairs that Harihar had arranged with such care. What are those? he said, finger trembling with age or indignation. You expect Chotte Sirkar to sit on those, those flimsy things?

Without waiting for an answer, he ordered the henchman to fetch an armchair. The man ran off and came back ten minutes later, directing three other men carrying a heavy, stuffed armchair. It was placed in the middle of the front row, and the Munshi ordered some of the low benches to be taken out. He was plainly unhappy still, and kept shaking his head, muttering, never, never if Raja Sahib had been alive, never on this earth. Then, finally about half an hour after he had first entered the tent, he sent a man to 'tell Chotte Thakur that the place is now suitable for his presence'.

The younger Thakur emerged with a retinue of family relations, all male and mostly young. Harihar sprinkled rose water on them at the entrance by shaking the lemonade bottle vigorously over his head, almost prancing with the effort as most of them were taller than him. There were fourteen of them and they sat down somewhat gingerly on the folded chairs and the front benches. The Munshi and a couple of senior retainers sat on a back bench.

Durga started playing the harmonium. Once the younger Thakur was seated in his armchair, she asked Ashok to run up and offer him a tray of paan, saunf and other ritual condiments. The Thakur declined it but his retinue took liberal helpings amid much back-slapping and laughter. After the usual nawabi style of greeting, Durga sang a bhajan by Meera. Harihar was particular about which song ought to be sung with a given film: bhajans for mythologicals, ghazals for historicals and simple popular tunes for anything contemporary.

While Durga sang, Harihar walked around the tent dimming the lanterns. Then he stood next to the single projector and slowly cranked the handle. Bars and spots fled across the screen and then suddenly the film began. Harihar read out the titles and the subtitles, which were in four different languages. Had he been rich enough, he would have hired readers to do this, or perhaps he wouldn't. This was the part that Durga never ceased to admire, for Harihar did not just read out the titles like all other readers, he concocted dialogues, mimicked sounds. Harihar was a gifted mimic, a talent that one could not associate with his nondescript clerical appearance. It was as if, next to a projector, he became not one man but many. And though he had been too ill to put his heart into the show for some time, that evening he performed as he used to when Durga first knew him.

★

Her mother had reacted differently from Harihar to her pregnancy. Or indifferently: she had hardly reacted at all. She had exhaled the smoke from the hookah slowly and given Durga a sharp but fleeting look. In that look Durga had read contempt and calculation, for Durga was the youngest of the women in the house and still well under sixteen, the age when, as her mother had often told them, 'the hole of a girl loosens and she becomes a woman', less attractive to a certain type of man. It had not surprised Durga when her mother had gone away for a day the very next week and returned with a scared twelve- or thirteen-year-old, introduced to them as 'a cousin from the village'. Relieved at being spared the ranting and raving that she had feared, Durga had welcomed the girl with more warmth than she felt for any of her own sisters. She had thought that the matter of her pregnancy had blown over.

But the matter had come to a head in her fifth month of pregnancy, when Durga could no longer bring herself to have sex with the men her mother sent to her. She had tried to explain, but her mother would not listen. I did it well into my last month when I was carrying you, and look at you, you are fine and well, limb and voice intact, arguing blithely with your very own mother, she had said. Besides there are men who pay extra for it.

Durga had known her mother would never let her marry Harihar: marry a Hindu, she would have exclaimed, suddenly becoming a devout Muslim – though if Harihar had the money, she would have allowed him to maintain Durga as his mistress. That very afternoon, while her mother slept, Durga had left the house with her bundle of jewellery and all the money – not much – she could find in her mother's box.

She was perhaps fifteen.

It had been difficult to get to the part of Howrah where Harihar had taken his show. The pontoon bridge across the River Hoogly had been sealed by the police for almost four hours. River and road traffic piled up on all sides, waiting for the police to wave them through.

The year was 1922. The date was 13 February.

It was an inconsequential day. A day earlier, and Durga's decision would have coincided with History: with the withdrawal of the call for Non-Co-operation by the Congress and Gandhi. Protests against the Rowlatt Act, the Montagu–Chelmsford Reforms and the Jallianwala Bagh massacre, the First World War when India had contributed 1.4 million forgotten soldiers to fight another people's battles, the Khilafat movement, the call for non-co-operation, it had been a turbulent period. The British were still jittery the day after the day when things ought to have officially returned to normality, which was the

day Durga stole away to find Harihar and the inconsequential day when an unidentified young man climbed
the highest building next to the pontoon bridge and, after
railing against the Congress and the British for almost an
hour, sent himself plummeting down to the asphalt
below. His last words, which have not entered any history
book, were: You like determination, Montagu? This is
determination. This is determination.

The man, whose scattered pieces were scraped off
the asphalt by the police, was referring to Montagu and
Birkenhead's warning that Indians should not dare to
challenge 'the most determined people in the world'.
He had meditated all night over the withdrawal of the
call for non-co-operation by the Congress, and he had
shed bitter tears of shame.

Very few in the crowd understood the young man
or what he had experienced, but many were strangely
moved by the sight of a human plunging to certain
death. It was not the protest itself that moved them, for
most of those standing by had not heard the man
shouting, rather it was the desperate intensity of the act
that fascinated them. The young man had launched
himself against the barbed wire of colonial authority, the
hard ground of reality, achieving fantastic yet fatal
mobility at the very end of his life. But many in the
crowd also felt a faint scepticism, a vague doubting in
the face of such an end.

The police took no chances. They sealed the pontoon bridge – erecting wooden posts with barbed wire on both sides – until every tendon and tooth of the crushed man had been picked up and the blood washed away with water jetted by a fire engine drawn by two impatient, heavy-hoofed horses.

It was this that had delayed Durga on her way to Harihar, her mind made up.

'Yes, my young scholar, this is a story about what happens in the mind just as much as it is a story about what happens to the body. Look at me. Look at my body. See, see, the skin fails to contract when I pinch it. See. Look at me, my pot belly, my hair. But once I was considered handsome. There were people who thought I was an actor, not a writer. And look at what has happened to this body, this face. But the mind, ah, the mind, how can anyone your age know what happens in the mind . . .'

By nine-thirty on the following night, they had wrapped up their first public show in Anjangarh. Harihar was very tired but in a happier mood than Durga had seen for months. Not only had Chotte Thakur given them fifty rupees as 'nazrana' the previous evening – money it would take them two or three shows to earn – but the show this evening had been packed despite the fact that Harihar had announced it in only three villages: he'd felt too ill to continue beyond the third village and had driven the cart back to the tent around noon. Still, more than a hundred people had turned out and most of them had paid in cash.

Feeling ill, Harihar had restricted himself to reading out the subtitles in Hindustani. Old Mehto was still missing and Durga had to help crank the projector. The villager they had hired was too untrained to help out with these matters. But most of the audience consisted of peasants who had seldom, if ever, seen a 'mythological' and they went into raptures at the sight of the Pandavas and Lord Krishna. Some of the richer ones even tossed one-paisa coins at the screen, which Ashok darted forward to collect. The climax of the film – when Bheema exacts a bloody vengeance by tearing apart Keechak limb by limb – was met with frenzied applause, even though the part had been heavily cut by the censors for excessive violence. Harihar was certain that news would travel and the show would attract sizeable crowds for the five nights that he planned to stay there.

Having assembled the folding screen and the equipment and put them in the middle of the tent – beside the two charpoys on which they slept – Durga went out to light a fire in the earth-and-bricks chullah that Harihar had made. They did not use the stove if they could use wood and other free fuel. While collecting firewood, she accidentally touched a toad, and returned wondering about its significance: her mother used to say that a

gecko falling on your clothes signified good luck. Or
money, for good luck was a synonym for ready cash in
her mother's mind. What did touching a toad signify?
She thought Ashok, who was sleepy and hungry, was
complaining and turned around to snap at him, but it
was only the sound of someone singing from the village.
It continued for a minute and then lapsed into the
trilling of crickets, a sound so shrill and constant that
one almost ceased to hear it after a night or two.

Durga squatted down, bending over the chullah to
blow into it, then straightened up, crying out in fright
when she saw three men standing there, one holding a
hooded lantern.

Harihar came running with the stick that he always
kept near him: the stick could be unscrewed to reveal a
long steel blade, not that Durga could imagine Harihar
using the blade. But it was only the Munshi and two of
his henchmen.

Chotte Sirkar has guests tonight. He wants you to
provide some music, said the Munshi to Durga. Here,
he has sent ten rupees as advance, he added, handing
Harihar a small pink cloth bundle containing some
coins. You do not need to take your harmonium-
varmonium. We have all you need in the haveli.

The Munshi did not look happy.

Durga and Harihar were not unused to such
requests. They were rare, but when they came they

meant a substantial income on the side. Usually Harihar and Ashok would accompany Durga, but tonight Harihar was too ill and tired.

I am too ill, Harihar said. But my wife will go with you.

He stressed the word 'patni', wife. Actually, he said 'dharam-patni', highlighting the heavy knot of religion in marriage, knowing these were men who would respect a married woman from the higher castes. They might take liberties with her in speech but they would never do what they might do to an unmarried woman or to a woman – married or not – from the lower castes.

In fact, they had never married. Durga had suggested it a few times in the first months. She was willing to be married as a Hindu, a Muslim, a British citizen, whatever. Harihar had postponed it and once Ashok was born it had ceased to be an issue, although it was one of the things Durga resented: she had wanted to be married; she had not met any prostitute, except her mother, who did not want to be married. Some were possessed by that dream.

Yet Harihar, while willing to pretend they were married and give his name to Ashok, would somehow not consider even the simplest wedding. Not even a Brahmo Samaj one. It was as if, having entered his dream world of films, he had no wish to be reminded of what he had left behind. Or was it because, deep in his heart, he could not imagine being married to a woman like Durga? This thought would cross Durga's mind once in a while, but she always pushed it away, sometimes in the process pushing away Ashok too as he clamoured for attention at an inopportune moment.

Instead, she had learnt to think of herself as Durga. It was a name she had chosen for herself. Harihar had not liked the name. Gita, he had suggested, or Smita, or Sita. There you are, Sita, now that is a good name.

No, she had replied. I will be Durga.

But it does not even sound like your Muslim name, he had observed.

'In different ways, all of them changed names. But I guess she was the only one who gave it real thought. And yet, a strange choice: the name of a goddess of vehement action, chosen by a woman who left hardly any trace in the annals of history, a woman who – if you film historians are to be believed – was a minor, insubstantial, ghostly figure in the glorious hard dream of Bombay films.'

The haveli was bigger than it seemed from the outside. It was also sadder. Not sad in the sense of someone who had experienced a tragedy, but sad in the sense of someone who was possessed by the tragic. It struck her as strange that she had hardly seen any member of the family other than the Chotte Thakur and his retinue of distant cousins. What about his brother and sister-in-law? Or sisters-in-law? What about children? All the children running in and out of the front gate were sons and daughters of distant cousins or family retainers.

The Munshi did not take her to the front gate. Instead he led her to a narrow side door; the doorposts were warped and termite-infested. From somewhere there was a faint clucking and stirring of feathered bodies, but the rooms overlooking the courtyard were so eerily silent that Durga felt as if they were holding their breath, watching.

She followed the Munshi across the large shadowy courtyard and entered a room attached to the haveli. The courtyard had smelled of cowdung and straw, but the room smelt of incense and agarbatti.

This room was not part of the main building. It was brightly lit with chandelier-stands and candles and seating running all along the walls. A huge punkah with tasselled edges hung with loose ropes – it was not being plied – from the ceiling. There were silver plates holding paan, saunf, nuts and fruits, as well as silver glasses and narrow-stemmed vases containing wine and water. In the middle of the room, on a low cushioned takht, there was an expensive harmonium, a taanpura and a tabla set.

There was no one in the room.

The Munshi indicated Durga should go to the takht,

waving her towards it as if waving away a bad smell. Then he closed the door behind him, softly, and she heard his steps and coughs receding.

Batin began his story from Anjangarh in 1929. That much is clear enough from my notes. But later, assembling the various strands of his narrative, splicing them together with other related stories, I often had a feeling of vertigo, of falling into the past and ascending to the future at the same time, of moving in different directions. Regardless of where Batin's narrative had begun, the story that I assembled over the years appeared to have a different beginning every time I looked into it.

When did the story I assembled, this tale, begin? That night in 1988, in a cold flat in Frederiksberg, where an ageing writer lounged on slightly worn, hand-embroidered cushions and spoke to an earnest young scholar over glasses of whisky, cups of tea? It had been blowing outside, where the hollow northern darkness was almost translucent; the windowpanes were glazed with moisture and melting specks of snow. Or did it begin that afternoon in 1992 when the same scholar visited a doctor – a lady doctor, she would be called – in Phansa, and she spoke to him of her father while the day of the North Indian plains slithered swiftly as a snake into night? Or in 1972 or 1973 when that doctor, then a gangly pony-tailed girl, heard her parents argue about seeing – or not seeing – a

film, that they would have called a 'picture'. Or did it
begin in 1948, when a gang of youths strung barbed wire
at the entrance of an old building, hammering in nails
and tying the twisted strands to them? Or in 1929, when
the Calcutta owner of a small travelling cinema met the
younger son of a feudal family in the village of Anjangarh,
or earlier when he had met the whore who would and
would not be his wife?

The strands of this story are entangled like the spools
of a film slipping from its reel, like lengths of curling
barbed wire. Barbed wire and photography: Batin would
refer to them again and again and often in the same
breath, the same sentence:

'Is it surprising, young man, that both photography
and barbed wire were born from the womb of the same
time? Photography finally came of age in 1880. The year
marked the decisive leap in its evolution. Gelatine emul-
sion and fast plates, in conjunction with hand and pocket
cameras, opened the shutters that year to thousands of
amateur photographers. No need now for the photographer
to have a darkroom and be thoroughly acquainted with
the rules of focusing, and the relation of lens aperture to
light, with the intricate science and art of developing,
fixing, printing, toning, mounting. Now any novice could
buy a pocket camera, have it loaded with a packet of plates
or films, push a button and freeze movement forever. The
modern camera had been born. Or our age had been

suction-pulled, bloody and squalling, from the body of the past, the past that we pretend is like a minor film character and conveniently dies on giving birth. A new century had been born, a few years premature. Meanwhile another device to fix movement was also gestating in 1880 in a very different part of the world – and like the camera, it could have been invented centuries earlier.

The camera could have been developed anytime after the invention of the camera obscura – literally the dark room – whose principles were familiar to the Arabs as early as the tenth century and described in detail by Hassan ibn Hassan, alias Ibn al-Haithnam. Ever heard of him, young man? Not even as Alhazen, which is how, in the twelfth century, he was known to your Roger Bacon, to whom the discovery later came to be attributed? Well, anyway. Like the camera, barbed wire could in theory have been invented centuries earlier. But it was only in the 1860s that the first barbed-wire patents were claimed and it was only in 1880, with the fencing, in effect, of the entire Texan Panhandle – a line of fortification against the North erected piecemeal by individual farmers – that the barbed wire came into its own. It was only in 1880, young man, that the effectiveness of fencing railroads was established, with the Washburn & Moen Manufacturing Co. beating down an anti-wire bill in the Connecticut General Assembly. The devil's rope had arrived. And from the enclosure of cows to the concentration of people would be a short step, just as it is a short step from the still photo to the motion picture, young man.'

So perhaps it is with the year 1880 that I should start weaving the strands of this story: the year of photography and barbed wire. Two tools perfected in 1880 to capture movement. But it is not in 1880 or in London or Texas that the story remains. For both barbed wire and the photograph travelled fast and came to the region called India almost instantaneously. I must have remarked on this to Batin – I am not sure, because I did not always jot down my own remarks – for in my notebook I scrawled this retort from him on the next page:

'But they did not come to India in the same way. No, far from it, my young scholar, far from it. Make no mistake: it is not the same story. If there are similarities between them, there are also differences. You say both of them do violence to life. But they relate to life, which is always mobile, in such different ways. And the story I will tell you now, young man, is about mobility, about how people move from place to place, time to time, name to name; and it is about barbed wire, how we are entangled in the barbed wire of history and our own pasts, how we erect in our minds the barbed-wire fences that leave our bodies bleeding, and it is about violence and about love. But is it one story? To be honest, young man, I do not know, for stories are impossible to fence in either time or

*space, and I was told this story by three different people,
from three different perspectives.'*

Imagine a fourth perspective: a day in 1992. Imagine
another place: a house with a red-brick wall lined with
pink and white bougainvillaea and perforated rusted-
iron rods sticking from the top of the wall, but, surprisingly, no barbed wire strung from rod to rod.
Imagine another person: a beautiful woman in her
thirties.

She is wearing a plain sari and no make-up. Actually,
her face has been so rigorously scrubbed of make-up
that it shines with the strength of circulating blood, has
assumed the beauty of youth and health.

She has just come back from work, from her 'dispen-
sary' as the servant described it: a successful private
clinic in Phansa. The grey Fiat that she drove is standing
there, outside the veranda where she is sitting in a
wicker chair, facing the scholar of films who speaks her
native tongue but works in another land (where was it
he had said he taught, Berlin?). On a chair next to them
lies the white towel with which she had wiped her face
and hands after washing: beads of water have marked
her progress, walking briskly, drying her face and hands
on the towel with the unconsciousness of a person used
to such busyness; drop by drop the water glistens almost

translucent on the mosaic floor, in a wavering line from the open door behind him to the chair facing the scholar that she occupies now.

Why is it that she opens up to him and talks about her childhood, asking the ayah to take care of the baby while she does so? Is it a bid to remember her father? Is it a bid to understand something only dimly comprehended? Is it the shared bond of films?

She casts her thoughts far back, decades back, to a year in the 1970s, to 1972 or 1973, she is not sure. It was before the Emergency, around the Bangladesh war, she says. I remember it was just before the Emergency because it was then that Papa had all the barbed wire taken down from those rods on the wall. It was his way of protesting. It was his way of learning to live with the past, but on his own terms.

This is what she says.

My excitement at the possibility of going out was always mixed with dread of those sudden fluctuations in mood and tone that could afflict the relationship between my parents and destroy an entire evening. Their quarrels never lasted more than a night or, at the most, until the next morning. They were like minor flash floods, the sort that occur during a monsoon, and they could be as devastating to our plans. A quarrelsome evening was sufficient to wash away an outing to the only good restaurant in town, or to postpone a long-promised trip to the cinema.

That time, I remember, it was indeed a trip to the cinema. But this quarrel had not blown over in a night; they had argued about it for a week, ever since the film was advertised for the matinee show at Paradise Talkies, and Ramesh Uncle, the owner, had called up Papa to tell him. Ramesh Babu was a friend, one of Papa's patients and a Phansa Club card-and-billiards crony, but Papa had received the news with ill-concealed displeasure. So ill concealed that Ramesh Uncle had started apologizing, using the affectionate diminutive, Ash, that Papa's friends would often employ. I could hear him say, the voice tinny through the receiver, But Ash, I thought you would have seen . . . you know, Ash . . . it is just a film after all . . . no one . . .

You don't have to explain, Papa said.

You see, Ash, Ramesh Uncle was stuttering, everyone knows . . .

I know everyone knows and I do not care, Papa replied. I have not seen the film in twenty years and I do not intend to see it just because it has been, what do you call it, re-released.

No offence meant, Ash, Ramesh Uncle continued to stutter. You see, I had no idea . . .

No offence taken, Ramesh, but let us drop the subject now.

And they had started talking about the coming elections for the Phansa chapter of Lions Club.

It was more difficult to get Mummy to drop the subject. She heard about it from a friend that very evening and, when Papa came back from the clinic at about eleven, declared her intention of seeing the film.

You can see it all week if you wish. I won't.

They argued back and forth about it, occasionally casting glances at the bed next to theirs where I was supposed to be asleep with my younger brother. Mummy was sitting at the dressing table, taking out her hairpins and undoing her elaborate jooda. Papa was fiddling with some sheets of papers in the box room and making occasional sorties to the clothes hanger. I pretended to be asleep, as I usually did.

Papa did not like the idea of going to matinee shows, although this time he was not objecting to the timing of the show but to the film itself. I couldn't follow their argument. I had heard about the film. It was old, called *Aakhri Raat*, a moderate success when released some time after Independence: two of its songs were still popular and sometimes requested on radio, particularly on Amin Sayani's *Binaca Geetmala*. It was said to be a 'family film', which meant they could not be arguing about the desirability of taking us. It was obviously a film neither had seen: it appeared Mummy had been much too young first time around, but Papa, who was older, had made a conscious decision to avoid it. And yet it also appeared that people expected my parents – particularly Papa – to have seen the film.

I could not understand what was so bad about the film that Papa boycotted it. It appeared to be the story of two friends who fall in love with the same woman and one of them sacrifices himself for the sake of his friend. Quite a safe formula. But Mummy and Papa were still arguing when I finally fell asleep.

It is just a film, I heard her whisper angrily as I dozed off. Why can't you let the past lie?

When Papa gave in, he did so with bad grace. And now he was standing on the veranda of our home, jangling his car keys impatiently. The two of us were already bundled into the back seat of the Fiat, and he was waiting for Mummy to lock the bedroom and then lock the back door of the house and come round to the veranda.

He did not dare confront Mummy directly, so he made general comments about the slowness of women. He jangled his key. Women, he muttered. Women, muttered Manik, my brother, arching his eyebrows and frowning at me. Shut up, I hissed at him.

Typical of boys not to realize the gravity of a situation.

Here we were on the verge of one of our few trips to the cinema and it could well be cancelled – or we might be late – if Mummy took just a few minutes longer in circumnavigating the house. Papa was about to blow the horn of the Fiat again – he had done so a minute ago – when Mummy strode into view, still giving instructions about the dinner to Bua, who was huffing and puffing, her hundred and twenty kilos heaving in various directions simultaneously, trying to keep pace with the slim figure of Mummy.

We will be late as usual, said Papa. Might as well cancel it.

We won't be late, Mummy replied. There's still twenty minutes.

And no traffic, Papa rejoined sarcastically.

And this is not Patna, Mummy said. She hated having the horn sounded to fetch her. Papa knew well. He opened his mouth to say something even more sarcastic, something so heavily sarcastic it would lead to an explosion and the cancellation of the trip.

Mummy, I shouted, Manik is pulling faces at me again. Mummiii . . .

It saved the day. And Manik got scolded too.

There is the squawking of an unseen parrot in a cage somewhere inside the house.

There are cracks in the mosaic floor of the veranda

and the scholar notes how they spread like veins on the back of an old man's hand. He looks down now, partly because the lady doctor's face has assumed an enraptured glow that, for the first time, makes him realize she is an attractive young woman. But he need not have looked away, for the lady doctor is lost in her recollection and hardly there on the veranda with him any more. So much so that her narrative lifts like a feather and seems suspended in time; it slips back and forth from past to present tense. The scholar notices this fluctuation of tenses, understands it achingly as a possibility denied to him, an option available only to those who, by some fluke of chance or conspiracy of events, have managed to grow up in the spaces of their childhood.

Her voice is like a thread knitting together the fabric of the past and the present, darting like a needle from one tense to another.

Paradise Talkies is perched, literally, on a nullah. It still looks the same as it did when I was a girl.

It was and is in the centre of Phansa and faces a small park, or anyway an enclosed space that contains a statue of Gandhiji and a few shrubs. Paradise Talkies itself is in a building that must have been built sometime in the nineteenth century, but definitely looks and acts older. Manik still claims that it groans once in a while. It slouches. It has not been painted for decades, as there is very little plaster left to put paint on. Instead giant hoardings add colour to the building and hide the spots where plaster has fallen away in a particularly sinister manner. Next to the nullah, there is a paan kiosk. It is a good spot for such a kiosk, and I have heard that Ramesh Uncle charges a 'minor fortune' for letting the space for the kiosk. There is a halvai's shop above the nullah, which is hardly fordable during the monsoon months (even though crowds of film fans do ford it on occasion, hitching up dhotis and trousers, holding slippers and shoes in their hands). The halvai pays good rent too; huge steaming cauldrons and earthen ovens, a few squat wooden chairs and tables and trays of coloured sweets and samosas fill up the cramped space of the shop, its walls dark with soot and grime, a naked bulb dangling from a wire in the middle of the room. Next door, a narrow stairway leads up to the balcony and the boxes while, behind, a shadowy passage leads to the cheaper 'ground-floor' sections. We used to call these sections the *chavanni* rows, though even the cheap tickets to the ground floor had long since cost much more than the proverbial twenty-five-paisa coin.

We took the stairway to the balcony where there is an actual popcorn machine, a square box with popcorn swirling in it like, we used to think, snow. It was rare in those days in Phansa – the popcorn I mean, not snow of course, which is unheard of here. Popcorn is sold only at this higher level. Downstairs one can get rassogulla, halwa, tilkut, jalebi, amritee, peda, barfi, samosa, nimki, kulcha, two kinds of chai and four types of cold drinks from the halvai, and paan, cigarette, khaini and bidi from the paan kiosk. But no popcorn.

Upstairs, we turned left, walked past a ticket kiosk and the popcorn machine, and into a narrow corridor, which was always damp and led to two rooms facing one another. One of the rooms had a door that hung off one of its hinges and wouldn't be closed: it was used by the two night-watchmen. Rolls of paper – posters – lay scattered in that room. In one corner, there was a stretch of barbed wire, tightly wound around two wooden posts, used to cordon off the entrance on occasions when the 'House Full' notice sparked a minor riot outside. Old posters had been spread like carpets on the floor and plastered on the walls; in places it appeared as if the walls were made not of brick and cement but of film posters.

The other room had a door that could be closed and locked. It contained a metal Godrej table and a number of aluminium folding chairs. The walls of this room were also covered with posters, but these were hung like portraits, framed and displayed. There were also some photographs of Ramesh Uncle standing stiffly with people whose faces were then vaguely familiar: actors whose star had described a short (and since) eclipsed trajectory in Bombay or Calcutta. Falling stars, we used to call them behind his back; my well-known actor friends, Ramesh Uncle would say in the course of almost every conversation in that room, waving a hand at them.

Ramesh Uncle was sitting on a swivel chair behind the large and many-shelved Godrej table, looking out of the only window in the room. He turned as we entered, the chair squeaking on its wheels.

Namaste Bhabhiji, he said to Mummy. Didn't see your car, Ash. Was getting worried.

Oh, I wouldn't let you lose four seats for nothing, Papa replied.

Four seats, what do you mean, yaar? I have reserved one of the boxes for you.

But I told you not to do so, Ramesh. We do not need fifteen seats . . .

It's on me, Ash. It is on me . . .

They argued back and forth for a couple of minutes, until Papa gave in: it was a ritual they enacted every time we went to see a film that was not 'House Full'.

Ramesh Uncle called one of the young men who work as cleaners, ticket collectors, bouncers and general handymen in whatever pies Ramesh Uncle might have a finger in at that moment – the hall was by no means his only source of income – and instructed him to take us to the 'reserve box'.

This is Doctor Sahib and his family. Take good care of them, he warned the young man, and make sure the children get all the thanda drinks they want. (I can tell you Ramesh Uncle was a favourite with Manik and me.)

The young man drew out a long tin torch from the folds of his kurtah and pointed with its yellow beam. This way madamssaar, he said. As we were being led up a flight of narrow stairs to the box, Ramesh Uncle shouted to another of the young men, Tell Rafiq to start the film. We are ten minutes late. Hurry up. Hurry up.

The young usher took his job seriously. Even though there was no one else in the box, he directed us with the beam of his torch to the middle seats in the first row as if the place were packed, before disappearing to fetch Coca-Cola bottles for all of us. Papa tried to pay him, but he declined and went away: these were small rituals that defined all our visits to Paradise Talkies. (They died with Papa's generation, I think, no one would go to such extremes for family friends or club mates today. But in those days such courtesy was expected in most circles.)

The hall was less than half full, but the third-class sections were getting restless and there were hoots and catcalls from below; my parents pretended not to hear the occasional lewd remark from the ground floor. It smelled of roasted peanuts and paan and sweat even up in the boxes. The metal fans moved with a dull clink, a certain heaviness of motion, doing little to disturb the air.

Why doesn't Ramesh do something about these infernal mosquitoes, grumbled Papa, and, as if on cue, the usher re-entered our tiny, suspended box and doused all the chairs with fumes of Flit. He sprayed with vigour, pumping until we were almost choking with the toxic fumes and Mummy was forced to rummage in her handbag for a scented handkerchief. As he retired, still 'flitting' until the door closed on him, facing us, moving backwards like one of those Mughal courtiers in films, retiring from the royal presence, a thin beam flickered through the hall, throwing dissolving numbers on the huge screen. A still – advertising one of Ramesh Uncle's many businesses – materialized, and the crowd roared in half-serious protest. The advertisements flashed by, each accompanied by a roar and the occasional curse from the third-class sections. Then the documentary news film – the final prelude to the feature film – came on, and suddenly the hall subsided into silence. Almost.

I do not recall all of the film. What I recall is this.

★

Manik is bubbling into his Coca-Cola bottle. He is muttering under his breath, doing a passable imitation of Papa when he does not like a film: terrible, he grumbles. Terrible. But Papa, who had started the show with similar muted remarks of criticism, has fallen silent, engrossed. I am closer to Manik's opinion. Not only is the film itself in black and white, with sudden jerky sequences, but the story has been progressing very slowly and the music sounds strange: thin, fluctuating and not as melodious as we are used to. Why are they singing like that, Mummy? Manik asks. Mummy hushes him and replies that was the way people sang in the past. Manik doesn't look convinced. He opens his mouth to say something more, and Mummy hands him a Cadbury's bar from her handbag. He accepts the chocolate, with a muttered, 'Terrible.'

By the time we get to the interval, the hero and the heroine have only just met. Well, they had met earlier – as occasional flashbacks inform us – when they were around Manik's age and sung a song or two, but then the hero's family had moved to a big city. The heroine had grown up in the village and was engaged to be married. But now the hero was back in the village and it appeared that he had remembered and looked for his childhood sweetheart all these years. The story confused me a bit, as I had assumed the hero always marries the heroine, but Mummy explained that in this film the hero finally realizes that he cannot marry the heroine and goes away, after saving the husband of the heroine or the heroine from some bad people or from drowning or something like that. It still seemed strange to me, like the music and the lack of colour.

Somewhere in the house, the baby has started crying. It is quickly soothed – the scholar can hear two women's voices – but the interruption appears to have disturbed the lady doctor. It has brought her back from the cinema. Her face changes subtly like a photo moved from shade to angled light, and her language registers the rhythms of daily life, of giving instructions to servants, changing nappies, shaking thermometers, writing prescriptions. She looks at her watch and when she looks up again at the scholar and continues her story, now seeing him once more, her narrative has returned firmly to the past tense.

The intermission was a relief. The doors were thrown open and people started shouting and talking again. The usher came back, this time with bottles of Fanta, which he opened with an expert pop and fizz. Manik and I insisted on going out for popcorn and, after an initial refusal, Mummy let the usher escort us to the floor below. It was full of people from the balcony sections, mostly smoking, talking or buying popcorn. Some college students near the popcorn machine were discussing the film in loud, public tones. They wanted to be overheard. No jaan, no dum, yaar, one of them said, shaking his head, no ras at all. No juice. Manik caught my eye and nodded in sage agreement. He put on the grave look of Papa disagreeing with some bit of political news: Terrible, he muttered.

We were still giggling when we returned to Papa and Mummy.

The lady doctor stops speaking. The call of the present brooks no delay: its message may be coded but the scholar understands, as does everyone else, that it is urgent. The dull thumping of the heart, the loud beating of time, which can only be borne because the present makes such small and insistent demands. Its tinny drumming drowns out the boom of eternity with the urgency of its petty commands: dinner, tea, salary check, appointment, shopping, borrowed book, letter to post . . .

The lady doctor goes inside to tell the servant to hurry up with the tea, taking the white towel with her. Sahib will be back any moment, jaldi karo, the scholar hears her say. Evening is falling, sharply. The mango tree outside casts a vague sense of its shadow onto the veranda. There are mosquitoes. The noise of traffic, never too much in this part of Phansa, has diminished still further. Small birds flit swiftly in the sky, darker jottings on slate. The scholar recalls a story that someone told him over a glass of whisky in a cold and narrow flat in a cold and narrow land many thousands of miles away. It was a story about a place not very far from here, about people not very distant from this young woman doctor, although she doesn't know it; the scholar has come here partly to tell her that story, and partly to hear her version of it. There are already three versions, or four, if the narrator is to be counted (and surely the narrator must count as a protagonist in every narrative?). He thinks about this, and feels more uncertain about his own role in this.

The ageing writer – in that cold and narrow country in the North – had spoken about a place not far from Phansa, a village called Anjangarh, perhaps not as far from here in kilometres as in years: for the year had been 1929. Anjangarh, he had said, and 1929.

'Do you know, my young scholar, that 1929 was the year we gave up our hopes of Home Rule? Following the British government's witch-hunt against communists, Marxists and trade-union leaders in that year, total independence became the only real option. By 1930, the sham legislatures were being boycotted even by moderate nationalists. The promise of Home Rule was exposed as the

carrot at the end of the Maxim gun. But at that time all this appeared to have little to do with the story that I am going to tell you, and if I see a connection today, the shadow of a connection between what happened to Hindustan and what happened to them, those various dreamers of one independent India, perhaps it is nothing but the meanderings of an old man's mind.'

I can see these words written in my Moleskine notebook. Strange, how he almost never referred to himself as anything other than an old man: only once did he call himself a writer.

Reef 11

Part II

Rasa Heroic

(24 January, 1948)

I am flying I am flying high over the second city of the
empire once the capital of British India I have never
been there but I am flying over it under this green wood
tree it exceeds the luminance of London on this particular night I know it is 1947 it is a few months ago it is
1947 this city I am flying over looks like one of those
schools of protozoan substances in the sea that light up
the water that I read about in school pinpoints of light
everywhere fusing into large patches of luminescence
patches of cloudy iridescence in the dark sea of India
not even London which I have not seen will not see
even London cannot rival it on this night which is a
night in the night of my night tonight then I start falling
from the skies falling into Calcutta and I notice that the
lights are mostly fires are from torches being carried by
screaming mobs flaming torches running across darkened alleys as if of their own volition and they fuse in
my dream in my sleep am I sleeping am I dreaming

under the green wood tree the torches fuse into the flare
of a hut or a house catching fire exploding simmering
exploding such beauty these are no electric lights such
terrible beauty is necessary says the Shakha head says
the Pramukh to me say I in my sleep if I am sleeping
necessary say I in my sleep to the villagers who will
follow me will follow me to terrible beauty but again
just as the fires pinpoint that man I know is a Muslim
a mullah I scream a Mussulman catch him kill him
I scream he runs through the dark alleys the torches
follow him he runs into a house and I scream in triumph
I urge the villagers on except that he is there again the
Sant the Shant of Shabarmati am I dreaming the Sant is
there in that room and he is saying he is saying shhh
shhh he is shaying I won't eat no I won't eat I won't
drink no I won't drink unless you promise me thish
man thish Muslim brother is shafe is shafe I laugh I
laugh but the people behind me the people holding the
torches I can now see they are not my villagers no they
are not my people the people with the torches and the
spears cast their spears down cast their torches down
and I am falling I am falling away from this city the
pinpoints of beauty receding extinguished I see Muslims
throwing their swords away I see Hindus throwing their
swords away I want to speak the word that will make
them stop the elusive word phrase that always eludes
me in my dreams if I am dreaming this casting away of

spears and swords this casting away of the possibility of action galloping action like a thoroughbred horse steaming the horse of my dreams the horse of the sacrifice not this not this shedding of weapons of manliness I see this in the land of heroes like Ram like Hanuman I weep at such cowardliness I weep at the beauty that will not be but I am falling away away from this city where the lights which were not lights are being extinguished one by one are falling into the pool of tears at the feet of the Sant the Shant the Sant of Sabarmati and I scream and I scream and I scream

The young man with the dented binoculars sits up abruptly on the charpoy, fully awake now, screaming silently.

The Panorama Box

*Face to face with Rizwan Hussain 'Batin', I took out my
notebook and ballpoint pen – always the diligent
researcher – but he did not pay them any attention. He
settled himself with infinite care on the sofa, carefully
pulling up his trousers by the crease before sitting down
and smoothing his shirt over his prominent pot belly.
There was just a touch of the prima donna to his gestures,
and it meshed badly with my image of him as a writer
and a Muslim who had, after all, chosen Pakistan, at
least for a few years. I tended to think of such Muslims as
Islamic, even though I knew from his writing that Batin
was not religious, and I associated Pakistanis, having met
only three or four who drove taxis or staffed corner shops
in Germany, with a certain roughness of gesture, an
element of mercenary coarseness.*

*Well, he said, after a pause. I guess you might as well
start asking your questions. We will be eating soon.*

*This confused me further, and I started to apologize for
arriving at the wrong time. He interrupted me: But of
course you are eating with us. We can continue the inter-*

view over dinner. I went through the motions of excusing myself, but he waved aside my hesitation. My wife has already cooked for three, he said. We do not waste food.

The subject closed, he returned to the reason for my visit: Go ahead, you wished to speak to me about films, didn't you?

About your years as a scriptwriter in Bombay: I am writing a PhD thesis on—

I remember, I remember: Bombay films around Independence. I am not yet senile, young man. Well, what is it you want to know?

Batin had by now seriously disconcerted me. I had come expecting a certain type of Urdu writer, a certain kind of Pakistani. But almost everything about Batin had run contrary to my subtle prejudices. For the rest of the evening, I decided to shelve my expectations and let him speak. The conversation, polite yet intimate, took us into the morning with only the occasional break to clear the table and brew tea or coffee from Nescafé packets. His wife didn't pay much attention to his anecdotes except to fill in the minor personal details that Batin tended to leave out – such as the profession of their two adopted children, who were both into computers somewhere in the USA – and went to bed around eleven. When she woke up at six thirty, we had just finished talking.

This is not good for you, she told her husband while bringing in the morning tea.

I haven't done this since I left Karachi, he said.

You haven't done this since you left Bombay, she replied, and that is why you are still alive.

Allow us old writers one last fling with Miss Vanity, woman, he retorted, stressing the word 'writers'. It was the only time he applied that word to himself.

She laughed, as if at a private joke.

An hour later, after joining them for their morning tea and biscuit, I left the elderly couple. The wife saw me off. Batin had already excused himself and retired; he was sleeping. Come back some day, she said, cryptically. He will love it.

I never went back. It is not that I forgot them, stranded – or so I thought then, slotting their past and present into my idea of it – in a place that refused to countenance the validity of their foreign memories, nor did I forget the stories Batin narrated that night. As the night grew darker and the wind rose outside, buffeting the highest branches of the trees which danced outside airtight windows as if in a film without sound, as the drizzle turned to powdery snow, Batin drank more slowly, his fingers quivering, from old age or the pressure of some remembered emotion, every time he reached out to grasp his glass or pour from the bottle. Stories crowded around him like the night, memories buffeted him like the wind. Stories were flutter-ing moths around the flickering candle of his memory. So many of them, all incomplete, interspersed with accounts of the picturization of the film songs – from Aakhri Raat mostly – he had composed, remarks about film technology or the rasa theory of classical Sanskrit literature or the history of barbed wire.

Indeed, the notes I took that night altered my consciousness of a time I thought I had studied and comprehended. And yet, copious as they were, there were such large gaps between the stories I'd jotted down that they could not be turned into anything scholarly. Some of these gaps I could fill with research; but still, my scribbles, like Batin's short stories, left one with a feeling of dissatisfaction, lack, incompleteness. They were not fated to contribute to orderly science, but perhaps, I thought over the years, art would find some use for them. What is art but the science of retrieval, of survival, of making sense, of making whole by telling a part of the story?

I read of Batin's death in a small Urdu literary magazine about three months after he had been buried – in a churchyard, the literary obituary mentioned with some venom, 'because Danish authorities and pressure groups have not allowed the construction of a Muslim graveyard even though Muslims are the nation's largest religious minority' (which made me chuckle – the thought of what Batin would have said about such indignation on his behalf) – and finally decided to fill the gaps in my

**notes, smooth the knots in the story he had told me. It
was a story that stretched across a lifetime and a subcontinent.**

Anjangarh was still, and so was the haweli, though the
sun was surprisingly strong and there were tiny heat
waves – rippling like water – near the horizon. Ashok
was sleeping, but Harihar was up, sitting cross-legged
on a reed mat. A long, narrow plank of wood, with two
spare stands for reels, lay in front of him. One bare foot
rested on the plank, roughly in the middle – toenails
cracked and grimed with dust – keeping it stable. He
moved the reel slowly in the slanted sunlight of the tent
opening, scanning the thin and dark pictures for the
flaw he had noticed last night. A roll of transparent
tissue, glue, a pair of scissors and a tin box of tools lay
to one side, neatly arranged like all his possessions.
Harihar's posture was that of someone spinning yarn on
a handloom or playing the sitar. His face was rapt.

Did you get some sleep? Durga asked, waking up
finally: she had returned when morning was about to
break. She fumbled about in her sari's fold and handed
him the twenty rupees that had been given to her by the
Chotte Thakur.

Some, he said, not looking up.

★

That evening there were as many viewers as the previous night but Harihar was unable to read aloud the subtitles. He tried and started coughing with the effort. Instead, Durga read them. Or rather, Harihar whispered them to her and she repeated them: she was illiterate; her mother had kept that one skill from all her daughters since, as she told them, it never gained me cash nor customer. So, Harihar whispered the Hindi subtitles – there were also subtitles in English, Urdu and Bangla – and, hands cupped around her mouth, Durga shouted them to the audience.

The Munshi was there again after the show to lead Durga, limping almost imperceptibly, through the same narrow door as before, across the watchful courtyard to the lighted room. Again there was the almost unheard cacophony of crickets from the fields; later, in the night, there was music. But the shadows of the haweli smothered the music, its walls rising stiffly against the slightly hoarse voice of a woman singing of unrequited love. The haweli was possessed by sadness; it hugged its sorrow and refused to open its window-eyes to the evidence of suffering across the fields and the ages. When the songs ended late that night, the surreptitious chirping of crickets regained the walls of the house, filled the fields around it like a flood.

Ashok, asleep with his left leg resting against Harihar,

heard this change in the quality of the night and woke to see nothing but a dark, star-stabbed sky outside the tent. He heard the laboured breathing of his father. He could see the hired man sleeping outside the entrance of the tent, under a small shelter. He fell asleep again before Durga got back.

What does a boy do when he grows up with images and movement? Ashok did not remember a home. And yet he could not forget it either, for his mother was possessed by the desire for one. For Durga that home represented the respectability – however spurious – of marriage and family, the possession of the different future that she associated with childbirth. It was a dream and, as such, did not have walls and windows. It did not have doors. But she still called it home, and that is the word she used in the stories she told Ashok.

Words are like shadows. They change shape. They grow. They lurk. Ashok would come to know that. But then he was too young to realize that his mother's word had changed shape in his mind. It had grown walls and sprouted windows. The doors through which they had passed for as long as Ashok could remember were doors he latched to that word, home. He wanted a home like the homes he saw, the homes he sometimes entered and invariably left. A home like the haveli or at least a home like one of the huts in the village.

Sometimes Ashok resented Harihar because he sensed that it was his father's dream that drove them from village to village, town to provincial town. Sometimes he ran playfully at his father and stabbed him with his wooden sword. Except that Ashok's face lost its playful look at the moment when he stabbed.

How was Durga to know that the home she had uttered as breath, a sound, a word, had turned into bricks for her small boy?

When Ashok first entered the haweli, he had been afraid of being shooed away. It had happened before: there was no space for him in other people's homes. And it almost happened on this occasion too. He inched past the studded door (the one he had tried to penetrate with a magic password on the first day), which had been left open for poultry to be driven in and out. Inside, there was a long damp passage, with yet more doors on both sides, leading to an expanse of light at the other end. Ashok inched towards the light at the other end, his back to one of the walls, hands brushing the cold plaster. He stepped out into the light and found himself in a large courtyard.

The courtyard formed a contrast to the cold and damp of the passageway. Bright, warm and dry, it was full of hushed sounds: a couple of men were threshing grain in a corner, there were people talking in a room upstairs, children playing, a hen with its yellowish brood, and, closer to him, two women grinding chilli. They had muffled their faces with the aanchal of their saris and were being supervised by a middle-aged woman, who reclined on a charpoy at a safe distance from the powdery fumes of the pounded chilli. Ashok was old enough to be able to tell – from the way she reclined and the way others deferred to her – that she was a person of importance in the haweli.

While he was contemplating this domestic scene, he felt a bony hand descend on his shoulders. The Munshi, who had emerged from one of the rooms in the passage-way, held him by the shoulder and peered at his face. Son of the bioscope-wallah, the Munshi muttered, and then raised his voice – What's your name, thief? What are you trying to steal, harami?

Even before Ashok could reply, he was slapped twice in the face. The slaps were largely theatrical, but Ashok was not expecting such sudden, rough handling and he started crying. The Munshi changed his grip to the scruff of Ashok's neck and started pushing him towards the passageway, abusing the boy's ancestors well into the ninth generation. Ashok, who did not know why he was being punished, tried to defend himself by answering the only question he could answer: My name is Ashok, he shouted.

Your name is Thief, scoffed the Munshi.

No, no, cried Ashok. He wanted to set this matter right. No, he shouted, my name is not Thief; my name is Ashok.

He twisted himself out of the Munshi's grip and ran to the matron on the charpoy. He did not know why he chose her. Perhaps because she appeared to be the only person who had the authority to stop the Munshi. My name is not Thief, he said to her. My name is Ashok.

The Munshi followed him, really angry now, swearing. But the woman raised an arm and silenced him. Then she turned to Ashok. What is it you said, boy? she asked.

Ashok stood sniffing.

What did you say your name was? She spoke firmly but kindly.

A-a-shok.

Ashok? she asked. As in Maharaja Ashok?

Ashok nodded.

The woman peered closely at him. Here, look at me, she commanded, tipping his face upwards with a finger. Poor boy, she said. Then as the Munshi started to speak, she added, sharply, Really, Munshiji, where was the need to terrorize this boy?

But, Maalkini sahiba, said the Munshi, all these boys are thieves: no home, no address, you cannot trust—

She silenced him with the same gesture she had used

the first time: a slight wave of the hand. That is enough, Munshiji, she said. We have allowed this boy to play here. He can come whenever he wants.

Then she got up and moved heavily towards the passageway. She turned once and looked at the boy. How strange, she said, Ashok ... and just as old, the same eyes ...

Ashok had the light grey eyes of his mother. But that is not what the woman was thinking of. She was thinking of a time fourteen years ago, when they had returned from the monsoon-swelled river carrying that which she had recognized even before she saw it clearly. Or she was thinking of a time before that, when she had lain on one of the beds in the side rooms of the first floor, clutching first the pillow and then the bed rods, trying not to scream – for the men were sitting just outside the room – bewildered that something she had been told was so natural could prove so difficult and so painful. But when the boy had been born and laid, hastily wiped, on her breast, the old village midwife had cracked her bony fingers on the sides of her temple and said: God be praised, a boy. You were lucky, Chotti Maalkini, a boy – and such an easy birth. You are blessed.

Later, they had made much of him: his lusty bawling, his light complexion, his grey eyes. My grandfather had grey eyes, her husband had told her, holding the infant tentatively, palms cupped and outstretched, as if receiving a prasad from the temple priest. And the temple priest had been called, pujas performed, all the rituals observed. Readings of the sacred texts had been ordered, even her husband taking out the family Mahabharata, a hand-written, gold-edged edition in Farsi translation, and reading a few pages from the Gita in his stumbling Farsi, a language the family was shedding like a discarded snakeskin.

At the back of their minds throughout was the curse. It was a curse that settled on the family every second generation, they said, muffling the walls of the haveli, enveloping it in a gloom that was palpable even to passers-by. Every second generation, it was said, the family produced no male heir. It had happened to her husband's grandfather, who had three daughters and no son; her husband's father had been adopted: he was the second son of his grandfather's brother.

And the curse had appeared to have struck her too, so when the boy was born after two girls, it was a matter of surprise and even more rejoicing than usual. And they took all the precautions they could – fed the poor of twelve villages around them, gave lavish donations to all the priests of all the temples in the neighbourhood, sent gifts to nearby Dargahs and mosques – and yet the curse struck. It struck, after seven years, when they had forgotten about it.

It struck like the early monsoon torrents, unexpected, interrupting a journey that many of the village men and children had undertaken to a fair eight kilometres away. In retrospect, all of them blamed themselves for not staying back. They blamed themselves for forgetting the story of the curse. They blamed themselves for taking life for granted. But what use is knowledge in retrospect? It is easier to talk of fate.

When she saw them bearing him in, bundled up in white cloth, she was reminded of how he had been given to her as a new-born baby, wrapped in a white blanket, wet and puckered up, yet beautiful beyond anything she could have imagined. He was wet again; his hair, when she held him, was encrusted with sand and weeds from the river. Outside, the monsoon rain had recommenced, a waterfall from the skies, raindrops hitting the walls and roofs of the haweli with the force of bullets, splattering the swollen, water-filled roads and alleys, fields and courtyard until everything outside was an expanse of liquid grey, broken by a wall or a tree here and there. All the land was possessed, the trees whirling like Dervishes.

They had come wading through the water, ten or twelve men, her husband carrying the dead child. They had walked into the haweli without wiping their feet, rainwater dripping from them. Those who had dived, braving the flooded river, had mud and grass and straw on their clothes and in their hair. They laid the dripping bundle on the Kashmiri carpet.

And all she had been able to do was to wipe his wet face with the aanchal of her sari, whispering his name: Ashok, Ashok, Ashok.

'Don't underestimate the materiality of the mind, young man,' Batin said, in the faintly argumentative tone that would creep into his voice once in a while, and then as suddenly vanish. 'Think of the connections the mind makes. I know you are a scholar of cinema, but I will tell you a secret about motion films. They do not happen in the projector or on the screen in front of you. They are happening in your head. Your eye connects the thousands of still photographs; your eye makes them move. Your mind turns the figures the right way up. No one knows why it does so. No one. But it does. You see, there is a lot in common between the magical darkness inside our skulls in which dreams fester and memories ripen, and the magical darkness of film theatres.'

Their days and nights had fallen into a pattern. Durga would return around two in the night and sleep until nine, by which time Harihar and the village would have been up for at least a couple of hours. During the show in the evening, she would read out the subtitles, whispered to her by Harihar. The villager they had hired at a rupee a day had been taught to crank the handle of the projector. He still could not join the reels, though.

(They had long since given up all hope of seeing old Mehto again, their curiosity occasionally exercised by the question of his fate: whether their Raleigh cycle had been sold to pay for an extended stay in the palm-frond toddy joints that he frequented across the land, or whether the cycle had been taken from him and Mehto left in a trough somewhere, not drunk but dead.)

Durga no longer played or sang for the show. She saved that for later. Watched by the younger Thakur, slowly sipping his wine, speaking very little except to ask her whether she knew this tune or the other, following her with large, slightly kohled eyes . . .

He was a strange man. Not much older than her, perhaps even younger: it was hard to say, he had such a gravity of demeanour, such self-possession. Unlike most of the men in the haweli – including the bearded elder brother who ruled over them from inside the haweli and who was evidently more of a father than a sibling to the younger Thakur – he was clean-shaven and even late in the evening there was no telltale blueish shadow on his chin, just a small mole, almost like a beauty spot.

But when she mentioned this to Harihar, Harihar only looked at her, strangely. Later, he shouted angrily at Ashok for some small fault of the boy and Ashok, not used to being scolded by his pitaji, took refuge in her lap, crying.

She could sense, for the first time, a current of jealousy under the surface of their relationship. Harihar suspected she was not telling him everything. He had grounds for his suspicion: she was *not* telling him everything. How could she tell him that late on the second night, as she was singing a thumri, the young Thakur had stood and, without a word of warning, launched into a skilful dance? How could she tell Harihar that the Chotte Thakur had put on a pair of ghungroos and danced every night after that, while she played and sang and, increasingly, instructed? (For though she had been born with one leg slightly shorter than the other, she had been trained to dance and could, while dancing, erase her slight limp in the rhythm of movements.)

How could she tell Harihar that the younger son of the Thakur family saw her more as an ustad, a teacher, that he asked her to demonstrate mudras he could not perform? How could she tell Harihar all this without making a mockery of the confidence that the Chotte Thakur had placed in her?

'I can see, young man, that you do not understand how any of them could have revealed something like that to a man they met

years later, in another place. But they did. I had that capacity to draw out the stories of others. All of them. It was a burden. I had to keep their stories out of my stories. I felt I owed them that. I owed it to myself and the people around me. Perhaps I was old fashioned; perhaps I was not enough of a writer to stop caring. That is what Saadat Hasan Manto told me once. You are not inhuman enough to be a great writer, he said. You have the talent, but not the remorselessness. I didn't know then what he had in mind. Until 1955, I did not even know, or understand – in spite of his growing drunkenness – what an effort his remorselessness was for Manto. But that, young man, is another story.'

Chotte Thakur sensed his brother knew of the nights and suspected he did not approve of the arrangement. His brother – Chotte Thakur had always called him Bhaisahab – was deeply religious, though attracted more to the reformative Brahmo Samaj than to local versions of Brahminical orthodoxy. Never having been sent to Calcutta or anywhere else for his education, Bhaisahab had reached his thirties in the shadow of their father. It was a heavy shadow, for their father had been a big man, so big that the title applied to him by the villagers – Raja Sahib – was not claimed by either of his sons, even after the man himself had succumbed to heat stroke, having insisted on inspecting some fields in the middle of June a few years ago, or almost two years from the day when his bloated, incensed face had torn through the curtain calls of his younger son's amateur theatre company in Calcutta, had pulled down the curtain on his son's education at Hindu College.

When Chotte Thakur had returned to the haweli (with the ignominy of his theatrical associations flying ahead of him like the banner that his father's pet henchman would carry on a pole through the villages to herald them) and to occasional beatings and whippings and a blanket ban on music of any kind, his mother had refused to come to his aid. But Bhaisahab had. Bhaisahab had put on weight in the intervening years and seemed to be more his father's twin than his eldest son; they even spoke the same kind of language, an old-fashioned Urdu that the rest of the extended family was discarding in favour of Sanskritized or Anglicized Hindi. But there was a world of difference between the two men. Bhaisahab never raised his voice, not even when he was angry. And though his father had the sharper look, his large eyes gleaming with perception, and Bhaisahab had inherited his mother's placidity and bifocals, Chotte Thakur knew it was a mistake to consider Bhaisahab slow or unperceptive. Years of working as his father's unpaid private secretary had ensured Bhaisahab knew all about not only their inherited lands and revenues but also legal or official matters in general. His father, in spite of his physical violence and bluster,

depended on other people – people like the Munshi –
to run his affairs. Bhaisahab simply humoured such
people; he could manage on his own, if necessary.

Bhaisahab, and to some extent Bhabhi, the Chotti
Maalkini, who was circumscribed by her position as
daughter-in-law, had come to Chotte Thakur's aid, once
even wrenching a whip from his father's hands. But
their mother had stayed silent, as if atoning for the fact
that she and Bhaisahab had talked Raja Sahib into sending Chotte Thakur to a Calcutta college. Not once had
she embraced him as she would when he was a child,
not once had she consoled him. She had stood there
like a person turned to stone, only occasionally wincing
when his father turned to her and roared, This is what
comes from listening to women: you and your Kulkutta,
you and your Bombaywali Mausi have turned my son
into a dancing-prancing-cooking eunuch! Even after his
father died, she had kept away from him, largely staying
in her room, reading from her Bhagwad Gita, served by
the two now-old crones she had brought into the house
from her parents' when she got married.

No, Chotte Thakur had no doubt that his brother
knew about the wife of the bioscope-wallah. Bhaisahab,
though he seldom left the haveli after the death of his
son, knew more about what was happening around him
than most people assumed. And, anyway, the devious
Munshi would have informed him. Would his brother

take it up with him one day? Or had he decided to ignore it, having long given up his attempts to arrange a marriage for his younger brother? Had he decided to ignore it just as he had ignored the music coming from his younger brother's room just one day after their father's shraddh funeral ceremony?

The house had been reverberating with silence, emptied of the old man's shouts, curses and beatings. Chotte Thakur had taken the gramophone and the records out from the cupboard where he had hidden them, afraid that his father would wreck them in one of his rages. He had wiped the dust off his gramophone and installed it. He had inserted a needle, put on a record and turned the handle. The gaping mouth of the gramophone had filled with a thin sound. It had grown fuller and filled the room. But it had echoed hollowly in his rejoicing, bewildered heart. Then suddenly, riding home one day, he had seen the crowd at the gate, the woman clutching the Munshi's leg and the cart in the field, and he had felt the music swell in his heart, each note fall like rain on the parched soil of his desires.

Four nights in a row she had been called to the haweli. Harihar had been pleased the first night, had not minded too much the second night. But tonight he was irritable. It was typical of rich people to imagine they could take liberties with people like him. And people like her.

Harihar felt the irritation growing into a bitter taste in his mouth. He stood at the opening of the tent and spat into the trodden grass, the scraped earth and fine pebbles.

His irritation sharpened his senses, made him work more energetically than usual, putting away the chairs and benches and pulling out the charpoys they slept on. The hired man had gone back to the village after the show that evening. One of his children was ill, he had claimed, and it was a claim that Harihar had to pretend to accept.

Everyone appeared to have somewhere to go in this village. Durga went to the room to do God knows what for the Chotte Thakur. The hired man probably lay under the palm-leaf shelter of some toddy-joint on the outskirts of the village. Even Ashok, now sleeping in the tent, had been fetched earlier on with a peremptory summons: Maalkini wants him. As if he was a piece of property, a dish being passed around a table. At least twice in the last two days, Harihar had heard that summons and had been surprised, pleased, irritated by it in turn, as with Durga's visits.

The tent was like a balloon. He could anatomize its smells: sweat, dungcake and bidi-smoke, stale trapped air, just the faintest trace of incense. Suddenly, he could not bear it any more and rushed out. Being outside did not help: the breeze bore the smell of recent cooking from the haweli and the village, or so he imagined. Everywhere the pure draft of possibilities appeared polluted with the smoke of human intention.

It was a moonless light. Harihar could not see into the fields. The play of images that the camera of the sun had cast on the screen of the heavens was no longer there to orient Harihar: he could be anywhere. He could be nowhere. The one lantern still burning in the tent could not give him sight. It was like his projector still standing in the middle of the tent: indifferent to all that existed around him, against him. He felt dizzy, weak with the recurring illness that had plagued him for weeks. As he walked back into the tent in the half-light of a single lantern, he stumbled against a folded chair and fell heavily.

Don't call us Maalkini, she had said the second time she saw him. Ashok had been playing outside the walls of the haweli – too frightened of the Munshi to breach them – when a maidservant had emerged and beckoned him to follow. She was sitting on the same charpoy in more or less the same position in the courtyard, an older woman putting oil into her thin hair, massaging it onto her scalp. She had spoken to him lying there, occasionally interrupting herself or him to instruct a servant. (There were people working all around her in the courtyard. Doing things in a strangely hushed manner, speaking in low tones, grinding carefully, washing clothes, drawing water from the well without letting the bucket drop sharply.) She had asked him what he could remember of his past, the surname and caste of his father – the answers to which seemed to have pleased her. She had been surprised by the fact that he had not met any of his mother's relations. She referred to him by his name, pronouncing it with care – unlike most other houses where they simply called him ladka or chokkra (if they did not employ the more colourful epithets used by the Munshi) – and she referred to herself in the royal plural: we. Her sentences were always formal, fully formed. We want you to tell us this. We want you to explain that. And then after about an hour of such conversation, she had said in response to one of his answers: Don't call us Maalkini. All children here call us Badi Ma.

Ashok knew by now that the children of her extended family called her Badi Ma but had not heard any of the children of servants calling her that and doubted that children from outside her family would dare claim the intimacy of referring to her as their 'elder mother'. He hesitated.

But I have a Ma, he replied, finally.

She smiled, patiently, perhaps even sadly.

She is your Chotti Ma. From now on we are your Badi Ma.

Then she rose from her squatting position and put her heavy legs on the ground. For the second time she touched Ashok, again turning his face up but this time by holding his chin between thumb and forefinger.

The same eyes, she said, the very same eyes.

'Eyes. What do they see? How do they see? What is it in us that knows in advance, so that an inverted image is righted in the mind, so that we grasp the kettle by the handle, we see people walking on their legs and not on their heads?'

Ashok had been called into the courtyard a number of times, but this time he was invited to watch the show of a passing Bahuroopiya in the actual haweli. He entered one of the rooms of the haweli, the first room to the right of the main door; it was more hall than room, used as a baithak by the male members of the family. But today it had been taken over by the women and the children. It was a damp, dark room, with a high, heavy-beamed ceiling. It was vaguely illuminated by light from the four narrow windows on one side. No lantern had been lit.

Charpoys and chairs had been amassed, mats and gotakiyas spread around the room. At one end three charpoys were arranged in a crude semicircle, standing vertically on their narrow sides, just high enough to hide a man, and draped with dark cloth by the Bahuroopiya, who was at that moment rummaging through a trunk behind the screen. He was dressed like a magician, replete with a flowing black beard, false but impressive.

Once the room had filled sufficiently, the Bahuroo-piya took out a dungaroo and played an intricate quick-silver roll of beats on it. Then he launched into his act, frequently disappearing behind the charpoys, sometimes – it appeared to Ashok – for less than a couple of seconds, only to reappear as another person, with another voice: magician changed to old man, old man hobbled off to the screen and suddenly Hanuman – half monkey, half god – jumped out, gibbering, snapping at the women servants and sending them scuttling with shrieks and giggles. He turned from man to woman to eunuch, from the wise Raja Harishchandra to a bear to a frightening rakshasa. He became a Babu businessman and an English officer with a cane and, suddenly, a half-naked toddy-tapper. As a moustachioed dacoit, he chased the small children in one corner of the room; as a topee-wearing policeman, he asked the Maalkini for bakshish. In less than an hour, the Bahuroopiya had become so many people and beings, assumed so many voices and faces, that Ashok was alarmed.

The other children were also frightened, but only when he assumed a frightening disguise and made a horrible noise. Ashok was frightened by the Bahuroo-piya's ability to assume such mercurial personas. He reminded Ashok of his own father reading out subtitles. There was something disturbing about that ability to be so many people. More so, in the case of the Bahuroopiya, for Harihar had a voice he returned to after the film shows. But with the Bahuroopiya, Ashok could not be certain of any core identity. He came as a magician; he left as a king. In between, he was so many people that Ashok could not tell who he really was.

After the show, as the Bahuroopiya went around collecting tips, Ashok plucked up his courage and put one question to this changeable, mythic being. Where do you live? Ashok asked. The Bahuroopiya, dressed now as a king, gave a booming, royal laugh. Little boy, clever little boy, he replied. I live wherever there are children like you; I go from village to village for the pleasure of good little boys like you.

Ashok had feared the Bahuroopiya's answer. It confirmed his suspicion: people who have too many faces and too many voices do not have a home.

Harihar picked himself up. His elbow was bleeding. He felt groggy, his head heavy with the weight of something immense, shapeless and liquid. His vision seemed to darken to a colour that was not black but all colours together and no colour at all – like the times when Ashok mixed colour into colour from his treasured watercolour box until he had obtained something indefinably dark.

Harihar groped his way to where Ashok was sleeping, wrapped in a chaddar, exhausted from the Bahuroopiya's show earlier that day. Ashok turned in his sleep and murmured something that sounded like, What is he now? What is he now?

'Like dreams, films are a happening in the head, young man.'

The Chotte Thakur had just started putting on his dancing bracelets when there was a commotion outside the room. Someone beat a frenzied tattoo on the half-latched door. The Thakur took the bracelets off and flung them in Durga's direction just as the Munshi burst in. He apologized profusely to the younger Thakur and added, But I had to come, huzoor. Her son is knocking at the gate. He says her husband needs help.

Harihar was delirious by the time Durga got there. He was running a high temperature, murmuring about coins and colours.

She had run to the tent, holding Ashok by one hand, dragging him along, her sari hitched up, and had not noticed Chotte Thakur following at a slower pace along with some servants. She was surprised when she finally registered his presence. The Thakur took over, ordering Harihar to be carried into a vacant room in the servants' quarters of the haweli, sending for the village hakim and deputizing one of his servants to sleep in the tent and watch over their possessions. Durga was grateful for such kindness: this was not what she had been told about people like him.

Two days later, Harihar was looking better than he had for weeks. Food from the haweli's kitchens and no pressures of running the show had restored him to some vigour. He was talking about moving on. Durga, for once, was not certain. Her nights of music and secret dance-instructions were still fetching her as much as most of Harihar's shows did. Ashok was happy, pampered by the Maalkini, and even Harihar was now better than he had been. She wanted to ask him to stay a few more days, to wait as long as the Chotte Thakur required her – except that she could not say that to him without confirming his (mistaken) suspicions about what the younger Thakur did with her every night. She was figuring out the best way to phrase her request when, suddenly, the Munshi came out of the haweli, and behind him five or six of his henchmen dragging a village youth. Durga and Harihar had seen the youth; he was one of the part-time village workers employed by the haweli, a man who – in dress and language – appeared to be more educated than most of the other servants. Now, as they watched, the Munshi had the youth's legs and hands tied to a post in the middle of the courtyard. The youth was weeping and calling out, Mai-baap, I won't do it again, Let me go, mai-baap, I won't do it again.

Some other servants and family members came out to watch.

The Chotte Thakur was the last person to come out. He was wearing his riding dress and carrying a whip, longer and thicker than the one he used for riding.

He lifted his arm and whirled the whip in the air, expertly, like a lion tamer. The courtyard reverberated with the sound, like the crack of thunder, and the hens and ducks scuttled away. Then he stepped closer to the tied youth and lifted the whip again. This time he brought it down on the naked back of the youth. The man knew how to use the lash. He whipped the youth five times, flaying skin and flesh from his back with every blow. Each stripe took a second filling with blood, as if flesh was surprised and needed a moment to find the appropriate response. After five lashes he stopped and said in a high but impassive voice: This was for stealing. Then he whipped the boy three more times and added, That was for lying.

Tossing the whip to one of the henchmen, in exactly the same way he threw his riding whip to someone at the gates after his daily ride – there was something theatrical about the gesture – the younger Thakur went back into the haweli. The Munshi, hunched low, a scuttling crab of venom, spat in the dust and followed him. After both had left, the servants' faces changed from that of moralistic condemnation to expressions of sympathy and camaraderie. They untied the youth and an old woman applied some crude salve to his wounds, asking him as she did so, What's the use of reading for the likes of us? What can we get out of it but trouble? And a book like that! Even I have heard of it. I told you, I told you not to read books like *Bandi Jiwan*, that bastard Munshi would find some way of punishing you. If he could not get you whipped for reading the book, he will get you whipped for something else. I told you.

It was a reference that Durga did not understand, but she realized that theft was not what was being discussed.

It was then that Durga remembered Ashok, who must have witnessed the brutal scene. She looked around for him, but Harihar had already taken him into their room and must have done so as soon as the whipping began. When she found the two of them, Harihar looked at her pointedly and then looked away. Durga realized there was no longer any way she could object to his plans. They would have to leave.

That night the Thakur did not call her to sing for him. The night sounded strange to Durga's ears, so used had she become to her own music and the jingle-jangle of

the Thakur's bracelets. She heard the crickets again –
their ceaseless music filled the fields and the mansion –
and had trouble sleeping. Harihar, lying with his back to
her, was also restless. Only Ashok slept soundly, tired
out with playing all day, full of the rich food and sweets
that the Maalkini fed him almost every mealtime now.
He hardly ever ate with Durga and Harihar, she had
even overheard the servants gossiping about how the
Maalkini would feed him with her own hands at times.

He insisted on calling her Badi Ma. Badi Ma! This
was a matter of some resentment to Durga, but she had
tried to hide this from Ashok, for she was – uncon-
sciously at times – shading him from the shadow of her
own mother. Her mother had been jealously possessive
of her children, including the ones she brought – or
rather bought – into the brothel. In her own way, she
was committed to their well-being, but she could only
imagine them as wanting what she herself wanted for
them. She would possess not only their bodies but also
their thoughts, their likes and dislikes, hopes and aspirations, dreams and nightmares, all in the genuine
conviction of wanting only the best for them. This
experience of parental love, 'ma-baap ka pyaar' as her
mother called it, had determined Durga's relationship
with her own son, a relationship in which she refrained
from preventing anything that might be good for Ashok.
And hence, she simply pursed her lips whenever he

shouted 'Badi Ma has called me' and ran off to the haweli.

Most of the rooms of the haweli frightened Ashok. They were hung with the hides and heads of animals: snarling tigers, glazed-looking deer, even a lion head, fangs bared, lips pulled back, emitting a silent roar. There were swords and studded shields, spears and daggers, muskets and guns on the walls. And outside the Bade Thakur's room, which Ashok had never entered, there stood a four-foot bear, stuffed.

It was only in Badi Ma's rooms that Ashok felt completely safe. There was no trace of an animal in her rooms, or that entire wing, which contained the rooms of the women. Once he pulled aside the bamboo curtain and entered that space, Ashok entered another world. The furniture was lower and less alien. Even the script on the calendars and books changed from Arabo-Persian and Firangi to Devanagari, which was the only script Ashok could decipher – he knew it as Hindustani – and this partial legibility was also reassuring. There was an occasional portrait of a god or goddess Ashok could recognize, and the smell of cooking. Not all servants could enter this section. They had to be of the Brahmin or Kshatriya castes. The Munshi never walked in; his position was usurped by the Brahmin head cook, a small, fat man, with dimpled cheeks, many chins and the voice of a woman, who would doze off if left alone for more than ten minutes: he was very different from the eagle-eyed, bony-handed and abusive Munshi.

In the cool shadows of this section, Ashok felt for the first time the kind of security he had always associated with the word 'home'. It was this – apart from the prestige – that made him want to call Maalkini 'Badi Ma', even though he could sense that his own Ma, Durga, did not approve of it. Or did he recognize, with instinctive empathy, the child-shaped vacuum left in the home of Badi Ma and Bade Thakur by the drowning of their son eight years ago, and the refusal of the younger Thakur to get married?

It is time to thank the Thakur sahibs and tell them we will be leaving. This was the first thing Harihar said on waking up the next morning.

Since moving to the courtyard, they had gotten used to waking up late and it was well after eight. The first glimmerings of life – the shivering flocks of sparrows, the servants brushing with datwan-twigs, the muffled collecting of water for ablution and cooking – had long given way to a more robust rhythm. (By seven thirty or so, the members of the Thakur family were also up, and the activities in the courtyard gained a decibel or two even as servants lost the fear of waking their masters.) Nevertheless, the scene still presented a strangely muted look to Durga and the only time the place lost this look was when the Maalkini came out: she would emerge around eight or so. For the next four or five hours the courtyard would fill with the bustle of daily chores, as the Maalkini sat on a charpoy and instructed. Sometimes she would be joined by guests from the villages and other women of the extended family. Tea would be constantly brewed in a huge, blackened kettle (referred to as Katlu Khan), on an open fire in a corner of the courtyard, tended by the oldest woman living in the courtyard, Miriasin Maiya, who appeared to have only that one chore.

Maalkini would retire to the haveli around noon – probably earlier in midsummer and later during the winter, Durga thought – and after that the activities in the courtyard would become more and more muted once more until, just before the godhuli hours of dusk, they would subside into a mournful, hazy silence, pierced by the ineffective rays of the first lanterns being lighted.

The senior Thakur hardly ever entered the courtyard. Around the time the Maalkini appeared, he would descend the steps and walk into the hall near the door. This was the baithak room and here, for the next three or four hours, the Bade Thakur listened to complaints from villagers, dispensed a rough justice to those who came to him (rather than the British courts in town or the village panchayat) to settle minor disputes and received guests. He was always surrounded by at least a dozen men, nodding their heads in absolute agreement. The younger Thakur was sometimes called in to join a discussion or implement a decision, but much of the time he was either out riding or in his rooms, listening to the gramophone or the radio.

When Harihar walked into the baithak room that morning and – after respectfully sitting around for an hour or so – asked for the Chotte Thakur, he was directed to the stairs on the left. He sent a message to the younger Thakur through one of the servants and was called up after about half an hour. Durga, watching this from the courtyard, expected him to reappear in a few minutes, but the time ticked away and there was no sign of Harihar. The baithak disbanded, the Bade Thakur went up the stairs, lunch was carried in from the kitchen in brass trays, a sunny silence fell on the courtyard – broken only by the occasional pigeon or crow – and still Harihar did not come down the stairs.

The afternoon deepened with summer warmth. The sunlight reflected off the puddles of water next to the well, attracting the odd mynah or sparrows, their throats throbbing. A kundoo – the golden oriole – flew down from the courtyard wall, frightened by this proximity to people, but beak open, drawn by the water. It drank hurriedly and flew off – a streak of yellow and black. As Durga sat there, waiting for Harihar – and for Ashok, who was also somewhere in the haweli – she heard the bird's rich mellow whistle: pe-lo, pe-lo. Drink it up, drink it up, it was crying to other kundoos.

The sun had started sinking in the west, and both birds and people were out again in the courtyard – the growing bustle in the yard had somehow made the haweli seem even more silent and sinister to Durga – before Harihar emerged from the haweli.

Durga hurried up to Harihar, but he had an absorbed, far-away look on his face. Before she could formulate her worries into queries, he said: A great man, the Chotte Thakur. So knowledgeable. And what a collection! What a collection!

He shook his head in bemusement and smiled for the first time in many days.

'Was it then that they started planning, the man who had followed his dream across hundreds of miles and the man who sought to distract himself from the reality of his own self with whips and ghungroos, riding and dancing? Was it then, when for a while they felt they shared the same desire? Or was it later? They never told me. But surely they must have discussed it, planned it, spoken at least to Maalkini and Bade Thakur in due course? Or did all of it – even that sinister bargain – did all of it fall into place naturally, like a tree fills with fruit, because the time was right, the place was right?'

★

Durga would have left the haweli then, yes, she would, for she felt its walls encroaching upon her life; its broad, cool walls represented everything she associated with home, and she could feel that this security, this solidity had started coming between her and those close to her. Not only Ashok, but also Harihar who, having long been separated from her by their diverging desires, had finally found someone who shared his desire, his love of films. But now it was Harihar who refused to leave.

He showed no inclination of renewing the evening bioscope shows. The equipment remained under its tarpaulin cover. Instead, he spent much of each day with Chotte Thakur, while Durga waited for both her husband and her son to return from the haweli every evening: the one singing the praise of Chotte Thakur and the other glowing with the love of Maalkini, or Badi Ma as he insisted on calling her. All through the deepening afternoons, she sat in their room in the servants' quarters and waited. She was not accepted by the other servants. They sensed in her a kind of foreignness, or they were wary of the strange relationships that her presence had introduced into the haweli. They did not know what relationship she had to the Chotte Thakur, and she knew they gossiped about the evenings she was called to play to the Thakur, still unaccompanied by Harihar. They could not tell what her status was: servant or visitor, dependant or guest, prostitute or performer? When she entered any of their gatherings, they fell silent. When she spoke to them, they switched to polite forms of address. And so she waited, as she had waited once in her mother's kotha for customers, she waited for the return of the intimate strangers that Harihar and Ashok were becoming to her.

Harihar was building a 'panorama box' with the Chotte Thakur. They had sent for material from Gaya and Phansa. It was meant to be a present for Ashok on his birthday, but Durga sensed it was more than that: it was a way for the two men to meet. There were too many differences between them – of class and age, position and personality – for them to meet naturally; they needed an excuse to talk about that which had made them seek one another. Their tongues were free only when their hands were busy. In the process of assembling and angling, hammering and adjusting they assembled a dream from which, Durga felt, she was excluded. But that was not really true. The dream included her – Harihar would come back and talk about it every evening – but in a certain capacity; she was necessary for their stage but in the same way as a central prop is necessary to a set. It would all revolve around her, but she could not move.

Durga could not express it in so many words, but she was disturbed and intrigued by the two men's persistence. It intrigued and disturbed her because she, in her own way, was just as persistent. She had through all these years of travel retained her vision of home: that desire to be respectable and housed. It drove her just as his dreams drove Harihar. And like Harihar, Durga had been close to despair too; she had come to suspect the only home permitted her would be the mansion of Harihar's dreams, that insubstantial, many-roomed house. And that was one reason she had not called Ashok away from the haveli, for what had she to offer him instead?

But Harihar's retention of images and ideas glimpsed in talk and book, experience and dream was a more delicate flower than Durga realized. It was easily bruised. It needed to be nourished by other dreams. Like a stream it needed to seek out similar streams before it could turn into a torrent and defy the terrain. It had finally found one such stream in the hidden shrubbery of the Chotte Thakur's desires and despair, those once rich patches of green that had been twisted and withered by a father's scorn and a mother's silence.

'Strange, isn't it, young man, how we are brought up to believe that sameness is good? If you want the same as I do, surely we will get along. What can be better than that? But it isn't true. If different desires create friction, so does desiring the same thing.

How can you desire the same thing and not come to blows over it?'

And so the torrent of one desire and different talents was poured into the construction of a box-like instrument for a boy who, it appeared, had no need for such play of shadows. Ashok had discovered a world so real to him that he had started believing in it: Durga shuddered at the thought of the day when this world would be taken away from him at a word from the Maalkini or the Bade Thakur. For surely, he did not belong there. Surely, he could not.

But in the meantime the box continued to grow. It swelled with images; it filled with darkness and light. When they finally unveiled it – to Ashok's rather uninterested gaze – it had become something else, their original plan of making a 'panorama box' having metamorphosed several times into the final reality of a picture-holder attached to a magic lantern. It was a large and heavy twin box, constructed partly by the village carpenter, with an aperture on one side and a reflector centred on a candle on the other. There were slits and slideways and two switches, a series of still pictures – depicting a woman threshing grain – which could be arranged and exhibited sequentially with the help of the slideways, creating the fluid motion of a woman threshing grain, projected onto the screen of a bedsheet by the means of the light source and a system of lenses in the magic lantern.

Harihar explained all this to the gathering in the courtyard – even the Bade Thakur was there – and gave the gadget the name of their original intention 'panorama baksa'. There were exclamations of surprise and admiration. Only Ashok looked unimpressed.

Aren't you happy with your present? the Maalkini asked him.

He shook his head, unhappy and noncommittal.

What is wrong with it? asked Harihar. Don't you like it?

Ashok did not say anything.

Harihar was irritated. We did it all for your sake, and you . . .

Oh, he is just tired. The Maalkini came to Ashok's defence.

Then Ashok spoke.

I don't like it, he burst out. It is just a trick.

'The camera, Director Hari Babu once told me, quoting from one of those lectures by foreign film-makers that he would attend with ritualistic diligence, is an enchanted box: it can photograph thought. Would it have photographed the thoughts that crossed that homeless young boy's mind at that moment? Or the thoughts that must have crossed his mother's mind, desperate as she was

for anchorage in a fluid world? Who knows: years later she would give me that story. It was one of the very few she ever recounted about her past. And she only did so in a moment of distress, of upheaval and resilting. She did so to justify her past, his past, their present. She did so to learn to belong in a different way. But all that, of course, was sometime in the future. We will come to it. The future is just as difficult to escape as the past.'

The next morning the haweli covered its eyes. Summer had arrived. Tightly woven carpets of fragrant khus – which the servants called khus ki tatti – were put up against all the windows and some of the doors on the ground floor. An army of servants was deputed to draw water from the well and toss it at the khus every hour or so during the afternoon. The Thakur family now started living downstairs for much of the day, and Ashok hardly ever left the haweli. It is too hot outside, he said in explanation, as if he had not wandered from village to village with his parents' travelling bioscope during most of the summers of his young life.

The mango trees outside the haweli had burst into clusters of yellow buds, like spots of sunlight bunched together, while the sun beat on the roofs with something of a physical presence. From outside came the shriek of the first loo of the year. It sounded like a woman wailing.

A small bird dropped dead in front of Durga the next afternoon.

And then Harihar came with the offer. (Or not an offer at all, because it had already been decided between the Maalkini and her husband, between Chotte Thakur and Harihar; and even though it appeared natural at the time – and such a piece of luck for them – Durga was to learn, years later, that it had been, like almost everything else, artificial and arranged. But she was still young then and had not fully realized the extent to which life can be artificial.)

Years later, when finally aware of the extent of Harihar's deception, she had blamed him, accused him not just of weakness but of premeditated evil. Later even that vehement condemnation had crumbled away and she had come to see her own culpability, her own responsibility, as well as the ways in which Harihar and Chotte Thakur were blind to all but their dreams, dreams that held each other and bickered and fought and grappled and kissed like two illicit lovers. But that was all in the future, which at that moment was darker than the nights that fell on Anjangarh. At that moment, all she had was the offer – and a feeling that she could not say no. How had Maalkini put it? A mother's sacrifice? A mother's sacrifice, she had said, handing Durga a paan. And she had added in her elaborate manner, We who have wombs are used to sacrifices, sister.

The rest of it was simple. All Durga had to do was

to lie about her past. She thought it was a small lie, a white lie. For years she thought it was the only lie.

It must have been at this moment that the first shadow of doubt crossed my mind. Was it all true? How much did Batin remember and how much was he making up? What was it that he wanted to hide, for why else should he have told the stories in such a patchy manner, so that I later recalled the narratives as one feels the moon on a cloudy night, a luminous presence hidden behind dark patches of cloud, its presence indicated by the moonlight, the silver of the clouds' edges, fleeting glimpses of a silver orb as it slipped from one dark cloud to another? This feeling of something not fully told grew with the night and added to my slight irritation with Batin, an irritation I could understand only in retrospect. Around this point of his story, having left it suspended on the thread of a ghostly lie, Batin took one of his frequent turns down a narrative side-alley and started talking about what appeared to be – at least initially – a completely new bunch of people in Bombay in the 1940s. Unlike the stories of Anjangarh, Durga, Chotte Thakur and Harihar, he employed here a slightly different register: that of a witnessed, at times even autobiographical, narrative.

Barbed wire demarcates the edge of this property, a colonial-looking building some distance from the village of Dallam, situated in a valley narrowed by rising rock and reached by the serpentine Poona–Bombay road. A long curving driveway, covered with sand and fine pebbles, which must have been trucked to this spot, and bordered by unusual-looking palms, leads up to the high-pillared veranda.

If you look closely you will see different structures and enclosures spread around the extensive and rocky compound. Some of the enclosures are also bounded by barbed wire, as if they were used to pen animals. The wire looks unusual in the rural setting, though this is a region between Poona and Bombay and, as such, carries more marks of urbanity than Anjangarh. Also, this is not 1929. It is 1948.

'Do I need to remind you what 1947 and 1948 meant to my generation, my young scholar? They meant barbed wire. It was being stretched across both sides of Hindustan, or it would be soon enough. That was the final gift from the British: they drew lines on a map and, hey presto, barbed wire appeared on the land. Papers published charts of this magical transformation. Here, let me get it for you, I still have the cutting from the Dawn. *Wait a second . . . Here it is. I came across it in a pile of old papers when I moved to Pakistan, and I have kept it ever since. Here, a boxed item, dated 18th August 1947. Boundary Demarcations At A Glance, it says. So that you could look in the day's paper to see whether your bedroom was still in the*

same country as your toilet. This thana to Pakistan, that division to India; that district to Pakistan, this village to India. And barbed wire to make all of it real. There are nights when I wonder whether the British would have drawn those lines on paper if barbed wire had not been ready and available. And profitable, young man, profitable.'

It is a thin fragile silence, stretched like the surface of a lake on which small long-legged insects walk. No, it is a taut hard silence, stretched like barbed wire across no man's land.

Saleem Lahori waits for the stone to come crashing, in slow motion perhaps, without the soundtrack initially, until the strange music surges back, the songs of violence from last year, eerie chants that had sounded in so many places in the North and the East, and the shouting, and the screaming, and then again the silence. He remembers it from the time he had toured and performed with the Aakrosh troupe. He remembers it from the time he found the two children huddling in a corner of a charred building, caked in filth, and he remembers the months before that. This is how it always begins: with a few stones, a single scream.

It has been like this all night.

He does not know how many there are outside. (And they do not know how few there are inside the house. Had they known, they might have thrown more

than the occasional stone.) Who does? He is not so
sanguine about it as Rajkunwar or Hari Babu. He is not
chained to the mansion by paper hopes or shadow fears
like Bhuvaneshwari. No, he is not – in spite of Bhuvaneshwari, in spite of Kabir and Rosy, those two
orphaned children who have returned him to life. He is
not, he tells himself, he is not and he will not be buried
in one place before he is dead.

He shakes the curtains at the two windows in this
room. (One of the window panes is broken, there are
glass splinters like flower petals on the floor. Some of
the panes have been pasted over with newspaper cut-
tings, mostly pictures of actors and actresses but also
one surprising front page, more recent than the rest,
announcing the independence of India in huge block
letters.) Then he walks through the other rooms in this
wing, randomly fanning the curtains or shutters as the
case may be. Sometimes he doubles back and creates
the impression of movement behind the same window.
He is careful never to reveal himself. Saleem Lahori is
playing the role of his lifetime: he is a dozen different
heroes, a dozen watchful defenders who peer from
chinks and curtains.

This is all the protection they have, the eight or nine
people left in this vast, cavernous half-Victorian building: play-acting.

★

Though dwarfed by the reddish-black rocks of the hills behind it, the building – not very far from the slate-roofed huts of a small village – looks as if someone had decided to make a defiant fist at the sky. Land has been hacked and perhaps blasted away, rigorously levelled for this gesture. It would have been a pseudo-Victorian kothi, but for the strange cardboard-like structures, resembling a flattened town street, erected at some distance around it, and the American ranch-like enclosures and sheds on the other side.

A tall and broad heddi tree rises on one side of the building, its outer branches touching the walls.

Even from the narrow, winding Bombay–Poona road it is possible to see the building, its strange enclosures and the low huts of Dallam, about two kilometres away, and to wonder. What is it? people would ask. (Even today, when the building is just a charred shell, blackened and broken, when the village of Dallam is almost part of Khopoli's suburbs and a six-lane highway overshadows the old single-lane Bombay–Poona road, it is still possible for the eye of a wearied commuter to or from Poona to linger on the heaps of stones and bricks, the broken beams, the sun glinting off glass particles, the silent shout of this destroyed, out-of-place building.)

But that night, in 1948, the building is still standing. The board that had been hung on a wooden gatepost has been ripped down only a few hours before. Made of heavy tin and wood and rusting at the edges, the board spells out the words RAJKUNWAR STUDIO in vivid red on a yellow background.

Two kilometres away, the village of Dallam is as still as a cardboard cutout. It is so still that it can only be dead or pretending. It is so still that Saleem Lahori can hear the rustle of the large heddi tree outside the studio building.

Saleem had often boasted that love had no place in his dictionary. Sex, yes, he had a reputation there, romance too, yes, he was a romantic at heart, but not love of the sort that leads to desperate acts of commitment, ending in death or marriage. No wandering around in the desert, shrieking Laila, Laila, Laila, for him, though he had played that role in the past, and quite convincingly.

But at that moment, surrounded by the prowling hate of those figures in the dark outside the studio building, Saleem was forced to ponder his reasons for staying on, for returning – as he told himself – in spite of the state of his foreskin. He could have left with the rest of the actors and actresses on Monday, the night after the first incidents. But he'd stayed to help Rajkunwar cut the film (or had he?). And when he did finally leave with the last lot, the hired hands and technicians who drove off only this morning, he had abruptly changed his mind and returned in the deceptive safety of daylight.

Would he have come back if Bhuvaneshwari had not stayed on? Was he there because Bhuvaneshwari had hugged Kabir and Rosy, the two orphans, to herself and refused to leave? So that now everyone was gone except for Raheeman Cha, the old guard carrying his one-barrelled gun, perhaps too senile to understand what was happening outside, and Hari – Hari the Husband, as he calls him in his mind – and one or two of the local hands. Rajkunwar had stayed, of course; Bhuvaneshwari was tied to Rajkunwar in some strange way he has not yet managed to decipher. The two children were there too, silent and large-eyed: they had been, in a way, his contribution to the company. That was it, just nine or eight people, counting two small children who woke up crying at sudden sounds, left in a building that had a few weeks ago contained close to fifty people. And, at the last moment, Saleem had surprised himself by getting off the bus, turning back from the anonymous safety of Bombay. He had chosen to return. Until then he had not known that he was in love.

Saleem Lahori is stopped in his slow deliberate act of shaking curtains and shutters by a sound from downstairs. He is standing in one of the small rooms that used to serve as a dressing and make-up room. As he pauses to listen, he automatically, unthinkingly, moves to the large dressing table – a wooden, many-compartmented thing, with swivelling full mirrors – next to the windows and looks at himself in the light of the candles that burn in those rooms with no window panes of glass. It is a gesture that comes naturally to him, after almost three decades as an actor. But these days he is surprised by his reflection, the stubble, the double chin, the bags under his eyes, the occasional grey hair. Sometimes the only thing he can recognize is the strange, unearthly glitter in his eyes, a glitter so mesmeric that some women have cried out in fright on coming across him suddenly and men never hold his gaze.

He listens. The sound comes again, like water cascading down the broad marble stairs that lead to this floor. It is a snippet of a song they had canned and discarded because a conversation had filtered into the recording. He knows Rajkunwar has put it on to give the impression of a recording taking place. Not that Rajkunwar believes this play-acting to be necessary. Rajkunwar has too much blue blood in his veins, or so he thinks, to comprehend the bitter violence of peasants, of people whose ancestors have, for generations, served his ancestors. But Rajkunwar does not want to leave the building unattended: there have been rumours of a possible ownership rift with Seth Dharamchand, and when the Seth wants something you have to guard it with your life.

Saleem Lahori makes his way to the stairs now, flapping a curtain on the way. They have agreed to meet in the editing room and perhaps Bhuvaneshwari will be there too with the two newly found waifs. Perhaps Rajkunwar will call, as he often does: Saleem Bhai, Bhuvaneshwari has made some chai, Saleem Lahori, where are you?

Bhuvaneshwari, such a non-filmi name.

'Once, young man, I visited a man I had come to know through Bhuvaneshwari. I visited him for her sake. This was not before Independence, when I hardly knew Bhuvaneshwari; it was sometime later. Bhuvaneshwari would not come with me. She could not. So I went to see the man alone while she waited in a hotel room. I went as her eyes, so to speak. I promised to be a truthful reporter, to write what I saw in the sheets of my memory and read it all for her on my return, word by word.

I won't tell you the name of the man: I promised her that a long time ago. I promised her not to let the past claim the present. So I won't tell you the name of that young man or the town in which he had made a life, raised a family. I had heard so much about him that I thought I knew him. But when I met him, he turned out to be as much a stranger as anyone else, even his name was half strange and half familiar. He, his family, his career, all were rooted in the past Bhuvaneshwari had told me about but when he spoke of that past, I realized it was another past altogether to him. He had made his own past, and that made his present possible. He had grown into the name he had assumed. But, of course, young man, there are ways of making the past again. You can lie about the past to destroy the present and you can lie about it to make the present possible. The lie you tell matters as much as the truth you champion.'

The lady doctor has come back, carrying the tray of tea herself. It is now so dark that you can hardly see the sky. Her mother, wearing a white cotton sari, has joined them for tea. But the doctor continues the story, switching to English, perhaps because her mother does not really understand the language when it is spoken quickly, though she can read it well enough. A servant brings a mixture of cowdung and herbs, burning on charcoal in a clay boarsi. Its pungent and not unpleasant smoke drives the clouds of mosquitoes away. If there are birds in the sky, the scholar cannot see them any more.

The doctor continues her story.

It was quiet in the car when we drove back after the film. Both Papa and Mummy sat quietly, thoughtful and distracted, and the mood so communicated itself to us that even Manik curbed his natural high spirits and hardly said anything until we reached home. But then, he was also tired and had slept through the last quarter of the film. So had I, almost. To be honest, I hardly remember much of the ending now. I know the film has become popular with film historians today, but we were young and we were the first generation to move from the redeemable villainy of Bombay films to the irredeemable, unalloyed evil of the Bollywood villain, from *Shri 420* to *Sholay*: we found the film boring. I guess we were primed for Bollywood, my entire generation, waiting for the slick violence of *Deewaar* and *Muqaddar ka Sikandar*. We were tired of the old family melodramas and social comedies, the love stories where the worst villain, apart from an obdurate father or a lecherous brother-in-law, was time. I guess even though we had not realized it then, the world had changed and we wanted to see a substantial villain like Gabbar Singh being bashed to pulp by some vaulting, limbless hero. We didn't want duets and lullabies, and that too without colour.

She laughs, and her mother, getting the gist of it, smiles happily. She looks serene and comfortable in her old age, wearing round glasses like those of Gandhi, and the scholar wonders what she would have been like when young.

The low bushes along the small lawn are silhouetted as light falls on them from the road; they are shadows

edged with silver. There are the headlights of a car, a
blue Maruti this time, at the gate, throwing the shadow
of the mango tree on them again, illuminating the
veranda, and the woman shouts, Shankar, sahib is here,
open the gate! Shankar! The mother gets up and goes
back into the house, carrying her cup of tea with her.
The tea in the cup trembles, and the scholar is reminded
yet again of the old writer in Frederiksberg holding his
glass of whisky, telling a story that had, in its turn, been
told to him in parts.

Reel 111

Part III

Rasa Erotic

Ugh ugh ugh I say thrusting my pelvis forward and backward in a lewd gesture why am I doing this in my sleep have I not done it awake just today just today am I awake am I dreaming ugh ugh ugh I gasp he gasps breathless moving as if leaning on a staff that cannot really sustain my weight his weight moving as if pushing into a woman I see in my sleep if I am sleeping I see the group of village youths from a corner of my eyes his eyes even as he seems engrossed in this caricature of an old man walking or making love I am counting on he is counting on the ambiguity of this theatrical kinesis the dented US Army binoculars sway back and forth on their strap around his neck ugh ugh ugh why are my binoculars on his neck is he me where are my binoculars I feel in my sleep under the bed I remember that I could not be dreaming I feel for the binoculars under the charpoy under the green wood tree it is there I know it is there I he thrust thrusts my his pelvis in my dream ugh ugh ugh I know I am satisfied with what he sees on the faces of the villagers around him there are fewer people in this group than there would have been a week ago when I he had started holding these impromptu talks ugh ugh ugh in a field just outside the compound of the studio I am thinking I cannot be asleep I know in my dream that a week ago such impersonation would have caused someone from the group to check him walk away in disgust it is different now I smile in my sleep the group is smaller but there is no dissidence no doubt on the faces of its members the young men in this group are looking at him at me with responding leers I know the leer it is the lustful disgust of young men who suspect an elder of doing what is often on their minds but seldom in their lives it is the hard intolerance with which the young separate age from the erotic so that the easiest way to mock the old is to accuse them of being sexually active I hear the voice of my Shakha Pramukh in my head it sounds clear it makes sense it has worked I see in my dream I am pleased they have come to see the Sant as I see him in my mind a disgusting and deceptive old man to reduce him to this caricature of animal sex is to make him vulnerable to replace the large words he spouts words like humanity forgiveness non-violence love with the swaying pumping motion that does not differ from what a dog does or a ram I laugh in my dream I see myself take out an issue of my

organization's monthly brochure it is hand-printed in
blotted ink on thin yellow paper I know its feel I know
its smell I read out an extract about the Sant the Shant
of Shabarmati sleeping with younger women I see the
old man I see him humping not leaning lecherous not
loving deceptive not struggling I know I have won I
know the villagers in my dream am I asleep the villagers
will lap it all up will lap it all up but in my dream if
I am dreaming I slip in that moment of triumph to
another time why why why again to another time to
another place I am a boy in a shed in a room I see
the movements hear the sounds coming from the corner
of the room that my parents share with me and my
brothers I am nine I am ten I am old enough to
understand but not to comprehend I see those movements the quilt throwing large shadows on the wall the
quilt is an animal it rears and grunts it has eaten my
parents up my mother and my father sometimes the
rearing quilt disappears and instead I see a horse pure
and savage a thoroughbred horse it stands there all
quivering muscles rain or sweat dripping off its twitch-
ing body its member huge and swollen and glistening
I turn my eyes away from the sight I want to utter the
word or phrase that eludes me that always eludes me in
my dreams I want to get back to the future where I
stand angry and leering ugh ugh ugh caricaturing the
Sant walking or humping ugh ugh ugh I want to return

to the leer of the villagers I will myself in my sleep and at first nothing happens at first nothing then suddenly I am there under the green wood tree ugh ugh ugh but the villagers around me are laughing now my heart swells with hope and hatred ugh ugh ugh what's the difference between the two my heart swells until I realize in my sleep in my dream I realize that the villagers are not laughing with me are laughing at me in my sleep I glance down and I see why why they are laughing at me I see the stain on the front of my pyjamas I feel the sticky wetness between my thighs no I have not escaped the past I am still there I am still there in that corner of that room with the animal quilt under my own quilt wet and sticky waiting to be discovered by my brothers by my mother by my father all in the same room with the ferocious quilt I want to be him the man in my dreams the man with the dented binoculars who has villagers following him I want to be him the man of the future but I am not I am not I am a small boy in a small room with an animal quilt

The Phantom Bird

The youth trains his pair of binoculars on the only window open on the ground floor of the studio. The binoculars are dark, MK21 army-supply ones. They bear the legend 'US Army', and under it 'Mark 23' and then the numbers '3138.1941'. There are other digits below these, but they have been rendered illegible by the friction of hands and the violence of war: parts of the instrument have been polished to the smoothness of marble, while other parts are dented and chipped. But there is nothing wrong with the lenses, and he likes the feel of the thing, he likes the notion of holding something so martial and modern.

It takes him only a few seconds to focus properly. He is no country bumpkin. He is the only outsider in the group of youths – most of them from neighbouring villages, not this one – who have been throwing stones at the Rajkunwar Studio building occasionally. Some of them are doing so because of what he and others from his organization have told them over the months. But most of them, he guesses, are doing so out of boredom and a sense of thrill: the building stands for all that their parents were taught to respect. (Of course, that was before they turned it into a cheap, two-cowrie studio employing Muslims and Communists.) And he can feel the excitement some of these youths get from tossing a stone at the building, and their sense of wonderment when no retribution – no gunshot, no lathi-wielding henchmen, no police challaan – results from it. He despises most of these villagers, and especially the two or three – all from Sarpanch Amrish Nath's family – who belong to this village. He knows that these men are there to settle some other account. They lob stones at the studio as if they were dropping them into a bucket, their eyes gleaming with greed, waiting for the water to flow over so they can lap it up. What is it they seek, that drink of their desires?

He resents the superstition of these village youths, their frequent refusal to go beyond the stables on the other side of the studio because – they claim – the stables are haunted by a dwarf on an invisible horse. They say he is immune to the dwarf because the dwarf is like his deformed twin, like his shadow: no, you do not really look alike, not too much anyway, they say, but he has visible birthmarks under both his ears, exactly like yours. Like teardrops. Like earrings.

He is ashamed of most of these men because they are so incapable of seeing beyond their own shadows.

Unlike them, he is not here from some personal hurt or for some personal gain. No, he is not. He is here to do his duty, to carry out the plans Guruji entrusted to the Poona West shakha of his organization. He feels removed from most of these callow, uncouth men, but he keeps this feeling wrapped up like his instructions in the deepest recess of his heart. He ribs them and chides them gently; he quotes holy verses at them and slaps them heartily on the shoulder, he derides the Sant and reads out extracts from certain publications; he does everything he can to hide his sense of separation, for he knows that he needs to keep their trust in order to lead them on. He is their leader. And that is what they call him, though he hates the word because it reminds him of those bastards in the Congress: Sardar.

His eyes have focused on the studio. The furry grey of its walls has resolved itself into clearer patches of cement, peeling chalk and paint, moss. (The walls are as reticulated with lines and borders as those mullahs have made of the map of India, of Akhand Bharat, he thinks.) He focuses a little more, and the bars on the open window materialize. He considers signalling to his followers to rush in and lob a few stones through the window, but he doubts that they will agree to do so in broad daylight. He has weakened the authority of the house, but it hasn't disappeared yet. If it had, he might have been on his way back to his children and wife in

Poona, his mission accomplished, this den of perfidies and immorality a smouldering ruin. If only his shakha or some shakha in Bombay would send a band of volunteers, of committed sevaks like him. He wonders why they haven't. He wonders why his Shakha Pramukh or some other Pramukh has not been in touch.

And meanwhile he watches. He still doesn't know how many people are barricaded behind the doors of that shockingly immense and, to his eyes, entirely alien building. It is in studios like this, he tells himself, rephrasing the powerful words of Guruji, that Bharat has been partitioned, broken off like the pieces of chicken that Hindus and Muslims probably share in such places, eating off the same plates, drinking from the same glasses, worshipping in the same room. These are stories that the Sarpanch's men have told him: how Rajkunwar ignored the request of some villager who wanted separate utensils for Hindus and Muslims and fired an assistant who did not want to cook for Muslims; how there was a room in the studio in which Hindu gods and Muslim relics were kept together; how there was even a mosque hidden somewhere in the compound, used by the Muslim studio hands to pray and plot. Yes, these are some of the same stories the men narrate to one another during the cold nights, sitting on their haunches, huddling around the boarsi glow for warmth, between bouts of stoning: stories of the decadence of the studio, and also ghost stories and love stories, stories of the actress who had come out wearing 'halfpants' and stories about the stables haunted by the ghost of a dwarf who had disappeared (been murdered and buried, one villager suggested) in the studio.

He watches through the lenses, focusing into the room with the open window.

He sees a man sitting on a cane bucket chair inside the room. This man is tall and wears a long overcoat even indoors. He looks middle-aged. His face seems vaguely familiar. Is he someone he has met somewhere, or is he a film actor from the days when he saw films regularly? Is he one of those mullahs this studio has continued to employ in spite of threats and warnings? Whatever, his instructions are clear. He has to wait until the Pramukh sends word.

A woman moves into the picture framed by the open window. She hands the seated man a cup of tea or coffee. It is a dainty cup, in a saucer. The man looks up at the woman. She has long lush hair. Even across the field and through the narrow apertures of binocular vision, he notices the change in the man's attitude. It is as if a statue has come to life. No, the man does not move much, but a charge of life – like electricity – passes through his body. He can see the expression on the man's face. It glows.

When the man extends his hand to take the cup

and saucer from the woman, his fingers rest momentarily on her fingers. Perhaps they rest for a moment longer than necessary. The man and the woman exchange a naked look that makes him – their audience of one – feel ashamed for the first time. He feels as if he is looking through a keyhole, as if he has witnessed a lurid peepshow. He is reminded of the first time his friends – he was in high school then – took him to a windy street corner which was favoured by admirers of women's legs and ankles. He feels guilty, as he used to when those noises came from the side of the room that his father shared with his mother. An old bed sheet used to separate his parents' side of the room from the side, also containing two charpoys, in which he slept with his three brothers. He feels guilty, confused, angry, and in the second before those mixed feelings change into manageable disgust, as they used to in his parents' stifling room years ago, he takes his eyes away from that naked scene for just a moment. Then disgust flows into him, thrills him with its legibility, and he feels like breaking down the studio building single-handedly, climbing on top of it with a pickaxe and hacking away at it as if it was the body of a Pakistani. But then even that feeling passes and he shakes his head: it is only a standing woman handing tea or coffee to a seated man.

When he looks again someone has closed the shutters of the window.

In Anjangarh, there were servants running up and down, and across the courtyard, slamming windows and doors shut.

At first Durga thought it was a freak of weather, until she was told by the other servants that a hailstorm or two was not unusual in the summer. But this year the storm is early, they said. The mango trees were hung with green fruit, not ripe enough to be plucked and put in straw if necessary. They fell in showers at times, hard and green and helpless. It will be a bad crop this summer, the servants said, shaking their heads, as if the loss was their own and not that of the Thakur family.

Or perhaps some of them had a tree or two of their own somewhere on their own little plots. She could believe that. She found it harder to believe that the summer in these parts – much hotter than anything she had known in Calcutta – could be split so swiftly by a hailstorm. The evening sky had darkened suddenly. Lightning cleaved the sky into two and crumbled away at the edges of the inky clouds. Grain, vessels, charpoys were still being dragged inside when the first fat drops fell, like hot tears. They stained the sides of the haveli, drew dark streaks on it. Then suddenly the asbestos roofs of the cattle shed behind the courtyard, and the tin roof of the hencoop in the yard, had resounded with the impact of tiny pebbles of ice, some as big as a thumb-print.

The verandas of the courtyard were crowded with people. The adults watched mostly in silence, breathing in the smell of rain, enjoying the slight chill in the air. They knew it would not last, just did not know what to do while it lasted. The children, meanwhile, were running helter-skelter across the courtyard, collecting hailstones, putting them on their tongues. They were full of the novelty of the event, and yet somehow behaving as if it would go on forever.

That, mused Durga, was the difference between Ashok and her. She and Harihar had been caught in a hailstorm in the middle of the dry summer of their bioscope shows. While Durga stood with her hands idle, waiting for the hailstorm to blow over or sweep them all away, Ashok rushed from haweli to courtyard to haweli, hands full of the gifts and sweetmeats Badi Ma gave him. Badi Ma, not Maalkini.

Durga did not stand with idle hands during the evenings she was called to perform for the Chotte Thakur. While they waited for their plans to be finalized and the main ceremony – a mother's sacrifice, Maalkini continued to call it, but only in her hearing – organized,

Durga still danced for Chotte Thakur. The difference was that Harihar would sometimes be there now, watching with the noncommittal gaze she had once taken for decency and openness, but had recently started suspecting was also something else. Harihar, she knew, was concentrating so hard on his dream that he had little time for the oddities of life; he had decided not to judge or comment because his eyes and heart were always elsewhere. She knew now that the intensity with which he had spoken to her of films – the intensity that had won her – was not reserved for her only, because she saw the glare of that intensity directed at the Chotte Thakur too when the two men sat and spoke.

Sometimes, they spoke till late into the night and the Chotte Thakur forgot to ask her to sing. Sometimes, they switched to English.

Durga knew that both men desired her, but in different ways. For Harihar, she was the younger woman who, perhaps for the first time, had enabled him to believe in his own dreams, realize the incredible power, the potency of his own storytelling. Recovered from his illness now, in their room that hardly ever contained Ashok these days, Harihar would make love to her more violently and brutally than he ever had: he wanted her to be his woman, something soft and useful, a receptacle for his ideas and dreams; wife and whore. Or perhaps he was angry about something or with someone else, and she was his punching bag, heavy with the sand of time that was running from the leaks in his dreams.

It was with the Chotte Thakur that Harihar shared his dreams now; Durga had become a means to the dream, only one of many. But this realization relieved her; she did not resent it. It was a relief to be released from the burden of sharing someone else's dreams, and she wondered whether any two people – even Harihar and the Chotte Thakur – could ever share the same dream. It was a disturbing thought, for without being fully aware of it she was living at a time when tens of millions were suddenly dreaming the same dream: that of Home Rule, autonomy, freedom.

And the Chotte Thakur? Harihar had been reassured by the knowledge that Durga was instructing the Chotte Thakur in kathak and thought his early suspicions had been unjustified. Or perhaps having found the Thakur to be so open to his own cinematic aspirations, Harihar no longer cared. Would he have cared if he had known how the Chotte Thakur beseeched her to hold him on the nights when Harihar did not join them? Hold me, hold me harder, the man who would on occasion whip servants for minor faults would cry.

She would let him sit in her lap, and rock him like a baby, this hard, trim man who wanted nothing from her but a few moments of strength. It made her realize how far she was – and had always been – from that which she sang about: prem, mohabbat, pyaar, love. But there was comfort in it, this slow rocking back and forth of a grown man, and arousal too, perhaps not untouched by the relish of knowing that Harihar was unaware of it, yes, there was arousal in it, just as there were days when she would respond to Harihar's brutal love-making.

They had come to share the same house, but they occupied separate rooms in it, rooms of their own making, rooms only partly visible to the others, rooms in which they had carried the distinctive and different inheritances of their pasts, familiar and flawed like old furniture.

I have, I must confess, filled in some of the blanks from hints that Batin dropped. It was only later – when I spoke to other people and especially after I had come to realize how intricately the main characters of the drama in 1948 were related to those of events in Anjangarh in 1929 – that I could join the dots of his remarks to make a legible narrative. But then I did not grasp the connections.

Who says that inhabitants make a house? It is surely a mark of the conceit of the human race that makes us attribute so much to our random presence. For it is not human beings who make a house full and complete, it is the objects that find their way to the house. Find their way – Saleem Lahori mutters to himself – for why should we assume that we are the ones who select and transport the objects? Perhaps, sharing as they do the elements of wood and earth and stone and metal and plastic – not sharing anything of our flesh – participating as they do in their dense objectivity, both house and the objects that come to inhabit it call out to each other, so that we – buyers, owners, sellers, subjects, human beings – are merely the means, the medium. We do the carrying and fetching, the buying and selling. But furniture chooses the floor, wall chooses the wardrobe.

He trails his fingers down the cool wood of a large cabinet in this room, one of the studio make-up rooms. It is built solidly, expanding like a Greek column at the top. There are deep scratches on its surface. It is clear to him that this piece of furniture must have been inherited or bought from an older owner. It has come to share this room with a cheap plywood dressing table and the aluminium chair in front of it. The dressing table has cloth tassels and a folding mirror. The mirror bears marks of lipstick and nail polish, various colours, too many to be inadvertent: it must have been used to demonstrate the colours to some fussy artiste. There are various shades of red running across one corner, like scars, deepening into a colour like maroon. Saleem Lahori remembers that colour.

He walks to the window and moves the shutters. He

is still acting. He is still trying to fool the watchers out there. But his mind is not in the studio any longer. It is winding back, like a roll of film, to a happier time.

He remembers that colour. Bhuvaneshwari was wearing exactly that shade of lipstick when he first met her. He remembers the date. It was five years, three months and eleven days ago. He remembers it exactly.

He is swept into the rawness of those years again, the hum and hustle of the streets and Bombay itself unfolding in glistening Monsoon humidity, heavy and fresh and suddenly green, the walls and buildings, the cars and trams momentarily washed into a deceptive newness.

'I was told just a few months ago, and not for the first time, in a letter, this time from an editor of a Pakistani journal, that I must have resembled Saleem Lahori as a young man. And now you have said it too, young man. Perhaps. Perhaps I did. I was not, as I have already said, unhandsome. But as to when I met Saleem Lahori, I am not sure. It must have been soon after the party that I am going to tell you about now, for (as everyone knows) I was working for Rajkunwar Studio around that time.

Perhaps I sought him out. Surely I must have, if I resembled him, if I resembled Saleem Lahori, hero. It is flattering to be told that you resemble someone on whom the angel of fame has waved his wand. I was hardly known as a writer then. (As you know, even those of my books that you find today are post-1947

editions. No one bothered to preserve a single copy of the first
edition of Bandish. Its current editions are all post-47 reprints.)
And Saleem Lahori had been a star, a silent star, but still. And
he had a circle in those days, a strange mix of Bohemian artistes
and artists from largely traditional backgrounds, at that moment
united by the dream of revolution and art, independence and
success, the dream that was to shatter, or rather that was to
splinter like a ray of light into its constituent colours: one day,
we discovered that time was vitrescent and the fused light of our
dream struck the prism of 1947 and refracted into the orange
and yellow of Hinduism, the green of Islam, the red of violence,
the blue of a disappointed hope, and into the indigo and violet
of subtle, unredeemable differences. But that was yet to come.
When Saleem Lahori met her, Bhuvaneshwari, hope was still
in the air, translucent, whole.'*

The heavy mist from the direction of Marine Drive had
seeped its way into the streets and even, it appeared, into
the building Saleem Lahori was about to enter. It was
thick as a blanket, so dense that he could not make out
the third storey of the houses. With the buildings decapitated by mist, he could not see what caused the bird
to fall down a foot from him. It was a pigeon and it
appeared to be dead. Had it flown into a wall, blinded
by the mist, or had it been attacked by a hawk higher up
where the sky was clear? He picked it up tentatively
with two fingers; its feathers were surprisingly dry. The

bird, wings spread out, dangled from his fingers. It felt warm but gave no sign of life. There was no obvious wound, only a drop of blood on its bill. Perhaps it had died of some sickness, something contagious, he thought, and almost threw it down again. Just then the bird tried, weakly, to struggle out of his grip before going limp again.

Was it dead, finally? Could he leave it here to be devoured by the mangy street dog that was lapping up some puddle water a few feet away? But what if it was not dead?

These were days when Saleem Lahori could not decide the simplest issues. Especially the simple issues, the minor ones, for the greater issues resolved themselves; there was always someone higher up, in the director's seat, pointing his finger at you and telling you what to do if the issue was momentous enough. He had not been like this in the past; he had not been known to worry inconsequential beads.

He knew that he was cutting an odd figure, a tall man wearing a fashionable trench overcoat of the sort made popular by recent war films, standing outside the entrance of a studio building, a bird hanging from his hand. Had the streets been busy, people would have stopped to stare at him. (Or had he done this even a decade ago, he would have made it into one of those new film magazines – 'Star Kills Bird' – for Saleem

Lahori had been a name to reckon with in the heyday of the silent films. But now there were very few who remembered. The language of the talkies was different from the language of the silent films; the stories that could be told in them were different.)

Saleem was not unaware of how one loses histories and memories with languages. His father had claimed descent from Mughal aristocracy and from the scholar al-Biruni; and though his father's claims were neither verifiable nor reliable (as a long list of debtors must have realized in his father's lifetime), this would mean that Saleem's family had cast off languages as easily as most people put on clothes. The Central Asian dialects of the early Mughals, the Farsi and Arabic that the Mughals picked up and that, claimed Saleem's father, was the language of Saleem's ancestors, the Urdu and Punjabi that Saleem grew up speaking, the English that he diligently polished (listening to the BBC and to all the great Indian orators of the generation) after becoming a silent star, his mother's Hindi that some Muslim friends had been telling him recently would consume his father's Urdu and Farsi . . . languages all. Sometimes Saleem did not care for languages. He thought it superfluous to use words when one could use facial expressions, gestures, postures, tics and tremors. Words pinned down reality to one interpretation; gestures opened them up. Allah, he often told friends, is credited with having authored

two ultimate realities: the Quran and the universe.
Which one, he would ask them, allows more possibilities: the reality of words or the realities of the world?
His friends would titter delightedly and look at one
another as if to say, Now, isn't that vintage Lahori? –
for Saleem had an exaggerated reputation for godless-
ness, which was largely the consequence of his relationships with a string of starlets, courtesans and even plain
whores.

Saleem looked around. He pulled his overcoat
tighter, huddling against the sudden chill and the damp.
No one had stopped to notice him or the inert bird still
dangling from his hand. He pulled out a big, spotlessly
white handkerchief and wrapped the bird carefully in
it, swaddling it like a child, leaving only the head
uncovered, and dropped the bundle into the deep pocket
of his coat. Then he entered the gate of the building,
part of a larger studio complex.

Matters that could not be settled could be postponed.

Silence, please . . . lights on . . . fans off . . . camera ready
. . . Mr Jagdeep?
  Yes, ready.
  Ready?
  Yes.
  Scene forty-one, take two . . .
  Saleem Lahori walked into the hall, exchanging a

few nods with the older hands. He cast half a glance at the scene being shot and filed it away as a family drama. Probably something to do with the newly married wife being persecuted by the in-laws, he thought, looking around for the man who had summoned him. He spotted him at the other end of the hall, sitting on a folding chair, being fussed over by the usual quota of chamchas. Saleem was familiar with the scenario. There was a time when his presence had attracted hangers-on, when they'd buzzed around him like flies around a lump of molasses. This man, thought Saleem, was one of those who had replaced him as their focal point. But while he could hardly bear the sight of the others, Saleem and he had ended up good friends.

Almost ten years his junior and from another part of India, Nitin Kumar was an up-and-coming star and, in some ways, the exact opposite of Saleem. A father of three at the early age of twenty-six and very much a family man, Nitin came from a middle-class family and had gone to English-speaking schools, whereas Saleem Lahori was a perennial bachelor pushing forty, with the reputation of a womanizer and with dubious educational and family backgrounds; it was even rumoured that his surname had little to do with Lahore and more with the Lahori Gate of Red Fort in Delhi, next to which his mother was said to have run an 'establishment'. There were other differences too: Nitin, in spite of his formal education, never read books while Saleem, as his closest friends knew, was a voracious reader and loved to quote obscure writers. And yet, the two men had gotten along from the very moment, five years ago – Saleem was still invited to important industry parties in those days, and Nitin had just had his second hit – when they met at the mahurat of a Bombay Talkies film.

Dada, two minutes, mouthed Nitin when he saw Saleem, raising two fingers to reinforce the silent words. Nitin gestured for a chair and some of the hangers-on rushed off to fetch one. Saleem accepted it with a nod, lighting up the Craven A cigarette, the only brand Nitin smoked, that the younger actor handed to him.

Another scene was shot. An old acquaintance brought Saleem a glass of tea. In between takes, Nitin made polite conversation but did not say a word about why he had asked Saleem to come to the studio this evening. Saleem knew from experience that people in the industry, even decent people like Nitin, liked to keep others waiting. Fifteen years ago, he would have done the same. He waited.

It was only when they were packing up for the day – after about an hour of shooting –that Nitin turned to Saleem and said, You are coming with me, Dada.

Where?

To a party.

Then seeing Saleem hesitate, Nitin added, A business party, Dada. There might be a role for you.

'To be honest, my young scholar, generosity is always hard to accept. We often accept it by attributing ulterior motives to it. Saleem baulked at Nitin's generosity and only accepted it because he attributed it to the young star's desire to show off, to add the gleam of condescending patronage to the glitter of his starhood. By attributing dubious motives to Nitin, Saleem overcame his own reluctance to pick up the odd scrap of a role from the star's table. It was only much later, perhaps as late as the letter that Nitin wrote to Saleem during his last days in Bombay, that Saleem came to see the narrowness of his own vision.

But anyway, young man, Saleem did accept Nitin's offer, and that is how Saleem met Rajkunwar, Hari Babu and Bhuvaneshwari.'

The hierarchy of Bombay had infiltrated the party. It was not as many-tiered as Bombay itself, for one had to belong to a certain class to be invited to parties thrown by PPK Joy Films in the first place, but it did have its circles. Three of them: the centre of the main hall was occupied by stars like Ashok Kumar, financiers like Seth Dharamchand and the German director Franz Osten; around them was a ring of people – Saleem would have been confined to that ring had it not been for Nitin –

who were insiders but not stars (either because they'd not quite made it or because their stars had been waning for a number of years); and finally there was a broad margin of hangers-on, minor businessmen and society types waiting for some stardust to rub off on their suited or sequinned shoulders. It was this margin that was most boisterous, most glittering, most starlike; compared to these people, the stars at the centre looked almost drab: it was as if dreams had crowded out reality.

At parties like this, Saleem knew from experience, Nitin somehow managed to turn the two of them into a social syzygy. He was seldom as deferential or close to Saleem as when he was in a big party, and Saleem had never been able to decide whether it was genuine concern for the sensibilities of someone who had been ousted from the limelight or a desire to display his own magnanimity to the public. A few years before, this would have bothered Saleem, but the continuing eclipse of his own star had taught him to accept the little light – and the few roles – reflected onto him by those who, for some reason or another, chose not to shun his company.

Despite wartime rationing, alcohol had percolated into at least the central two tiers of the party; if the war was anywhere in evidence – aside from occasional references to it in conversation – it was in the brands of the spirits being served, which were all Indian. Saleem, sniffing with elaborate suspicion at a local whisky he actually knew to be pretty decent, watched as Ashok Kumar and Franz Osten were escorted into a side room by one of the long-waisted sari-clad hostesses. He wondered how Franz Osten had avoided being quarantined: he knew that Germans and other supposedly hostile nationals were being picked up by the British and herded into concentration camps all over India.

Nitin, who had managed to disentangle himself from his admirers, grabbed the sleeve of Saleem's coat (which he'd kept on as he was wearing a rather old shirt underneath) and tugged.

Come, Nitin said. The real booze is elsewhere.

He pushed Saleem towards the same room the star and German director had entered. By the sides of the door stood two hefty men, dressed as cowboys, examining people's invitation cards. Not all cards were equal. But they did not stop Nitin.

At first Saleem thought the room had been decorated by someone who had seen too many Westerns. The walls had been freshly painted with semi-arid landscapes teeming with vultures, half-clad village belles and cacti: a Bombay poster-painter's idea of the Wild West and Chambal. But then he noticed the Western-style bar at the other end and waitresses dressed in cowgirl suits with cutout gun belts and pistols, and he realized it was a theme party. Someone had decided to throw a party within a party, a party for the special guests. He should have guessed when he saw the cowboy bouncers. Theme parties were obviously in again.

Nitin was swallowed up by people who rushed to greet him and Saleem was left alone for the moment. He knew many of the guests, at least by sight as their faces appeared in newspapers or on the screen quite often. The people surrounding these faces were mostly hangers-on and financiers. They looked alike, all loud and expensively dressed. All except Seth Dharamchand, who – as everyone knew – was not just a financier. Saleem could see the Seth in one corner, laughing in the slightly stupid way, a soft babyish gurgle, that, Saleem was sure, he cultivated on purpose. The Seth did not need to be loud to be heard. He did not stalk stars: actors and directors came to him, stood around fawning or, if they were big enough, being demonstratively friendly.

Saleem knew that many of these people recognized him, for he had worked with some of them. But most pretended not to. Only one man came up to Saleem. Short and fair, with an apologetic smile, and large bags under his eyes, he was wearing a cowboy hat, which was the only thing that distinguished him from the guests and relegated him to the rank of waiter. The man must have been in his fifties, but he had a jaded boyish look about him in spite of the wrinkles, the greying hair, the tired eyes.

Saleem Saab, he said, shall I take your coat?

Saleem shook his head. He peered at the man who smiled and said, apologetically, Amar.

Amar, stuntman Amar! Saleem exclaimed.

No longer, Saleem Saab. Too old for it. Went into business: Triple A Caterers now. You might have heard of us; we are doing well.

And what about your friend? Saleem remembered that Amar had shared a room – and it was rumoured more than that – with an aspiring actor from the Punjab. The three of them had opened the occasional bottle after shooting in the early years, before Saleem's career took off and he left many of his old pals behind.

Akbar? Still around. Staffing the bar at the moment. Calls himself Anthony, though. People prefer having their drinks prepared by Anthony rather than Akbar. That is where the Triple A comes from, actually: Amar, Akbar, Anthony. Can I get you a drink, Saleem Saab?

I will find the bar, Amar. And don't saab me. Look around: I am incognito. You are the only one who knows me here.

'That was what was irritating about Saleem Lahori in the early days, his greedy self-pity. In retrospect one can understand the wellsprings of that self-pity, for Saleem could frequent the kothas

of whores and courtesans but could never acknowledge his own background. That was how Bombay was structured, not just the Bombay of the vegetarian and intensely domestic Gujarati merchants, who might invest in films but would never hobnob with the filmi crowd, or the Bombay of England-returned directors like Himanshu Rai, but even the beer-guzzling, back-slapping, swearing-in-English-Marathi-Punjabi-Urdu Bombay that had accepted Saleem. Even that Bombay would celebrate his reputation as a rake but openly laugh at any vulnerability such as descent from a kotha, and that too brazenly acknowledged. In all his years in Bombay, Lahori told only one person about his mother, Gulabo Bai, and the Maulvi Sahab. But then, young man, the Saleem Lahori of those days was not the Saleem Lahori who stepped off the Rajkunwar Studio bus in 1948, disembarking with a slight wave of the hand, a gesture that was dismissive of the two things he had cared for all his life: fame and money.'

The same as usual, Lahori Saab? Akbar/Anthony asks, looking through him at the room in general, not really focusing on anything or anyone in particular.

Anthony has already picked up a bottle of Schenley and a metal ice scoop. He stands behind his fake wooden bar, all in black, his silk shirt, flaring buttoned trousers and studded broad-rimmed hat highlighted against the gleaming yellow of the desert scene painted on the wall behind him, a scene of sand and vistas, bones and vultures, he stands there, his youthful looks shrunk to a grim, perpetually unsurprised, pale Jinnah-like visage, and waits for Saleem to nod.

Saleem nods and says, It gets more crowded every time, doesn't it?

He says, It what?

Saleem takes the chotta peg on the rocks that Anthony has put on the counter and touches the whisky to his lips. He moves his tongue slowly over the slightly chapped skin, savouring the burn of the whisky, before he repeats the observation.

Anthony frowns, scratching his cheek. The world gets smaller, Lahori Saab, he offers diplomatically.

And crowded. Saleem pursues the point, but Anthony is already ministering to two young women in almost identical chiffon saris. They look sideways at Saleem through long false eyelashes. His face might appear vaguely familiar to them, but they seem to be unable to place it.

One of them says something to the other one, and both laugh. It sounds like the ice tinkling in Saleem's glass. They are bejewelled from wrist to neck. One of them even has a diamond tiara. Or a fake diamond tiara. Their hair, he thinks, are elaborate nests of the weaving bird, upside down.

As he thinks of weaving birds, the ghostly tugs that he has felt in the region of his pocket a couple of times earlier are renewed, and this time he knows what they are. He looks stricken as he puts his hand into his deep overcoat pocket. The fabric has come alive. He pulls something out. No one notices except the two young women who are watching him from under their false eyelashes. One of the girls lets go of her glass of orange juice and clutches her throat. O my God, she says.

Saleem Lahori is standing at the bar at a party where people have decided not to see him, holding a pigeon. He does not have a proper grip on it and the bird suddenly flaps vigorously and slips out of his grasp, landing on the polished floor in a shower of feathers. It hops twice and then, with a desperate effort, it takes to wing, describing a wobbling series of circles around the closed room until it has reached the skylight near the ceiling. It flutters against the glass of the skylight and gives up for a moment, perching there out of the reach of human hands.

Saleem Lahori stands below, a few feathers on his coat; he is no longer invisible. Saleem knows that Nitin Kumar won't come to his rescue; there are limits to Nitin's patronage after all. He wants Saleem to act the iconoclastic bohemian eccentric; he does not want Saleem to be a forgetful old man who collects things in his pockets and releases them at inopportune moments.

★

The young men laughing like hyenas in various groups are distracted from their forced joviality. Now they really come alive. They are all over the room, hounding the bird, shouting ribald jokes, slapping each other on the back. What a bird, yaar, they say, looking in the direction of some glittering starlet. They are circling Saleem, sniffing blood. This old lame buffalo, for of course they recognize him – they recognize everyone in the room and at least half the people in the film industry – and so they circle him, sniffing blood, waiting for that slight gesture from one of the famous and the powerful, the nod that will allow them to sink their fangs into him, hound him from the room.

But he is saved from that fate. A woman detaches herself from a small group and asks Akbar/Anthony to get someone to open the skylight. The suggestion is taken up by the hyenas and repeated like a charm. The skylight is opened, and the pigeon flutter-falls into freedom or the jaws of some mangy cur.

As the commotion subsides and the hyenas return to forced joviality in their circles, Saleem finds himself in the woman's group. There are introductions. He catches the name Rajkunwar and it rings a bell. (Rajkunwar Studio near Khopoli, well outside Bombay; he has heard of it. It was a surprise success a decade or so ago, a studio set up by almost complete outsiders – one of them, as the name Rajkunwar suggests, supposedly a prince.)

He has missed the woman's name, however, and he listens to the conversation, willing someone to utter it again. And someone does: Bhuvaneshwari He is taken aback by its lack of Bombay glamour.

Later Saleem realizes Bhuvaneshwari is married to Hari Babu, the director and co-producer of Rajkunwar Studio Films. Hari Babu is a senior man, who rarely speaks of matters unrelated to cinema, leaving the social talk to his business partner, the younger Rajkunwar. But it is Bhuvaneshwari who catches Saleem's eye, and years later, in the emptying besieged Rajkunwar Studio building, he can still recall the colour of the lipstick she was wearing.

It was Shahzaada Salim who left his favourite doves in the care of Anarkali, wasn't it, Rajkunwar asks. Have you heard the story? They were on the roof of some fort and he was called down. He handed Anarkali the doves and said, Hold on to both of them. When he came back, she had only one. What happened to the other one, he asked her. It flew away, she said. How, he asked. Like this, she said and opened the hand holding the other dove. Your namesake, Lahori Saab, no? – Shahzaada Salim, the future Emperor Akbar. No wonder you go about with doves in your pocket.

Well, it was actually just a pigeon, he feels like responding, but he only smiles in reply – because it doesn't matter and because Rajkunwar is simply trying to put him at ease.

'*Rajkunwar had a talent there: the man who was never at ease with his own self could somehow make others comfortable. That was the way they worked: Hari was the negotiator, the manipulator, the bargainer; Rajkunwar the pacifier, the communicator, the facilitator (though I guess both failed in their chosen roles finally, they failed faced with the steel of Seth Dharamchand, his dexterity with the barbed wire of business). And then there was Bhuvaneshwari. Would either of them have succeeded without her? Would any of us have clustered around that studio building without her, the queen bee? I don't think I realized it then, but in later years I have come to see her as the person who enabled it all. To her we brought the homage of our pollen, stealing from a hundred different flowers across the land, and she somehow turned it into the honey of our films.*'

Batin paused in his narrative and peered at me, his eyes narrowed, the skin around them crosshatched with wrinkles. '*How much will you scribble down, my young and diligent scholar? And what? For, you see, Saleem Lahori's story is like the plot of a Bombay melodrama: it teems with characters and names, episodes and incidents, but in the end it always comes back to one core romance, a love so swathed over by other emotions and events that you can hardly discern it: it is a brilliant sari laid out in front of you, like those small-shopkeepers lay out saris, one cascading over the other, and more and more, until you only catch a glitter of the fabric you had first noticed. You will have to reach under all that fabric to pull out the sari you wanted. Women are good at it. But we men, we get lost in the variety of fabrics, in the details. Keep your eye on the fabric of Lahori's story, young man; note his name, and that of Bhuvaneshwari, Hari Babu and Rajk-unwar. The rest of them? Well, the rest ought to have their own scriptwriters and directors – no doubt, if I had been a different person I would have laid out the saris in a different manner – but here, in this shop, they are nothing but items to be discarded, anecdotes, sub-plots.'*

They had offered Saleem Lahori a supporting role in a film they were already shooting. From this followed a similar role that came to be noticed in Mehboob Khan's *Taqdeer*, and this in turn marked a second coming for Lahori, this time as a 'character actor'. In return, he introduced Rajkunwar and Hari Babu to his friends: Dr Surender Singh, who had abandoned a general practice in Lahore to become an actor in Bombay; Ashiq Painter; Avik Sen, the photographer from Calcutta; Taan Kap-taan Hassan Ali Turki, who was definitely not from Turkey but spoke Pushto, Farsi, Punjabi, Urdu and English with equal epithet-studded fluency; and Bala (short for Balasubramanium), the journalist and editor. Sometimes they would be joined by Nitin Kumar, or by writers and musicians like Saadat Hasan Manto, Sheikh Taleb Deen Joshilla and Rafiq Ghaznavi, who had worked for Rajkunwar Studio in the past.

Like any such group, they had a repertoire of significant experiences, which could range from some mythologized slip of the tongue to elaborate stories like the one about the kirtan that Taan Kaptaan Hassan Ali Turki had taken over and conducted for three nights because it was being held at a temple not very far from where he used to stay and Turki could not bear badly tuned musical instruments and badly played music. They had jokes that did not need to be narrated within the group: one word would set them laughing, and not only when they were high. They had nicknames for politicians. They had a kind of belief in things changing, in words like 'revolution' that they had not really defined, in a visceral defiance of traditional roles, a bohemianism they were not always aware of. They knew, for example, that Lahori disappeared for days at a stretch at times, and could be located only on the kotha of a renowned courtesan. They knew of Turki's fine ear, of his intense, frenzied objection to any instrument being played even slightly out of tune. They knew that Bala had an affair going with a married woman in Karachi and would go to that city every six months – he told his wife that it was for work and managed to produce an article or two to show for it. He would book into the same room of the same hotel. Bala did not need to work; he was the only one among them who had inherited money, though once Hassan Ali Turki, the Taan Kaptaan, the Captain of Tunes, had said, high on marijuana, you do not know, La-La-Lahori yaar, what a pedigreed little mastiff I am. No one knew where Turki came from. But they knew that he claimed to be 'terminally incapable of leaving Bombay for more than forty-eight hours', even refusing assignments in Madras or Calcutta as a consequence.

That year they had celebrated Holi at the studio, Turki, Avik Sen, Dr Surender, Bala, Joshilla and Lahori driving more than three hours to get there, cramped up in Bala's dark-blue Austin. It was the only car they had between them, now that Lahori had finally sold his Master DeLuxe Chevrolet from 1936, its body a standard black, but the mudguards silver, with coquettish eyelashes painted by hand on the bulbous headlights. By the time they reached Rajkunwar Studio outside Dallam village, turning off from the Bombay–Poona road after Khopoli and driving in under the huge red-on-yellow board announcing the place, they had already emptied one bottle of rum.

The palm bushes along the long curving driveway had been hung with coloured ribbons and balloons and the small swimming pool on one side of the studio – it had been made largely for filming purposes – had been half-filled with coloured water. People were being tossed into it, a Hollywood version of Holi.

Later that afternoon, when most of the guests had left, a well-painted Ashiq Painter, looking like the abstract art he had started celebrating lately, after beating the drum of realism for the past two decades, pulled out the hemp they had brought and they had it prepared, mixed into minced meat, lightly spiced, in the studio kitchen. They ate it with rice and mango achaar. They were in no condition to drive back and had slept over in the small art-deco-type viewing theatre of the studio, sprawling in the chairs. It was the first of many nights Saleem was to spend at the studio over the years.

Over the next few years, Holi at Rajkunwar Studio became a regular fixture in the calendars of Saleem Lahori and his friends. But Saleem started turning up there with one or more of his friends on other occasions too. He would be there for Eid, in spite of the fact that Raheeman Cha and other Muslim hands at the studio always tried, and failed, to drag him to the Khopoli Eidgah for the Eid prayers. He would also be there for Diwali, when long card games were played well into the nights.

They mostly played flush or poker with the Western cards and ekrang, a trick-taking game without trumps, with the circular Ganjifa cards. Lahori was good at it, and the only person who could beat him was Bhuvaneshwari. Many of the others who played largely learnt from watching Bhuvaneshwari and Saleem. But not all played ekrang: Hari could never be interested enough to remember all the 120 cards; Avik and Ashiq declined to play with Ganjifa cards when they were there, the former calling them 'too Mughal-gaudy' and the latter considering them not 'modern' enough. Sometimes some passing studio hand or starlet would turn out to know the old cards and the game would last to dawn, the hours filling with cups of tea and jokes about the film industry.

'But looking back, young man, that was the time when their jokes began to turn sour. Bombay might not have had any major riot, like Amritsar or Lahore or Calcutta in 1947, but it was changed by the events too. All of Saleem's friends were changing with the times. Though they continued to slap each other on the back and swear in the familiar fiimi manner, calling each other saala, binchod and bastard in the usual fashion, and though they still met regularly for drinking sessions, the yeast of religion had been at work in some of them and their jokes had fermented and turned sour. I think I can recall the first time it happened.'

★

It was in Café Majestic at Dhobi Talao, down a side alley not very far from Kayani's, with its dark wooden chairs, its tables with white tablecloths held down by glass sheets, its round lamps and three-bladed fans on long white metal stems hanging from the ceiling, its walls hung with portraits, calendars and a large board: The Great Name in Cakes. In fact, Café Majestic was a poorer version of Kayani's, one of the most popular Irani hotels in the city. Perhaps Café Majestic just pretended to be Irani; certainly its proprietor was about as local as it was possible to be, his language replete with formulations like 'chalenga' and 'karenga' which are never used in any other dialect of Hindustani.

Café Majestic was a cavernous place, dimly lit, with a plethora of slow fans on long stems hanging from the ceiling and paintings of women in the Raja Ravi Verma style on the walls. A wooden counter stood next to the entrance, and behind it the framed sign: No mischiefs in Cabin, our waiter is reporting.

The cabins were the reason they came to this particular restaurant. The booths – wooden partitions roughly the height of an average man – lined the back of the hall. They didn't have doors but curtains, and once you sat down inside, nothing could be seen of you but your slippers or shoes. On the other hand, all you needed to do was stand up, perhaps on tiptoe, and you could look out. The cabins were popular with lovers, and people who wanted to drink. The latter were an exclusive clientele: the Irani owner did not serve or stock alcohol, but he did allow regular and favoured customers to bring their own bottles, and for a nominal 'overhead' (and the understanding that the customer would keep ordering plates of snacks), he would let them occupy the cabin for as long as they did not get too boisterous. If they did – and that was unusual – he would call his four sons, all cast in his massive mould, and threaten to have the customer thrown out. He never had to go beyond threats.

Lahori was sitting between Avik Sen and Bala that day. Opposite him, across the table cluttered with glasses, plates, a half-filled ashtray, and an almost empty bottle of whisky, sat Joshilla, Ashiq Painter and Doctor Surender Singh.

Bala had been telling them about the problems he was facing convincing his family that he had to go to Karachi 'on business' – 'on business' being his euphemism for his half-annual pilgrimage to his married mistress. Bala's family, unaware of the true situation, were objecting to the planned trip: it was just after the war, and there had been a few riots between Hindus and Muslims, a faint prelude to what was to come in 1946 and 1947; there were even rumours of Hindus leaving Karachi. These were dangerous times for Hindus to go to those regions, his family told him.

Avik Sen could not help teasing Bala. How did this saala-baldy manage to get a Muslim-lover in binchod-Karachi? he laughed, in his usual half-hostile, half-friendly manner. The question, Dr Surender interposed with a belly laugh, is how this saala-baldy managed to get a Hindu wife and six children in the first place. Only four, corrected Bala. Whatever, Surender guffawed, it takes something to get all that, you saala-baldy. He held up a finger and repeated, something.

Shut up, you filthy bugger, retorted Bala in English. I have a problem. I need to go.

Avik was not convinced. If I were you, I would give this a miss, he said. No time to go gallivanting in those parts.

What do you mean, those parts? I am from those parts, bastard, Dr Surender objected.

But you are no longer in those parts, saalé.

The doctor took umbrage. The notion he had left Lahore for any reason other than his love for films, and the free life he associated with them, was untenable to him. And he was a plain-speaking man.

You mean, Avik, that we should be sitting differently here. Lahori, Joshilla and Ashiq Bastard on one side of the table, and you, me and Bala Bastard on the other side. Or perhaps, being a bloody Sikh, I ought to sit on the table! What rot, saalé!

Times are changing, Doctor. Have you seen what

the *Dawn* carried this morning? Here, let me show it to you.

Avik pulled a crumpled newspaper clipping from his pocket, swept the table clear and smoothened out the clipping. It was a cartoon, not very well drawn, depicting a fat Hindu businessman sitting on a thin, bearded Muslim. In the background, there were three monkeys: the first had covered his eyes with his paws, the second had covered his mouth and the third had stopped his ears. The monkeys resembled M. K. Gandhi, Jawaharlal Nehru and Maulana Abul Kalam Azad.

This is Jinnah's paper, Avik. Why are you showing it to me? What do you think it will say? It is Jinnah's paper, dammit.

The doctor was incensed. And perhaps it was to calm him down that Ashiq Painter interposed his comment, a weak joke aimed at his own slippage from realism to abstract art.

And remember, Avikbhai, Ashiq Painter said, trying to joke about his own conversion. Remember, art has nothing to do with reality.

It is easy for you to talk art, Ashiqbhai, replied Avik mincingly, his voice barbed. What do Muslims know or care about the reality of Bharat?

Perhaps it was what he said, perhaps it was his tone, or perhaps it was his use of 'Bharat' instead of 'India' or 'Hindustan', but for a few seconds no one said anything, no one even swore, and soon after that the group broke up, as if dazed and distracted.

The husband of the lady doctor turns out to be a round-faced man of about her age, plump and with a broad close-cropped moustache, resembling a plain sparrow next to his beautiful wife. He doesn't have much to say, but listens to his wife's account with a good-natured smile. It is hard to imagine him without that smile: it denotes satisfaction with life but somehow falls short of irritating complacency, of smugness. They are a comfortable couple, and it doesn't surprise the scholar when the wife reveals that they had met in medical college and fallen in love immediately. But don't tell Ma, she adds. Ma thinks we had an arranged marriage. He got his parents to come to us with a proposal.

It is a story the scholar has heard before: there are always these marriages that were arranged in more ways than one. He wants her to return to the recollection of her childhood. He wants to return to his hotel before it gets too late. It is night now. The birds in the sky are just an occasional ghostly flutter of wings, the mos-quitoes a dull whining. And he is reminded of the story – an old man's recollection – that had, finally, brought him here. Then too it had been night. But that was in another place, in a cold flat in a narrow country far away, and what he had sensed there was loneliness, or lack, though in recent weeks he has come to question that initial impression. Perhaps the loneliness had been in him as much as in the aged writer, the writer whom he had gone to interview in both admiration and irritation. That hidden irritation had developed over the night, even as the writer spun out his stories with the greed of a spider, reminding the scholar of the nickname used by his detractors, Batuni – the talkative; and it had come to a head in a single sarcastic observation from the scholar at which the old writer had gripped his hands with desperate strength and retorted: *I did not choose to leave, I never chose to leave. I simply chose to live.* It is a line that has returned to worry the scholar and finally force him to begin understanding the many ways, all varied, some opposed, in which people choose life and the many ways in which they repudiate it.

But here, the scholar feels, and he feels it more fully, more surely, he feels a sense of companionship and warmth. Not loneliness. Something has been made in this house, something sustains its inhabitants. He wants to understand what has been made, and how. Perhaps it will fill the lack in him. And as such, he wills her to return to her recollection. And finally she does, but now there is a deeper personal note to the recollection, as if she is narrating it to her husband rather than to him.

Occasionally, the couple even steal glances that verge on the amorous, fleeting looks that accompany some modulated reference to sex and reveal to the scholar the young lovers they must have been and that they continue to be in each other's eyes.

Intermission

Night of 16th January, 1955

What? You too, my friend? Are you dead in that land you fled to last year, where you chose life for yourself (as you told me at the Coffee House on your last evening in Lahore, a week before you left Pakistan for good), and those two children and the woman, for whom you would have chosen – and once did choose – death with as little hesitation. Or are you alive and yet only a ghost, one of the spectres who have visited me nightly, much to the chagrin of my wife and daughters, who would preserve me from all kinds of spirits. They have always come singly, these ghosts, one at a time, which is the appropriate thing to do when visiting a deathbed. All of them came, from Bari Alig Saheb to Begum, all. But perhaps some of them were spectres of the living, for those alive cast ghosts as well as those dead. That we have known, haven't we, my friend? We have both known the fragile unity of bodies and shadows, and the murder and chaos born from their partition.

Look at the mess I have made of my body. Look. I can hardly speak to you; my throat is parched and it is not water I crave. Not water at all. This evening, coming back from the bar, I vomited blood again. The six-year-old son of my nephew saw it but I managed to convince the boy I had been spitting paan juice. Such petty lies I stoop to these days; I go begging for ten rupees from editors; I ignore the loving regimes of health and abstinence that my family devises to preserve me.

In your last letter you praised the bracing air of your new homeland. I have never smelled air that was purer, you wrote. Ha! How can that be, my friend? How can the air in the lands of infidels be purer than the air in the land of the pure? And what do we have to do, you and me, with purity, except perhaps the artificial purity of our art?

I can see you shaking your head. You believe that the art of life takes precedence over the life of art. If so, my friend, you have chosen a path very different from the one I took. Will it lead you to a greater flowering? Perhaps, if you are not already dead, I will return to sit on your deathbed and we will exchange notes – and insults, as usual.

Can't you find a drop of something for me to drink? Not water, my friend, not water. Not our element, that. We hardly ever drank water together, did we? Not with you or Joshilla or Ashiq or Avik or Doctor Surender or the Taan Kaptaan. Not even with Hari Babu, who was in many ways an artist like me, a man for whom art came first, and not even with Rajkunwar, who never got drunk – that man held his liquor even better than I could. But I would much rather not think of those two. No, I shouldn't. And I can see you do not want to be reminded of their end either, for you have always felt guilty for leaving – though did you have a choice there, my friend? – when you did.

Is that what life always does to art, my friend?

Get me a drop, please. I beg you. Get me something before my family wakes up. Oh, what's the use? You are a bloody ghost.

Or is it me who is a ghost? Did we manage to keep body and shadow together, my friend? And if we did, why am I here, coughing blood in my desperate search for death, and why are you there, driven so far away by your choice of life?

No, my friend, I cannot speak for you. But I believe I am still all here, still all here (as they say in English) in spite of getting myself admitted – was it once or twice? – to a lunatic asylum. No, I have kept myself together in the only way I could. I have proof of it, my friend, written proof. In recent years, in spite of imagined or real crimes of blasphemy and vulgarity that the Government of the Pure regularly hauls me to court for, I have managed to write more essays and stories than ever.

True, I have sold them for a pittance. I have walked into the offices of editors and written stories sitting there at their desks, demanding to be paid immediately so I could go and buy myself a half-bottle of whisky. Do you know, my spectral friend, my stories have actually gotten better, as if my craving for alcohol has focused my mind on both life and art. I will be remembered for these stories when my flesh is cold. These are not the ramblings of a mad man.

But what about you, my friend? Will you be able to write if you start living? And what do you want to leave behind of your stories – for you, my ghostly friend, have a story to tell that only you and the woman you call your wife knows. Even I and Joshilla know only a few chapters, only a few hints here and there. What a story you could tell, my friend, if you decided to. But I know you have pledged not to do so. It is part of your choice of life: what you write will only be fiction. But the facts of your life, you living ghost, what about the facts of your life that are stranger than any fiction? Will you, the writer and the showman in you be able to resist and take them to the grave? Or will you leave some clues behind, cryptic like those literary quotes with which you could pepper a late-night drinking round in Bombay?

What will the inscription on your grave read, my friend? (Or what does it read if you are already dead?) And in what language? What language indeed? Mine, I have already composed, and it will be in Urdu. You would have laughed at it and said it is typical of my big mouth and bigger ego. You were one of the very few people who would say that to my face, and it was this that made me forgive you, because, my friend, my ego and my mouth were never bigger than my talent. So this is what I have told my family to put on my gravestone: 'Here lies Saadat Hasan Manto and buried with him lie the mysteries and art of the short story. Under the weight of Earth he lies, wondering if he is a greater story teller than God.'

Don't laugh, saalé. Make a peg for me before it is dawn.

Reel IV

Rasa Marvellous

(26th January, 1948)

It is a dream I have had before it comes to me like the breeze of a fan on summer afternoons like the smell of rain in early monsoon like lamps being lit on the evening of Diwali I will it to come this dream for it is a dream about a place that makes me feel happy happy happy a place of many people all dressed in white like ancient monks like ancient priests all murmuring and walking around and around like performing a Vedic ritual it is a dream I know I am sleeping this is not something that happens in my life I have never seen it with my eyes open I have never known this slow camaraderie of chants the people all dressed alike as Hindus should be united united walking around a huge lingam a large black lingam that towers above them that is storeys high the people all dressed in white united in purpose united in effort as the India of my dreams as India as we would make it I hear the Pramukh say an India of Hindus one India of Hindus one people one

Hindu people the people all in white like Vedic priests like something from the reign of Lord Ram loose-flowing garments like dhotis like sheets the people walking around this gigantic black lingam except except it is square it is square the lingam is square

It is then that he usually wakes up, with the realization that it is a square lingam, and he wakes up not with the pollen of happiness from the dream on his lips but with the sour, stale taste of doubt and dissatisfaction, his head throbbing under the steel bands of incomprehension, his mind trampled as if by a herd of horses.

Sensation Shows

On 13th February 1922, Saleem Lahori, then a gawky young man of fifteen, walked out of the impressive portals of Victoria Terminal. It was his first visit to Bombay. It was also the first time he had left Delhi (he was to return to Delhi only twice, years later, for the very different funerals of his parents). Saleem felt it was a momentous day for him, a day with special significance for him and only him: the feeling would linger, remain with him in later life, even after he fell in love with a woman who – by some strange coincidence – considered that particular day just as important in her own life.

But that day, the feeling was tempered by a combination of both fear and exhilaration. He gripped his painted tin baksa tightly by the handle. The man who was supposed to meet him at the station was nowhere in sight, even though Saleem was at the gate the man had described in his letter.

Saleem had met the man twice before, as far as he could recall, and called him Satish Mama: he was Saleem's maternal uncle, though 'mama', in itself, did not mean anything. Saleem had grown up being patted on the head or tipped off for errands by an army of chachas, mamas and mausas; his mother had dozens of 'brothers', of whom some – like the Nautankiwallé Chacha, who had occasionally employed Saleem in his loud nautanki shows in Daryaganj – visited regularly over the years, while others came only once or twice. There was a Moté Chacha, known for his girth, a Hasté Chacha, known for his easy laughter, and a Talvarwallé Mausa, who never went anywhere, not even into Saleem's mother's room, without his curved sheathed sword.

A much older man, thin and white-bearded, Saleem's father was known as Maulvi Sahab in the neighbourhood not because he led the prayers or visited the mosque more than once every Friday, but because he was always buried in books and papers. In the evenings, when Gulabo entertained her guests on the second floor, Maulvi Sahab would collect Saleem and any other small boy or girl who might be around, herd them into a small room in a back corner of the ground floor, and instruct them in Urdu, Farsi, Arabic, mathematics and (ancient Greek and Arabic) philosophy in the light of two lanterns. Saleem had been a diligent student, with a talent for languages and an ear for accents, until his growing awareness of the world around him wrenched him away from the Maulvi Sahab.

In later years, Saleem was to wonder at his father and how he maintained the pretence that all the men going up to see Gulabo were her uncles, cousins, brothers. But that was later. At the time, in 1922, Saleem did not wonder at this self-deception on the part of his father; he detested it. He resented his father for it just as much as he resented him for being penniless: all the Maulvi Sahab's learning and intelligence did not fetch him a paisa. Occasionally, he was paid by a neighbour to write or read a letter, but even there it would be by default: he would read the letter out anyway without stipulating a fee, and it was up to the neighbour to offer him some money as a gift. Just as he would never ask Gulabo for money. Instead, he would say to her, Did I tell you, jaanam, yesterday in the market, Habib Darzi showed me a kurtah that reminded me of my younger days. And Gulabo would, later in the day, hand him a bundle of coins saying, I had this lying about and thought well, why not give Habib Darzi some custom. He is a good tailor. And Maulvi Sahab would take the bundle of coins saying, Yes, he is a good man.

By the time Saleem turned nine, he'd realized his father, the learned Maulvi Sahab, lived off the earnings of his mother. It took him a further four years, however, to realize how precisely Gulabo earned her money. When he did, he found himself getting into arguments with his father, being rude to the old man, even sometimes playing truant from the evening classes. He would see a cloud cross his father's face, his eyes flicker as if in shame or doubt, and he would feel sorry for the gentle old man, and even more angry at him at the same time. Saleem was torn by conflicting emotions, all churned up in the pottage of adolescence. As his chin grew a shadow and his voice broke, he struggled with his own sense of reality and respectability.

Other events took place in Saleem's fourteenth year. First, he lost his virginity to one of the girls who 'attended on' his mother in the evenings. (Unlike the neighbouring houses, Gulabo did not have other women living in her kotha. Instead she had a few – they called her Didi – who came to the kotha every evening and left the next morning.)

One night when the Maulvi Sahab was asleep and Saleem was loitering outside – he had started coming back late – a woman, much older than Saleem, emerged from the front door and beckoned to him. At first he thought she had been asked by the Maulvi Sahab to look for him, but when he entered the house, she closed the door behind them and put a finger to his lips. Then she led him into one of the empty rooms and squatted down on the floor, lifting up her sari. Saleem did not hesitate. He dropped his pyjamas, and entered her, haunch hammering against haunch. In a few seconds it was over and the woman stood so abruptly that Saleem fell backwards to the cold floor. It was dark. He could not see her expression. But he could sense she was laughing. Didi ka ladka aur anari! she giggled and dissolved into the shadows of the corridor. Didi's son and inexperienced!

Second, he fought with Talvarwallé Mausa.

The evenings when Talvarwallé Mausa visited Gulabo were usually filled with tension. The Talvarwallé Mausa had a loud voice and a combative attitude and it was seldom that he did not pick a fight with one of the other guests. Usually, he was talked out of it by the women or calmed down by the male musicians, who were in the pay of Gulabo. But on this particular evening, while Maulvi Sahab taught his classes below, the noise and bluster from above dragged on and on, until Saleem heard the voice of his mother raised in an angry scream. At this the Maulvi Sahab jumped up from the mat and shot out of the room, with Saleem and the other children following at a distance. As they approached the stairs, a bundle came rolling past their feet. It hit the corner of the landing, stopped and unfolded into a man. It was the Maulvi Sahab, trembling with hurt and frustration. The Talvarwallé Mausa was at the head of the stairs, his sword out. You, Maulvi, he shouted, leaving out the suffix of respect and making 'maulvi' sound nasty and demeaning, Maulvi, go back into your stinking hole . . .

You, sir, said the Maulvi Sahab, taking a step up, you

sir, have no right to speak like this to me in my own house.

He spoke softly, though his voice shook with fear or anger, and he did not swear. The Maulvi Sahab never swore.

The Talvarwallé Mausa met the Maulvi Sahab half-way, shook the thin man by the front of his kurtah and flung him down the stairs again, swearing and calling him a pimp. Saleem, unable to restrain himself, flew at the Talvarwallé Mausa and bit him hard in the sword arm. Saleem felt blood filling his mouth; the man flung him against the wall with a resounding blow but also dropped his sword, enabling the other men – onlookers until then – to hold Talvarwallé Mausa and cart him out of the kotha, swearing and flailing.

A week later, he was back, sword in place, with an elaborately wrapped basket of fruits for Gulabo; and when he stared defiantly at Saleem's father, the Maulvi Sahab simply looked away.

From that day Saleem stopped going to his father's evening classes. A week later, when Saleem began performing regularly for the Nautankiwallé Chacha and spending all night with a group of known trouble-makers, Gulabo and the Maulvi Sahab decided to send him to Satish Mama in Bombay.

Satish Mama lived alone. Unlike the other mamas and mausas, he had stayed at the kotha for more than a night – he had spent almost a month on each of his visits, sleeping in the room that the Maulvi Sahab used for his evening classes – but his stay was different from most in any case: he resembled Gulabo to such an extent that even Saleem, sensitive to deception, could not doubt their relationship. After an exchange of letters that took over six months to be completed, Saleem was bought a ticket to Bombay and sent off to stay with Satish Mama, though not without a sniff of deception trailing after him: in order to avoid the hostility that might accrue on both sides of the religious divide, Saleem – given his Muslim name and father – had to pretend to be the son of Satish Mama's Muslim raakhi-sister, not his actual, and hence Hindu, sibling.

Except that now there was no sign of Satish Mama at the designated gate of the terminal, where Saleem stood dwarfed by allegorical sculpture depicting not only such august personages as Progress and Queen Victoria but also the railway directors, the newly quantified castes of India and a profusion of real or imaginary flora and fauna. Saleem looked around, peering closely at people who looked vaguely, or at a distance, like Satish Mama. He had been confident of recognizing Satish Mama but now, faced with the flow of people in a strange place, he felt his confidence seeping away. Saleem was interrupted in his scrutiny of passing faces by an elderly man, and a boy who could not have been much older than Saleem.

They had been hovering around for sometime and now the man approached him and asked, Delhi?

What? stuttered Saleem.

Have you arrived from Delhi? You are Saleem, aren't you, son of Satish's raakhi-sister?

The old man explained that he was a friend of Satish – they worked in the same mill and lived in the same chawl – and he had been asked to meet Saleem.

But why isn't Satish Mama here?

He is away.

Away? That is not what he wrote. He said . . .

He is away, son. But we will take you to his room.

The boy had already picked up the tin suitcase that stood at Saleem's feet. Saleem grabbed it back from him. The old man and the boy did not look dangerous but Saleem had no reason to trust them. He was too much of a city boy.

I will wait for Satish Mama here, he told them. He can fetch me when he has time.

The old man looked dubious. It might take long, he said.

I don't mind waiting a few hours more.

Days, son. Then he added, after a slight hesitation, You see, your Satish Mama has been picked up by the police. He is in jail.

Saleem was too dazed by this piece of information to argue further and simply followed the old man and the boy when they picked up his suitcase and herded him past the recumbent Lion of Britain and Tiger of India into a tram a few metres away.

How does he know? I remember thinking. How can he know all this about Saleem Lahori? How much is the old man making up? Is that why his detractors call him 'Batuni', the talkative one? And I think the fact that I did not entirely believe his ramblings must have begun to register with Batin as well, for around this time he started justifying the veracity of his recollections, even questioning my responses occasionally, displaying his more argumentative self at times and subtly scoffing at my generation and its relationship to Bombay films – which irked me more than he realized.

They switched trams twice, once not very far from the gas works at Chinchpokli, and then walked a short distance to the chawl in Parel. Later, Saleem realized that they had taken a rather circuitous route, perhaps because that was the only route the old man was familiar with or because he had tried to distract and impress Saleem by showing him some of the sights of Bombay.

Like most chawls, this one (nameless, as far as Saleem could make out) was defined by vocational and caste loyalties. However, unlike in many other chawls, such loyalties were not inescapable and binding: while most of the inhabitants were UP and Bihari Hindus from the artisanal castes and many worked in the neighbouring textile mills, there were some Muslim youths, a few high-caste families from villages near Delhi and a handful of workers from the railway workshop at Parel as well as some hawkers.

Saleem had grown up in cramped quarters. The houses in his part of Daryaganj, not very far from the imposing bulk of Jama Masjid, hunched into one another, divided and connected by alleys that were sometimes only broad enough for two people walking shoulder to shoulder. He was used to dirt and mud and refuse, to the sun not reaching the dark and littered ground. But still, he was not prepared for Satish Mama's chawl, its bustle and filth.

Inside, Saleem had a feeling of claustrophobia that was unusual. The compound was after all wider than any of the alleys in Daryaganj. But the buildings around it diminished its width. The narrow staircases leading up, the verandas running around the buildings and overlooking the compound, the walls blackened with water from open drains, the pressure of eyes through windows and tattered curtains of sackcloth or newspaper: such was the presence of humanity in the buildings that it shrank the compound to insignificance, made it seem narrower and more cramped than any place Saleem had experienced until then.

The old man and the boy ushered Saleem up the stairs of the building to his right and into a small room on the second of its three floors. Then the old man pulled out a mat and tossed it to Saleem. The only good thing about Satish being in jail is that there will be more space for all of us tonight, he cackled. Though I guess we will have to eat at the Khanavali; I do not feel like cooking and Bhola here cannot cook to save his life.

It took Saleem a few minutes to understand that the two shared the room with Satish Mama.

They were woken up around midnight. Satish Mama had returned. He had been released earlier in the evening and had walked many kilometres to get back as the policemen had forgotten to return to him the little money he'd in his pockets at the time of his arrest. With Satish Mama's return the whole chawl began to stir. In ones and twos people came in and sat down, almost always in silence as if attending a solemn religious function. Some brought nimkis or biscuits. Soon the room and the veranda outside contained at least twenty-five men, sitting on the floor or, now there were so many of them, standing. It was then Saleem discovered what Satish Mama did. And in some ways, Gulabo's brother had chosen a career that was just as legitimate – or illegitimate – as hers.

★

'Why do you look so doubtful, my young scholar? Is it because I am recalling too many things? It is difficult, young man, for me to recount just one story, for each leads to another. You know, when I was your age I used to believe that stories had a beginning and an end. Now I know that they only have hooks, many hooks, and each hook is caught up by another hook. The Saleem who arrived in Bombay in 1922 was the same man as the ageing, almost-forgotten star who fought a losing battle in the Dallam Studio in 1948, but in between there had been so many stories . . . where do I begin? What do I tell?'

Satish Mama's room was filled with different human smells and sounds; outside, the night was dark, with only one gas lamp in the compound and a couple of lanterns in the room itself.

Though he listened to the conversations around him, Saleem could not always follow them. He gathered that all the men worked in the same textile mill, but what they did remained a mystery to him. It was not the dialects he was confused by; it was the words used: the men spoke of tarwalas and drafting rollers, spindles and bobbins, naikins and (here their voice assumed a sombre note) jobbers. They spoke of time rates and piece rates. The more voluble among them referred to the general strike of January 1920 and the Indian Factories Act of 1911. And again and again they referred to the new maalik, someone called Dharamchand, each time with bitterness. The English word 'lock-out' was used by a couple of the more angry young men.

'Dharamchand. Mark the name, young man. You have heard it before and you will hear it again. It is a name that, unlike the name of Satish Mama (or, for that matter, Saleem Lahori), has grown with the times: from Dharamchand to Seth Dharam-chand to Dharamchand and Sons to . . . who knows what it might be today. I stopped keeping track decades ago . . .'

Satish Mama changed his posture and one of the men sitting on the charpoy next to him held up a hand. Suddenly, the room subsided into silence, which merged into the silence outside. A dog howled somewhere. But Satish Mama ignored the howling and began to speak.

Many of you, he said, looking at the old man next to him, who nodded slightly, many of you will remember when I came to this chawl. It was the same day that I started working in the mills, which were owned by Seth Dwarkadas in those days, of course. I came to this chawl (and here I have stayed) less than a month after coming to Bombay. I spent that month on the wharf and I distinctly recall, on 9th January 1915 – I even remember the date – watching the arrival of Gandhiji and his family while carrying loads to an adjoining ship. He still looked very young then, almost a boy, but there was a crowd with garlands to receive him. I did not know who

he was. I was told later by one of the older coolies. The
coolie told me how Gandhiji had led a large army of
men and monkeys, like Lord Ram, against the British in
Africa and almost destroyed them single-handedly. I
found it difficult to believe, not just because I do not
think our times are the same as the days of Lord Ram,
but also because there was around Gandhiji and his
family a certain aura of being that, I thought, was very
removed from my life. As such, when I urged all of you
to join Gandhiji's movement some months ago, I did so
not because I believed it would succeed, but because it
was the right thing to do. And my doubts were right.
You all know that the movement has been withdrawn.
That is not a tragedy for us as mill hands; the tragedy
is that this call has coincided with Seth Dharamchand's
attempt to increase, in effect if not on paper, our
working day by an hour. This, as you know, is against
the law. But Dharamchand is not Seth Dwarkadas; we
would not be in this predicament if Seth Dwarkanath
had not been forced to sell many of his mills in recent
years. The days of working with Seth Dwarkadas were
not without their problems, of course, but at least you
could talk to Seth Dwarkadas. He might, if he considered it necessary, employ his money (and God knows
he had money then) to get his way; but he would never
employ force or criminal tactics. Not like this Dharamchand, who has bought up so many of Seth Dwarkadas's

businesses. Dharamchand, I hate to say to those of you who want a strike, is a first-rate harami; he will employ everything against you. He won't just try to break the strike; he will break you.

There was a pause, as Satish Mama waited for the murmuring which his words had caused to die out. Then he raised his voice and said, using the English word 'smash' – that Saleem gathered had an extra meaning in the language of mills – He will *ismash* you so badly that no binchod weaver will be able to draw in your broken threads and reshuttle.

In response to a louder hum from his audience, he raised his hand and said, Do not misunderstand me. I am not asking you to be afraid; I am asking you to be cautious, to be prepared. Listen to me. Listen to what happened to me when I was picked up by the police yesterday after work. For no reason whatsoever. But the bastard Dharamchand had found a reason. He had also heard about the meeting we held here two days ago to discuss a protest strike and heard that all of you had entrusted me with the responsibility of organizing it. You know I am not a Gandhi man; I am not a communist either. Yes, I have walked in crowds of Gandhi's men and I have applauded Comrade Mirajkar's speeches: who won't applaud the Punjab Mail in full flow? (This reference to the fiery communist leader as one of the fastest and noisiest trains running through the mill areas drew a ripple of laughter from the audience.) But I am not one of them. I am one of you. I am not even a unionist. I am here, like you are here, and when I fight, I fight for a better life, not for some abstract principle. Principles, we know, do not fill an empty stomach. You cannot clothe your children in principles. You know all this, and Dharamchand, who knows what we are about to do even before we do it, surely the bastard knows this too. But somehow the police had come to believe that I was a communist: I was interrogated for hours about Mirajkar and Ghaté and the Gaya Congress. Don't ask me how Dharamchand got the police to believe this, whether he bribed them or whether he played on the government's fear of the communists in Russia. But believe him they did. And if we have a lock-out tomorrow, we will be seen not as fighting for our legitimate rights, but as agents of communists and per-haps even 'foreign powers'. That is why I ask you, don't be afraid but be cautious. We are up against a vicious enemy this time.

But what is it that you are actually saying, Satishbhai? one of the young men burst out. Are you asking us to abandon our strike even before we have struck work?

Yes and no, said Satish Mama with a somewhat mischievous smile. I am asking you to abandon the strike and organize a tamasha instead.

A tamasha? The old man sitting next to Satish Mama

was visibly startled. You mean with music and plays and all?

Yes, a tamasha. I have not just walked with the Gandhi men, Gajanand Kaka. A tamasha, with perhaps Ram Katha in the evenings for the next three days. Surely, if the chawl has a tamasha, we cannot be expected to go to work? We are not communists or foreign agents; we will not strike. But we are workers and Hindus; we will have a tamasha and Ram Katha. Even Seth Dharamchand cannot deny us that.

Gajanand Kaka laughed, as did many of the other men in the room. But then one of them said, How, Satish Bhai? How do you expect us to get a tamasha organized in a few hours? It takes days to organize one, collect funds, get people . . .

The funds are up to us, said Satish Mama, rising from the charpoy. I have one rupee and two annas in my box here.

He walked to a corner and took the money out of a large metal box. He spread a towel over the charpoy and dropped the coins onto it.

Here, he said. Leave whatever you have on this bed. One anna, a chavanni, a rupya, whatever. As for the tamasha, don't we have young men like Amar in the chawl? They are actors; they know artistes. Surely, they can find us some group by noon?

I will call Amarbhai, a voice from the door said. And

a few minutes later Saleem met a bleary-eyed Amar, still rubbing sleep from his eyes. It was a meeting that would, along with his involvement in the tamasha, change Saleem's career – and life.

'It was from the various tamashas organized at the chawl and his growing friendship with the actors living there that, over the next few years, Saleem gravitated to films. Not immediately, you understand. Over about three to four years. At first, he began working as a badli after the first tamasha ended. Dharamchand gave in after two days, perhaps because he was still new to the game and could see that he had been out-manoeuvred. With the mill running again, Satish Mama took Saleem to the Jobber in charge of employing and training labour – he was also the man who ran the Khanavali to which Saleem had been taken by the old man, Gajanand, for his first meal in the chawl – and after some discussion the Jobber agreed to list Saleem as a badli, that is, a worker who would stand in for an absentee worker. Mills had a high rate of absenteeism and being a badli could mean work for days at a stretch if the Jobber favoured you. But it was not regular employment and on the days when Saleem had no work he would hang around with Amar, Akbar and their actor friends, sometimes picking up odd assignments as a film extra. He preferred working as a film extra to his mill jobs: an hour or two of shooting earned him more than an entire day at the mill. Moreover, the sets were places of light and colour, very different from the mills with their tall barbed-wire

walls, their grey rectangular buildings, their damp darkness, their leaking, polluted water tanks and dirty, crowded canteens, their humming and grinding machines, their frequent alarms when the loom's moving parts collided – this was a 'smash', Saleem was to find out – or the yarn broke. Well, young man, yes, I know sets are noisy places too, but in a mill the noise is that of souls trapped and punished, and on a set, well, on a set the noise is that of a party getting out of hand. Or that is what Saleem used to say, anyway. He is there in a number of films of the early 1920s, a tinsel-studded courtier in Star Films' Chandragupta, *a Rajput warrior in B. P. Mishra's* Veer Durgadas, *a greasy lawyer in Naval Gandhi's* Bombay ki Sethani. *By 1925, when Satish Mama was forced by circumstances and his own nature to become all that he had not wanted to be, Saleem was landing bigger roles. He had been luckier than Amar or Akbar, perhaps because of the fact that he had grown into a remarkably handsome man and had some histrionic ability – his rhetorical style of acting was noticed quite early on and sometimes Amar or Akbar teased him by calling him 'the future Henry Irving of India' – or perhaps (as it was also rumoured) he had the luck of becoming the lover of a series of older women who, either as mistresses or actresses, had some say in the industry. One of the women he was linked to was almost famous: I won't mention the name, young man, but I will say that she was one of those actresses who had the vulgar 'Bai' suffixed to their names before they became stars and the respectable 'Devi' afterwards. But whatever the case, in 1925 Saleem*

*got his first proper role in a film, what would be called a
supporting role now, and was paid fifty rupees for it. He had
never seen so much money in one place before; the average
monthly wage of a millhand was around thirty rupees in those
days and a badli earned much less. Soon afterwards, he took on
the room in the chawl that his Satish Mama vacated that year
because . . . well, let us leave that for later.'*

The heddi tree outside the studio building is wet after
the sudden sharp downpour; water glistens in its hollows. The pools, seen from the vantage point of the
window that opens into the branches of the tree on the
second floor, reflect the sun that has come out again.

Saleem saunters into the only room on the second
floor that had been a set. (The other rooms on the
second floor had been for storage, make-up, guests, and
the southern wing was being used as private quarters by
Hari, Bhuvaneshwari and Rajkunwar.) He can hear the
voices of the two children coming from that direction,
intermingled with Bhuvaneshwari's laughter. They are
playing some game. It is only recently that the children
have started laughing, and they still do not laugh in the
company of anyone except Bhuvaneshwari and, occasionally, Saleem. In spite of the brusque manner that he
has cultivated over the years, his matter-of-factness, his
caustic quips, Saleem has been deeply touched by the
children's response to him. From the moment he dis-

covered them hiding in a corner of the burned house – at first he thought it was a couple of stray dogs – and picked them up (once it was a pigeon, now it is children), they clung to him, followed him with large, hurt eyes.

He looks up and can see the muslin stretched across the ceiling, diffusing the light from the thick glass panes that form half the ceiling in this room. The glass ceiling of the roof is scattered with pearldrops of water. This set had been made to use natural light in the days when the studio lacked lighting facilities, as it does again at least during the nights – now that the electric connection has been cut and they are too few and too insecure to go out to the generator next to the stables after dark.

The diffuse light beats softly on his face, turning the few greying hairs a venerable silver. The room still contains old instruments once used to make the magic of films: a man-size camera that resembles two bulbous eyes on three alien legs, like some space creature; a discarded single-system Tanar recording equipment. In such surroundings, Saleem cannot but think of his days as an actor. Acting had filled a hole in him. By enabling him to step out of his own skin, it enabled him to live with unanswered questions – what had happened to Satish Mama or his parents, whether what Gulabo and the Maulvi Sahab had shared was after all love, if . . . there were so many questions. He realizes now that

Bhuvaneshwari and the two children have made it impossible for him to escape the issue of responsibility and choice, indeed perhaps to live comfortably, which is not a gift to disdain.

They had been heady years. In spite of his imploding stardom, in spite of the war, in spite of the growing rumours of Partition. When did they end: in 1945, when Avik made that remark? In 1946, when Bala was murdered? Or as late as 1947?

Saleem Lahori's nostrils fill with the acrid smoke of things burning which were not made to be incinerated in that manner: beds and chairs, plastic and rubber, books, film, flesh. He can still smell smoke from the time, only a year ago, when smoke and fire had become their neighbours: when he had roved with the Aakrosh troupe from village to town in the North, distributing pamphlets, performing 'amity skits', seeing things that were unimaginable in Bombay. He smells the smoke and doesn't know, for a confusing second, whether it is a fire burning in his memory or whether the nightmare of the past has come alive again. But the smoke cannot obscure the bright realms of his memories of the years before the riots. They appear through the rent shreds of 1947.

His mind, used as it is to the idiom of cinema, often replays scenes from that time. They come back to him

and with each viewing lose a bit of their colour, each
time becoming more jumpy and jerky and disjointed.
They come back to him day after day now, like the
stones that land on the studio walls and roofs night after
night. Each stone is a memory. Each memory is a stone.

Standing there in the dim light of the shuttered windows
of a besieged and almost abandoned studio building,
Saleem Lahori recalls the rectangular room in which he
had started his film career, a career that had come to
him almost by accident. He had lived like so many
others, narrowly. The calendar on the wall; the sounds
of the chawl ranged around a littered compound, teeming with excrement and vermin. He had occupied a
room, two metres by four, on the second of its three
floors, reached by a veranda festooned with washing, the
air tangible, heavy with smoke from stoves and chullahs,
the ceilings damp in the corners with drain water from
the floor above.

But there had been companionship then, Satish
Mama and Bhola to begin with, then friends like Amar
and Akbar in the next room, the passageway divided by
a disintegrating sackcloth curtain; and next to that
another room, shared this time by three brothers who
sold peanuts and other snacks from three different
portable bamboo stands in Chowpatty, shuttling for

hours by tram and train every morning and evening, and next to them another room and another, and more below, and more above.

There were entire families, and lonely bachelors. There were pundits and whores; there were university graduates, rickshawpullers, businessmen, technicians and, above all, a sprinkling of actors. Aspiring actors. Extras, fillers, walk-on artistes, faces in the crowd behind the hero. He remembers their faces. He can even recall their names, all of them men . . . One or two continued after the first three years or so, but the rest went back to their hometowns or found other professions. Perhaps he and Amar and Akbar/Anthony are the only ones still left in the film industry.

These, he knows, are private sorrows: for public traumas have passed him by and left nothing more than conventional regret. He recalls hearing the blast that had marked the sinking of *Fort Stikine*, when limbs and heads and wood and gold bars and metal pieces had showered over much of Bombay. The ship had been carrying bales of cotton, which had caught fire in the summer heat, and had ignited the cargo of explosives – it was wartime – which the ship had also contained. When the main explosion came, it had tossed into the seething summer air not just human bodies and bits of the ship, but also silver and gold bars, which was the secret cargo being brought by *Fort Stikine* to stabilize the war-hit Indian rupee. There was some talk of sabotage, but the British were quick to scotch that rumour.

About three hundred people had died, some of them blown to bits on the docks, some decapitated by the metal sheets and shreds hurled into the city by the explosion. For months afterwards, Bombay talk would return to the explosion. It was the lodestar of all polite conversation: those aspiring to wealth talking about the gold bars that had showered on the city (the marvel of sudden riches) and those already affluent horrified or pretending to be horrified by more gory happenings, a flying metal sheet slicing the head of a man going to the market, a horse skewered by an iron rod. But all that talk – even the talk of war, with its great losses, or of the first riots in 1946 in other parts of India, had evoked in Saleem, as such news does, a kind of abstract regret and sympathy. It was only when the public strife assumed a private face that Saleem's world started emptying of colour and sound.

He associates this turn to the *Aakhri Raat* story sessions, which mostly took place in Hari's dark, curtained bedroom with Joshilla and Rajkunwar. It was summer, the heat was unusual, like a wall, and the sunlight seemed almost geometrical and physical outside. Inside, the fan circled overhead, water dropped from a mechanical arrangement on the khus at the windows. Hari handed Joshilla the lined exercise books in which he had apparently been keeping a sort of diary: there were seven in all, the first three tattered and broken and held together by string or rubber bands. Hari said, This is the story of my life and I want to make a picture of it. The frown on Rajkunwar's face. These are jottings, Joshbhai, but you can make a screenplay of these. It is all there.

The frown on Rajkunwar's face.

Hari said, I want to call it *Teen Ajnabi*. Rajkunwar snorted. Three Strangers! Who will go to see a film with that title? And finally, at the end of two hours of barbed negotiations, the name had been found: *Aakhri Raat*. Last Night.

'I was there: Josh always involved me in the scriptwriting. It was then that I noticed the tension between Rajkunwar and Hari Babu. Perhaps, I thought, their different preoccupations had in the past obscured the hate, the dislike that had accumulated over the years. But once they were working together on a film about the trajectory of their own dreams, their common desire, they finally realized that they were not collaborators after all but competitors. Have I asked this before, young man: how can you desire the same thing without coming to blows over it? It is strange they did not ask themselves this even in those years, when the common desire for independence was tearing through a land, rending villages and families asunder, ripping apart human bodies like some mythical demon, this common desire, this good

*desire, this peaceful desire for a breath of freedom, a nation of
one's own, independence.'*

What Saleem Lahori saw enacted during the filming of
Aakhri Raat did not surprise him entirely. Over the
years, Saleem had come to see filmmaking as a sacrificial process: it involved a certain sacrifice of personality
on the part of the actors. The exaggerated actions and
mannerisms of some actors and industry people was a
consequence of this constant killing of one's own self
on the altar of performance: they tried to pretend that
they still had what had been sacrificed, and this pretence
could only be sustained through an exaggerated sem-
blance of personality. But more than that, the way a film
developed was sacrificial: it involved the ritual slaughter
of various components of the original idea and plan.
Facts, lines, images, camera angles, characters, themes
described in the original masterplan could subsequently
be sacrificed. So a corny line would be retained because
it appealed to the star or the producer and an apt expression would be slashed to shreds. It was the same with
people; the victims were always weaker, and often sur-
rogates: conflict between two stars, or between director
and producer, would be enacted through the whittling
away of lesser roles, a bargaining of cameos and extras,
with – finally – the weakest, least-connected actor seeing
his two-minute role axed from the finished film.

Saleem was used to this process, but what unfolded during the making of *Aakhri Raat* went beyond such rituals. There was real violence – though sometimes only in words – between Hari and Rajkunwar, both straining to fit their facts into fiction, both grasping at details of desire that were invisible to everyone else, both calling for greater and bloodier sacrifices. And there was a symmetry of violence in those days: what was happening in the studio was also happening outside, as sacrifices were being demanded elsewhere too.

That is how he came to see it when Dr Surender Singh took to mysticism, growing his hair long, disappearing for days into temples and dargahs and gurudwaras. Around the same time religion came out of temples and mosques and gurudwaras and started running rampant on the streets. (What had he hoped for, what had you hoped for, you gentle giant, you medical misfit? Did you think you could stop all the madness by going to the roots of religion? And where are you now? In what temple or dargah or gurudwara? Or if with your usual obstinacy you persisted in going to all three, then – and Saleem thinks the thought bitterly – in what unmarked grave?)

That is also how he came to see it when they waited and waited and waited for Bala to disembark. (That was also when the marvels stopped altogether and the night-mares began, and Saleem came to realize that neither fact nor fiction, neither truth nor lie has a patent on violence.)

The long wait in sultry April when Bala did not turn up. The train emptying of passengers, a beggar crawling through an empty compartment, evading the vigilance of the Anglo-Indian guard, collecting everything that had been discarded during the long journey from Delhi but still had value in his world. Dr Surender interrogating the Bengali ticket collector and managing to find out, after a hurried consultation of clipped charts, that Bala had not boarded the train in Delhi, despite an advance booking. And later, as they had done the rounds of railway offices and police stations and Bala's editors, the growing anger in Avik Sen's voice as he muttered, spitting, I told him, I told him not to go into those mullah regions. And the irritation in Ashiq Painter's voice as he countered, how do you know it was a Muslim who killed him? And finally the day Saleem stood in front of Bala's widow – the mystery of Bala's murder still unsolved but the body having been fetched from Karachi by sea (after much pulling of political and administrative wire) – and wanted to know when the cremation would take place. The day Bala's widow hesitated and finally Bala's eldest son, an angry and bewildered youth of seventeen, answered for her, blurting out the words without looking at Saleem: It is a Hindu ceremony. It is only for Hindus.

It was a new world, the promised era of freedom, but somehow Saleem could no longer imagine the future. Perhaps Avik could, and Ashiq, but could people like him and Bhuvaneshwari? For he had slowly come to faintly comprehend what he shared with this woman who ran the studio and whose name never appeared in the credits of the films made here. He shared with her a space that was being gradually erased all around them.

They had called her Bhuvaneshwari, which was as good a name as any and reminded her of the Durga she had once been, for it was the domestic form of the Goddess, though of course Durga carried no echo of the Muslim name she had borne before that. From Durga, wife of Harihar the Bioscopewallah, to Bhuvaneshwari, wife of Director Hari Babu, so many shifting roles and relationships – Ma, Didi, Mausi, Bhabhi – in so many different accents, dialects, even languages spoken by the people who had come to the studio and to whom she had been mother or aunt or sister or daughter.

She had seen them come, and she had seen most of them leave over the past two years. They had trickled into the studio as rivulets of rain trickle into a puddle or a pond during monsoon, some invisible arrangement of the landscape leading them in that one direction. Each stained the colour of his or her trajectory, those lines they had traced across the deceptive flatness of the earth to this place. Red as moraine were the two brothers from the foothills of the Himalayas, who had come seeking work as actors and stayed on as clapperboys and extras. Pale as sand was Singh from Rajputana, who had joined Raheeman Cha as the other guard, both full of the martial myths of their manufactured clan memories. Dark as the stones of Chotta Nagpur was the Munda gardener. There were so many of them. Rather, there had been so many of them. Before the troubles started, before the downpour of cinematic success slowly petered out to an increasing drought in the studio, while outside it started to rain blood and screams. They started disappearing then, some back to the homes they had left, some to new homes in places of safety. And some just disappeared altogether. Like Yusuf, for she remembers his disappearance most. What colour was he? What was he?

Yusuf had turned up one sunny morning, not carrying anything and dressed in an oversized shirt and pyjamas, which made him look smaller than he was. He was small. No bigger than a normal-sized child of ten or eleven, though he claimed to be thirty-four years old. The exact age surprised her: so few of them knew their own age, or wanted to reveal it. She herself was not sure how old she was. So Yahunf (as he pronounced his own name, for the boy-dwarf suffered from some kind of speech deficiency) had come to them, certain only about his own age and the fact that he could work with horses. (She feels certain that they gave him a chance because of his name, for Rajkunwar had burst out laughing, Yahoo, he had said, Yahoo, we will try you out with the horses for a week. But we will call you Yahoo, he had added, guffawing for some reason Bhuvaneshwari could not comprehend, and Hari had smiled too.)

They had four horses in those days and needed a stable boy; Yusuf had proved to be a wizard with animals. He had been less successful with the other workers and actors and technicians. His deformity and speech had removed him from them. And the fact that he was always enveloped in a horsy aura, the smell of dung and straw; even his voice had the nasal note of a neigh. And he had slept in the stables. Stories had percolated about him: it was said that he was an orphan of unknown origin who had been found, as an infant, in the stables of a local raja, that he had been allowed to live there, reared on what he could scrounge and the food sent out to him from the kitchens when anyone remembered; it was said that even now, when he could not sleep on the reed mat that he spread out over a pile of straw in a dry corner of the stables, even now when the dark horses of sleep eluded him, he would climb onto the back of his favourite mare, an old nag, and instantly fall into a comfortable slumber.

And then, some months ago, when dreams and nightmares were raging across the land, when Pakistan and India were taking shape in a cascade of blood and screams, Yusuf had disappeared. It was the night before the mare was to be sent to the butcher. At first, Rajkunwar and Hari and their various lackeys had asked in a joking manner, Where is Yahoo today? Haven't seen the Lilliput all day. But then news had trickled in from the stable that not only Yusuf but also the mare had been missing all morning and well into the afternoon. Rajkunwar had flown into a rage and telephoned the Khopoli police station to register a case of theft against Yusuf. A prize-winning stallion, he had told them.

Perhaps the police were too busy with other thefts, other disappearances; nothing had happened. For some days, rumours abounded in the studio: rumours about how Yusuf had decided to ride the mare all the way to Pakistan, or how he had run away with her to some nearby forest. Even, in the slow evenings, talk about how he was still somehow in the studio compound, he and his mare, how there was sometimes a smell of him in the corridors, or the sound of invisible hooves, lame trotting. Then, gradually, Yusuf had disappeared from their talk. But for some reason, Bhuvaneshwari has never forgotten the boy-dwarf: she recalls his neighing speech, his easy understanding of horses; his marvellous appearance and his unexplained disappearance signal to her a change in the story of the studio. His leaving was, she feels, a sign of lack, of drought, or of a monsoon that rains something other than water.

But then she thinks of the two children brought to her by Saleem Lahori only a few months after Yusuf's disappearance, and she is no longer certain whether lack or drought is the appropriate word for the change that was taking place across India, across West Pakistan and East Pakistan, but most of all in those hidden aspects of people that trail along inescapable and unobserved like shadows.

'Yusuf, a small man, a deformed dwarf – not someone who would ever enter a history book or feature in a film about those times. And in that way, young man, not so different from Bhuvaneshwari, who, I am sure, never appears in any of those books on Bombay films that you have read. And yet, jot down the name: Yusuf, the boy-dwarf, the ghostly rider of horses. Yes, write his name in your diary, my young scholar; it is more important in its own way than many of the things you have written so far. Like Bhuvaneshwari, Yusuf is not just an extra in my story, oh no, far from it, far from it.'

★

Why is it that she was the only one capable of recognizing, however fleetingly, the change that took so many people unaware? She could see it happening. But not in the studio. In the studio, somehow, all external fractures were healed; the internal tensions had their own logic and were not the same as the forces that were fracturing the land outside. In the studio, a different reality – with its own cracks and fissures – reigned. But elsewhere (and that is why she hardly ever left the studio any more) for that fraction of a second that might take place in the mind or outside of it, shadows would detach themselves from bodies. At first, there would only be a hairline crack or a gap of an inch or two, but the gulf would widen; with some people, shadows would disappear altogether. Bhuvaneshwari – frightened by the way her pretended ability to read shadows was coming alive – would look away, then back, and everything would be back to normal. But just when she least expected, it would happen again. Not to everyone. Some – like Saleem – seemed unaffected. With others, though – Ashiq or Avik, for instance . . . For a shadow without a body is a frightening thing; a body without a shadow can only be ruthless.

'Listen to this, my young scholar. I am translating it from memory, but I remember it well. Saleem Lahori used to quote it

*in the Farsi. It was one of the extracts his father would read out
to him from al-Biruni's tenth-century book on shadows. I think
I can recall it almost verbatim: The greatest length of the shadow
extended along the ground is at sunrise and sunset and hence al-
Khali used to say that whenever an affair reaches completion, its
decline approaches.'*

It was not something she could mention to the others,
for it happened only fleetingly and only in her eyes, and
surely anyone else would attribute it to a flaw in her
vision, perhaps even see it as a sign of incipient lunacy.
But, quite early, she had begun to see it as a sign of
what was happening to the land, and as such she was
not surprised when the stones finally started landing on
the studio, thrown by shadows in the night. And because
she did not consider it a simple error of sight or a
complex slip of sanity, she had shut herself up in recent
months in the studio compound, for this was one of the
few places that, she felt, remained conjoint. And now
she held on to the studio building with a desperation
that went beyond her original desire for a home, a
desperation that she felt was vindicated when the studio,
emptied of its horses and birds and monkeys, emptied
of Yusuf, emptied of most of its regular servants and
studio hands, suddenly filled with two children: Kabir
and the nameless girl, recovered from the charred build-

ings, so frightened that Saleem had to carry both of them to the van, like they were stricken birds, his fine silk kurtah muddy with their fear, so frightened that she still needed to sleep with an arm around them . . .

She had once sacrificed a child to make home possible, now she was unwilling to abandon the two children that had been given to her.

Durga had woken up with a start and not known where she was. The slant of the daylight was wrong; the feel of the charpoy was strange. This had never happened when touring with Harihar. Somehow, she had always known where she was: under the blue roof of the sky or the grey roof of the tent, she had known. But today it had taken her a minute to recall that she was in one of the rooms of the Anjangarh haweli's courtyard. (They had been living in this room for almost two months now, in the pay of the Chotte Thakur, the projector standing in a corner, the tent, cart and other equipment stored away in one of the sheds attached to the courtyard, the bullocks let out to graze with the haweli's kine. And now they were all gone – much of the equipment on its way back to Calcutta, the cart and bullocks sold to a villager.) That was all it had taken Durga to reorient herself, just a minute, but for that minute she had no sense of her place in the world. She turned to look at the room, her neck humid with perspiration, and she noticed a line of red ants crawling across the dusty floor in a tidy zigzag from the doorpost to a crack in the wall.

Her lips were dry and crusted. Her mouth felt stale. Harihar was sleeping on her right in a separate charpoy, as he used to. It was early, so early that the courtyard was still silent. Almost, apart from the twitter of birds and the gargling and spitting of a man performing his morning ablutions. Durga felt around for Ashok and experienced a moment's panic before she recalled that he had slept over in the haweli. Then the day fell into place in her mind and she remembered.

How had it come to this? And so soon. Less than two months ago they had been in the bullock cart, trundling up a narrow dirt path to an unknown village and a haweli wrapped in a faint but palpable aura of gloom. Less than two months ago, Ashok was running after the cart, imitating bird calls. Less than two months ago, he had banged on the metal-knobbed door of the haweli and she had clutched the Munshi's thin hairy legs, begging. What had Ashok shouted at the gates? Why does that memory come back to her so vividly?

She looked at Harihar, so soundly asleep, and was irritated. How could he sleep through the oppressive heat of the night – she had fallen asleep after hours of tossing and turning in bed – continue to sleep, so soundly, this morning of all days?

Ashok had shouted, Khul Simsim, khul Simsim.

Sesame had opened for him. There were no thieves in that cave, no, not thieves, but people with gifts, or at least one woman with gifts, the gift of sweets and toys and clothes, the gift of a new relationship. And then the gift of this ceremony, this honour Durga would be a fool to refuse.

This sacrifice. The glory of it, O, the glory of it.

When the hidden truth was revealed to her much later, years later, she found it hard to forgive Harihar and Chotte Thakur for using Ashok as the pawn in their game, for persuading her in terms of what was best for him rather than what was desired by them. For how could she have refused their appeal to her mother-hood? Wasn't it expected of the mother, for what do mothers do in films but sacrifice? In all the ancient stories and myths Durga knew, the mother stood silent, eyes brimming with tears, sacrificing herself for her child, sacrificing her child for the status quo: Krishna's mother, Karna's mother, Rama's mother, Kabir's mother. What choice did she have after such epics of sacrifice?

The morning was rent by the cries of the moorhen

from a bush outside the courtyard. It sounded like an animal in pain.

The ceremony had been explained to her by Harihar. Hiranyagarbha, is what he called it. An ancient ceremony, a Vedic ceremony still practised in the house of the Thakurs. Or the house of Maalkini's ancestors, she forgets which.

It involved a golden vessel. A large golden vessel. It involved pundits and Brahmins and fire and hymns. It involved putting a man into that vessel. He had to lie there curled, as if a foetus in a womb. It involved the chanting of hymns and verses, the pouring of rice and petals. It involved the death of the man; it involved the rebirth of the man inside that vessel, born into a higher caste if necessary.

It was unbelievable to her and, she could see from their faces, also to most of the villagers, who had never imagined the possibility of escaping caste in one lifetime. But the Bade Thakur had caused the Vedic verses and descriptions to be read out – first in sonorous Sanskrit for the effect and then in Hindi translation – and who were they to argue with the wealth of the Thakurs and the learning of the Brahmins? And the Brahmins had agreed too, but only after pointing out that in this case the transfer of caste remained confined to the twice born: after all, Hari was a Brahmin and so, they assumed, was she.

Perhaps the Brahmins had been so accommodating because the golden vessel was always given to the officiating Brahmins in the past. But this was not the Vedic age. This was Kaljug. A silver vessel would have to suffice. A silver vessel was enough. And a silver vessel had already been procured.

The silver vessel that was the golden womb of death and rebirth.

Who was Durga to object to religion and rebirth?

'Religion, young man. None of us ever objected to it, finally. Not one. We found reasons to titter at it, to ignore it, to excuse it. We forgot that at the heart of all religions there is a little man facing a big god. And we who were neither big nor little, ignored both in different ways. So that when the two forged an alliance, when the little man armed himself with his big god, all we could do was run.

There are things to be said in our favour too, young man. Of course there are. After all, we were hoping for a secular rebirth. But then again, how can there be rebirth without death? Hundreds of deaths; millions of deaths. The rituals of modern sacrifice in which entire peoples are put on the stone slab and killed for the sake of the wellbeing and unity of the nation.'

★

Anjangarh has been awake for sometime. Perhaps it did not sleep that night. It is that kind of night after all. But now even Harihar, who did sleep, is stirring.

Miryasin Maiya pokes her head round the door. She is chewing on a datwan twig. She chews on it for some time until her eyes get used to the shade of the room. Her cheeks work like deflated balloons. Then she takes the twig out and speaks.

Awake, daughter? she says. Take a bath. I have had Phaagu draw a bucket for both of you. Maalkini's asked me to make sure that you do not have to do such things anymore.

Then she shakes her head and mutters, What a blessing, what a blessing, who can read the play of fate? She goes away chewing vigorously on her datwan twig, even though she doesn't have a single tooth left to clean.

The women are singing. They are singing in a rustic dialect. Their song has a harsh but rhythmic quality. Durga understands only a word or two in every other sentence. But she knows that these are the songs that are sung in this region after childbirth. These songs herald the birth of a male child.

Harihar is dressed in a silk kurtah and dhoti that the Maalkini has sent. He stands next to the Chotte Thakur, who is also wearing a silk kurtah and dhoti. They could be father and son. What are they thinking? Are they thinking of films and music, of the sensational screen that has captivated both of them in different ways? Or have they finally noticed the sensation of this event happening around them, this thing, for it is palpable and alive, this act they have so easily agreed to on her behalf, this act she cannot say no to?

The haweli has woken up. It has dropped its aura of silence and gloom, is filled by the chatter of people. The kitchens are busy, cooking food to serve at least eight hundred guests from the villages in the neighbourhood. Tents have been erected all around the haweli. It looks as if an army has come to camp.

Later, as the bluster of the summer day declines into the soothing currents of evening, there will be entertainment. But not provided by Durga: Harihar will not hold his bioscope show; Durga will not sing. Never again in this village and never in the villages around it. That is part of the deal, a legal document, stamped and attested, bearing her thumbprint and Harihar's signature.

'I didn't realize then, but it would involve more than one death and more than one rebirth, she told me later.'

She looks across the mat to where the Badi Maalkini sits on a decorated charpoy. Its cover is of pure silk, embroidered with silver thread.

Apart from the Bade Thakur, who sits next to the Maalkini, inscrutable as ever, and Harihar and the Chotte Thakur and one or two other men – and of course the seven Brahmins who lead the ceremony – it is women who fill the room. From the doors and the windows there peer a hundred heads and hundreds more crowd the haweli and mill around the courtyard. Something exceptional is happening. Something sensational.

She clutches Ashok more firmly to her breast and feels him stiffening with resentment. He feels he is too old to be sitting in her lap.

Harihar has his own qualms about the ceremony. He is not even sure whether it was sanctioned by the Vedas, and if it was, he is certain it had some other significance originally. But the rich can invent religion. And he has no doubt about the Maalkini's intention. The matter had to be put to Durga in a subtle manner, of course; he doesn't think he has lied to her. No, he has just made it possible for her to realize her dreams for Ashok, whittled away all the other words to leave only one: 'home'. Isn't that what she has always desired?

And then, in spite of a sense of unease, a dull ache when he looks at Ashok, he starts thinking about the future, the future that suddenly seems possible.

★

'It was then, he later told me, that he started working on the love story contained in his diaries, the one we finally filmed as Aakhri Raat. I don't think he realized, even years later, the irony of writing about love at the very moment he had bartered it away. The story was originally meant to be narrated from the perspective of a single night, but all that remained of that idea in the end was just the title. He commented on that, though: he laughed and said, This is what happens to dreams in reality, they leave only one image, two words.

What he did not comment on in that light-hearted manner, what – I realized later – made all his petty differences with Rajkunwar turn so intransigent and disruptive, was a darker issue. In his story, the heroine had been betrayed as a child, and the film was in part about redeeming the past. There was, no doubt, an artificial and sentimental aspect to this redemption, for it assumed that the past can cease to haunt. At first, I thought this was the reason Rajkunwar objected to the story. But later, I was to realize my error.

As it is, the film as it exists now hardly has anything along those lines, and for the flimsiest of reasons: the distributor insisted on the film being solely a love story, without any serious angle to it. But the fact remains that Hari had written it as a negotiation with the past. He had worked on it for years. He gave us the lined exercise books – of the sort used by school-children – filled with his close, crabbed hand-writing in ink and pencil.

*This is what I want you to work on, he told us, handing
Joshilla those exercise books, two of them falling apart and held
together with rubber bands.'*

The scholar puts down the spoon with which he has
been eating rice, daal and chicken curry.

The lady doctor has finished eating; her husband is
helping himself to more rice and daal. He likes to finish
his dinner with one last helping of rice and daal, with
a slice of onion to go with it. The mother pushes back
her chair and gets up. I think I will go and lie down
with Munnu a bit, she says. Munnu, the scholar knows
by now, is the baby. She smiles at the scholar, as if to
say goodbye, and he makes an incomplete namaste
gesture towards her. She leaves, walking slowly, her
rubber chappals slapping on the tiled floor. It is only
then that the lady doctor resumes her story.

I must have fallen asleep. But I woke up to Mummy
and Papa's murmured conversation under the mosquito
net in their double bed. They were discussing the film
we had seen that day.

It was a windy night. The lamp outside was throwing
floating, haunting shadows of trees and leaves on the
bedroom walls. The shadows changed shape. I did not
want to see them. If I did I would cry out and Mummy
would come into our bed to comfort me and they would

know I was awake and they would not discuss certain things. I pretended to be asleep, huddling under the wool-stuffed razaai.

I couldn't always hear. They were talking in hushed tones; the razaai also muffled their voices. But I did hear my father say: They never tried to hide it from me. I knew I had another mother; I even had faint recollections of bullock rides and bioscope shows. But, to be honest, I never felt any desire to look her up. Badi Ma filled all the need I had for a mother. It might sound heartless, but that was the way it was. They became my family; they were my family. They *are* my family. I sometimes sent a letter to Dallam, mostly because Badi Ma insisted, but I never wanted to visit them. I think she returned to Anjangarh only once, a couple of years after they had established the studio in Dallam. I don't think she liked coming back either. Not that it was easy to travel in those days. Anyway, I was too busy with my new life, my new family, school, friends, and then the move to this town, for Badi Ma wanted me to go to a better school. You know how remorseless children can be. Years later, you know, on my way back from England, people asked me whether I wanted to see the, see the, you know, but what was the point . . . ?

I could hear Mummy comforting him. I was afraid; I remember I was afraid of the shadows on the walls. They made me feel as if I was in a storm-tossed ship, as if the solid stability of the house was an illusion. But I lay still in the cocoon of the wool-stuffed razaai, willing myself into silence. I wanted to hear more.

And after a second Papa continued, more softly now.

But I am glad I saw it finally. Their last film. Not that she had anything to do with it. And it is not true. There was nothing of that nature between the three of them. People used to whisper behind my back, I know they did, but it was all rot. Sheer spite. I guess they had some sort of a business understanding, you know we had that mansion near Bombay . . . nothing at all between her and him. You know, those were different times; they were different people. Whoever heard of affairs in those days? This was India in the 1930s and 40s, not Hollywood! Then they started all that talk of the film being based on a real story – a real-life love triangle, is what they called it – and I guess that added to the popularity of the film. But it was all talk, gossip. And anyway, my father had known Chotte Thakur Uncle in Calcutta; they had gone to college together. Badi Ma told me that. But you know how it is with the film industry . . .

It was just a film, said my mother. Just a film. One has to let the past be, Ashok, let it lie.

She called Papa by his first name only on occasions of great tenderness and vulnerability. I knew that. Some-how, the way she said it and the way Papa had been speaking and the shadows on the wall, all of them combined to make me feel uncertain of what was and was not, what was dream and what was reality. I wanted to be reassured of the world I had taken for granted and could no longer hold back a tiny cry of fear.

They heard it, and immediately Mummy was in our bed, holding me, asking, What is it, baby, what is it? Did you have a nightmare?

The wind was still raging outside. I could hear it whip the asbestos sheets on the shed of our neighbour's garage. The shadows writhed on the walls of the room and reached out with pointed fingers and made faces and changed shapes, but the house grew solid and rooted again. I breathed in Mummy's perfume and smiled and held her arm between my hands and fell asleep again.

'I hate to concede this, young man, but there is something about religion that needs to be respected. It is like memory. You might not believe this, for you are too young and still think of memory as something to be retrieved, to be recovered, as if we can delve into the box of the past and pull things out of it, as if the past was a box of chocolates. Actually, my young scholar, the word 'recovered' is not too wrong: memory is always re-covered. It is covered again and again. And religion, to the extent that it is necessary, is like that. It covers what would haunt us. It protects us from our own violence by taking it out of our hands. It distorts reality, misinterprets everything. But religious

misinterpretation can be a positive force: it purges us of the suspicions that would poison our lives if we were always fully conscious of each crisis. Memories can be sacred and religions are memories, and just as unreliable, just as vital, just as much a part of the present. Both are attempts to define the same borderless reality – two different names for the same elusive person.'

Reef V

Rich!

Rasa Pathetic

(27th January, 1948)

I am walking in this dream I am walking sometimes I
am walking down familiar roads roads I knew as a child
know as a man I am walking but I know I am not really
walking I am pretending to walk I am running I am
running I am trying not to run but I know there is
something behind me I can hear a sound like galloping
hooves but I can see nothing nothing but the familiar
road I want to call out its name or some name I want to
utter the phrase that will save me I know the phrase
almost but it eludes me always it eludes me and so I turn
and look look in my dream I turn and look but I see
nothing I am walking in this dream I am walking I am
trying not to run

Waking up with a jolt, the man with the binoculars
sits up and looks around. It is almost dark. There is still
the sound of birds, but only from the foliage of nearby
trees: a varied assortment of chirps and chatter as the
birds settle for the night. The shadow of the earth has

expanded and now covers everything, chill with the winter cold now there is no sunlight to warm it.

His men should be here any moment. The men he has trained, harangued, joked and argued with, led. They are from different villages in the vicinity, all except the three young men – one of them hardly more than a teenager – from Sarpanch Amrish Nath's family. Those three don't count.

He prefers the waking hours of the night to his bouts of daytime sleep, for during the day he is plagued by a confusion of dreams, dreams that buzz around him like mosquitoes and insects, talking in a thousand half-understood tongues. So, yes, he prefers the night. He sees better at night. He sees a studio festering with Muslims, communists, traitors, immoral men and women, so that even the light from the chinks in its windows seems to him to be viscous and yellow, oozing like pus, and he is convinced.

A Kiss in the Tunnel

'On 28 July 1925, the Millowners' Association of Bombay decided to reduce the dearness allowance of the workers by 20 per cent, bringing down total earnings by more than 10 per cent. This was one in a series of measures (including diversification and what would these days be called 'rationalization') that Bombay millowners had taken since 1920, when productivity and profits had peaked. Since then the mills had undergone a gradual decline, partly because of competition from upcountry mills and Japan and partly because of the loss of foreign markets, especially China. The tamasha that Saleem helped organize on his arrival in Bombay had been only one of many subsequent lock-outs and putative strikes that spread, like the influenza epidemics of the period, from mill to mill in the 1920s. On 29th July, though, a general strike broke out – the fourth in recent years – and it was this that decided Satish Mama's – and to some extent Saleem's – future. You have to remember, young man, you have to recall before you judge him that Satish Mama had become a kind of organic labour leader. He was literate and urban, unlike most of the workers, but was also someone who, perhaps because of his background, was suspicious of

respectability and the respectable. He could neither be a Gandhi man nor a communist without ceasing to be who he was, and that, young man, is the answer to why he did what he did.'

But it is a general strike, Satish, the older Gajanand was saying. It is a general strike and you need the unions for general strikes.

It was a smaller version of the impromptu gathering that Saleem had witnessed on his first night in Bombay, except this was daytime, and the air was steamy with the sun and humidity of July. Outside, the compound was full of women and children, sitting here and there in the shade of verandas and two spare trees, or walking through on some errand. Their voices – a couple of them raised in a blistering argument full of obscenities – and the relentless cawing of a flock of squabbling crows drifted in and out of Satish Mama's room where twelve men were holding forth, their faces beady with sweat. Saleem was the youngest and he was there less in his capacity as millhand and more because, over the past three years, he had become the person everyone came to if they wanted to organize anything cultural in the chawl.

I don't trust them, Gajanand. I know you worship Gandhiji and there is much I respect about him too, but he does not strike me as a person who likes industry or industrial labour. If we wove clothes on handlooms or splashed about barefoot planting paddy in fields his heart would bleed for us. But we work with machines, dammit; we live in fucking cities . . .

One of the younger men broke in: That is why, Satish Bhai, we should go with the unions. They are dominated by communists and you know the communists swear by industrial labour.

And who are your precious communists, Pratap? Don't misunderstand me. I worked shoulder to shoulder with Dange and Mirajkar during the epidemic; I know they mean well. But who are they, these communists of yours? Lotwala is a rich merchant, Parvate is a journalist, Nimbkar and Dange are Brahmins, Ghate is a graduate and a cashier; come to think of it, the only communist leader who does not seem to be Brahmin or affluent is Mirajkar, the fucking Punjab Mail!

I think, Satish, Gajanand interposed, I think your personal feelings are prejudicing your judgement. It does not matter who they are. What matters is the cadre and the organization. And we are talking of the unions, not of the communists. The unions contain workers, Satish.

You know what I think of the unions.

I know that you do not trust anyone but yourself, Satish, said Gajanand with a hint of irritation in his voice.

No, Gajanand Kaka, I trust you. I trust us. I don't trust them.

But we have to be with them if we want to get something done this time. We are not fighting for our mill; we are fighting for all . . .

I am fighting for my mill, Gajanand Kaka. That is what matters to me. If we have to join the strike, let us do it indirectly – let's organize a tamasha or something; that is why I have asked Saleem to join us. Let us not join them directly: what is the difference between being ordered about by Seth Dharamchand and being ordered about by some union leader in crisp dhoti?

A hell of a difference, Satish Bhai! What do you mean? the young Pratap exploded.

After that, the discussion got more and more bitter and personal, and as it continued into the evening, Satish Mama swore more and spoke less. Finally, by the time the gathering had decided to join the general strike and nominated Gajanand and Pratap as their representatives (pointedly and – for the first time in Saleem's recollection – leaving Satish Mama out), Satish had lapsed into an angry silence. He looked older and grimmer, the lines on his face deep, his forehead furrowed with thought. There was only a mutual exchange of nods when the men left.

What happened next was uncertain, though perhaps only in Saleem's mind, for the other people in the chawl had no doubt that Satish Mama betrayed them, that that night he walked out of the chawl and went straight to either the Jobber or Seth Dharamchand to alert them to the meeting. And later that night a police party descended on the chawl and, with planned precision, arrested Gajanand and Pratap. (They were released after a couple of days, but that was enough to disorient the workers, so that Seth Dharamchand's mill was one of the very few mills in Bombay in which the strike was not total.)

Satish Mama defended himself against the allegations when he returned the next day, obviously the worse for drink. Why should I have told them? he shouted at no one in general. When is it that the fucking Seth did not know about our plans?

The next morning Satish Mama woke up late: his relationship with the chawl had changed. They turned their faces from one another. He pretended not to see the others and they pretended not to notice him. Even when something had to be said, people relayed it via Saleem rather than speaking directly to him, and it was the same in the mill, from what Saleem could see on the few days he went to work after the strike was over. Satish Mama, who had earlier responded to the talk of the chawl with warmth, now responded to its silence with coldness; before, he had opened himself up, now he rolled himself into a ball, hard and closed, and that was how Saleem often found him sleeping at night, curled into a foetal position.

It did not come as a surprise to Saleem when, sometime in September that year, Satish Mama said he would be leaving the mill and Bombay. He was going away. He did not – would not – say where.

Gajanand and the boy had already moved out of the room – that was almost the first thing Gajanand had done on his release from jail, and it had been the last time Saleem had seen Satish Mama react to anything said or done by anyone from the chawl. That evening – for the last time during his days in Bombay – Satish Mama had come home drunk. After that, he simply came home bitter and silent. He walked slowly, dragging his legs, as if his shadow was metal chained to his ankles.

In later years, when time had made him more conscious of the ease with which people can be abandoned and more aware of the ghosts spawned by every such act, Saleem had a recurrent vision of the last time he saw Satish Mama in the mill. There was a deafening chatter from the weaving shed. The air was floating with fibres and dust. Satish Mama stood in the middle of the room – alone, the other workers somehow contriving to keep a certain distance from him when they were not forced to work shoulder to shoulder. Saleem could see fibres sticking to the sweat on Satish Mama's face, like white cracks creeping through his skin: the shed was warm during winters, heated by the presence of too many bodies and machines and with the windows kept shut to save the threads from being damaged by the wind, and now, in late monsoon, it had turned oppressively humid as well. There was such an expression of loneliness on Satish Mama's face that he appeared to be caught in a bubble of silence, as if the hubbub of the mill broke around his aura: a man standing under a cascade of water, starch dry.

At that moment, Saleem felt an impulse to go to the older man, reduced to a poverty that was greater than that reflected by the grime of the window panes, the plaster of the cheap building, the narrowness of its doors. But someone or something – Saleem could not recall in later years – had come up and the moment, with the opportunity it offered, had passed forever.

There was a room behind the Khanavali to which Gajanand Kaka and Bhola had taken Saleem on his first night in Bombay for the standard thali of rice, roti, daal and vegetable curry.

If the Khanavali was an unprepossessing place – a spare room, walls blackened by fumes from the kitchen, filled with low, stumpy chairs and tables, illuminated by kerosene lanterns rather than electricity for some reason – then the room behind was worse.

This was where the Jobber, who also owned the Khanavali, met with his cronies – and anyone else who had the money – to gamble, mostly with Ganjifa cards.

The Jobber would occupy the largest, middle table, and run a game of naqsh, in which he would be the banker, with the traditional advantage this involved stretched to unprecedented levels, while the other tables might contain smaller groups, usually the Jobber's cronies, playing Hamrang. Apart from the gambling, the Jobber's adda was where regular mill workers came to exchange news and gossip. The conversation would flow from table to table, sometimes merging into one stream, sometimes collecting in various pools.

When Saleem entered the room that night – having recently been paid more than he had ever expected for a role – conversation stopped for a minute. Then it continued, but slowly, taking some time to build up again, as if the speakers had switched topic and needed time to get back to full volume. It was obvious to Saleem that they had been discussing Satish Mama and, sitting down, he said – a bit too loudly – to Bhola, who was also there, Bhola, I won't stay long tonight; I have to get back and help Satish Mama pack.

He did not have to make that remark. Satish Mama had told only him that he would be leaving, and not even mentioned when . . . At the time, Saleem reasoned that he had said it in the hope of getting some of them to patch things up with Satish Mama. But he also knew deep down that his comment was intended to distance himself from Satish Mama, to indicate that from now on he would be his own man, that he would come occasionally to gamble and relish the glow of his success but without the shadow of Satish Mama falling on them.

In later years he would consider that remark as false – not because it was a lie but because it was a truth stained with his relentless greed for more in life, a selfishness that blinded him to the lives of others.

And do you want me to believe that you, Writer Batuni, were the one he recounted this to? I remember thinking this with growing irritation. I had the feeling that Batin was playing a strange cat and mouse game with me, telling me a lot but not enough. And then there was this distrust of someone who had, after all, moved to Pakistan. Perhaps I was also a little disoriented and resentful: it is hard not to resent people, especially people we admire and think we know from a distance, for turning out to be very different from our idea of them. Apart from the alcohol, Batin was not the kind of Urdu writer I expected him to be; he was not my idea of the sort of person who would move to Pakistan, if only for a few years. It was a combination of all this – distrust, resentment, confusion – that must have betrayed me, that finally forced Batin to grab my hands and say in his own defence: I did not choose to leave, I never chose to leave. I simply chose to live.

*

It was New Year's Eve. 1946, the first new year after the war. (And perhaps, it was rumoured, the last under the British Raj.) There was a touch of reckless optimism in the air, though Rajkunwar Studio was in financial trouble and surviving largely by offering its services to other film-makers (not many of whom were interested in its ageing equipment and remote facilities). Hari and Rajkunwar had already started raising the money for *Aakhri Raat* – they had decided on the name by then, and been assured of substantial backing by Seth Dharamchand – and it was clear to everyone that this might be the last film produced at the studio.

It was also becoming clear to those close to them that the relationship between Rajkunwar and Hari had frayed. Perhaps cognisant of the effects of their bickerings, however, and the need to put up a united front – at least for the benefit of financiers like Seth Dharamchand, who was not a man to tolerate weakness – Rajkunwar and Hari decided to spend New Year in Bombay; Bhuvaneshwari did not go, preferring to stay on in the shadows of Dallam.

They arrived at the New Year party together, Rajkunwar, Nitin, Joshilla and Saleem Lahori, Hari joining them a bit later after calling on Seth Dharamchand. They had taken Nitin's second-hand Auburn Cord 810, its powerful V-8 engine much repaired and patched up with makeshift spare parts but its shiny body still glistening and replete with retractable headlights, wraparound grille and chromed exhaust headers. Nitin always drove it himself, and often so slowly and carefully that drivers in less powerful cars would honk at him in impatience.

It was unusual for Hari Babu to drink more than a peg, but when he arrived at about eleven, it was obvious he had decided to make an exception this time. Saleem could tell something was troubling him, and that the relationship between Hari and Rajkunwar was not as good as it had once been.

The table was full of empty and half-full glasses and overflowing ashtrays. Nitin was the only man not smoking (or drinking, for he never drank) at the table: his Craven A cigarettes, which had almost disappeared during the war and were still available only through the black market, had long been exhausted, mostly pilfered by the others. The hour struck. Their host set a gong ringing and the lights went off for a second: people jumped up and raised a toast and clasped whoever was handy and pounded each other on the back. A huge egg was rolled in on a trolley – an inappropriate Easter egg – and suddenly it went to bits with a puff of smoke and a bang and a bellydancer hopped out of it. There were loud cheers and they could hear fireworks outside. The bellydancer had a tired, heavily mascaraed face and a belly that danced without too much effort on her part, but the men generally acted as if she was the most desirable woman they had ever seen. It was a fiction sustained by their wives and female companions, some of them scintillatingly beautiful, who frowned theatrically or pouted and complained to other women at their table when the man got up to prance for a minute or two with the bellydancer.

Nitin stood up. Too late, have to get back, he said. He was uncomfortable on occasions like this.

It was agreed that Nitin would drop them at Saleem's flat, not very far from Brabourne Stadium, with a view of Churchgate Station. This flat (which Saleem had finally put up for sale) was often considered by visitors to be the last remaining trace of Saleem Lahori's years of success as a film star. They would drop broad hints to that effect, sometimes in admiration, sometimes in surprised envy. Saleem never disabused them: the large amounts – Ashok Kumar was reported to have charged Rs 110,000 for his latest film – paid to stars in the late 1940s had not been on offer in Saleem's heyday; he had never been paid more than five thousand for any role and the flat had been purchased by selling his mother's jewellery, following the death of his parents. A lifetime of prostitution had paid for that flat.

By the time Saleem unlocked the front door, it was past two. The fireworks had died out; the sea was almost audible. They trooped in – Nitin had already left – and made themselves comfortable in the sitting room. Saleem fetched two bottles of whisky – one imported and the other deshi – and some glasses. He poured Johnnie Walker into two of the glasses and handed them to Hari Babu and Rajkunwar. He poured the deshi Nasik whisky into another glass and handed it to Joshilla.

Joshilla drained it in a gulp and reached for the imported bottle. Saleem removed it from his reach.

C'mon, yaar, Joshilla laughed, pass us the Johnnie Walker.

You have the deshi, saalé, Saleem replied.

We want the imported too, Joshilla laughed, speaking in the royal plural.

What will you do with the imported, Haraami? The mutual insults were a sign of their closeness, though sometimes misunderstood by others. Has a single member of your family for the past seven generations seen anything other than toddy and tharra?

Then he relented, as Joshilla knew he would, and poured a glass of the imported whisky. But you don't get any more, saalé, he said, handing it to Joshilla. You drink whisky like Coca-Cola. Good stuff is wasted on you.

Rajkunwar took the bottle from Saleem and started

pouring himself another peg. You know, Saleem, Hari Babu here might prefer deshi too. I doubt that his ancestors were much accustomed to imported stuff.

He said it with a smile, and Hari Babu laughed it off. But there was a slight edge to the exchange. And it got worse later that night.

By four thirty, the Johnnie Walker was empty and rolling on the floor and the Nasik bottle was less than half full. Saleem suspected that Joshilla had sneaked more than a glass or two out of the imported bottle when he had not been looking. He had fallen asleep on the settee.

Hari Babu was in as bad a state, lolling about on the sofa, blabbering and singing love songs. Rajkunwar, who had grown steadily morose, had shouted at him to shut up once and now he shouted again.

Shut up, Rajkunwar shouted into the room, looking at no one in particular.

Hari Babu rolled over and looked at Rajkunwar, his beady eyes bleary. Yes, yes, scold me, scold me, I am a bad man, he blubbered.

You are not a bad man, said Rajkunwar, taking a sip from his glass.

Yes, I am, I am, I am, I sold my own son, my own son for a handful of silver. My own flesh and blood. Judas, I am Judas, I should hang myself.

I will hang you if you don't shut up, bastard, said

Rajkunwar, still speaking quietly, as if discussing the weather.

Yes, hang me, said Hari Babu, suddenly getting up and standing – tottering – arms spread in the posture of theatrical crucifixion. He looked older than his sixty or so years. Hang me, hang me, hang me, he sang. Tell Dharamchand you have hanged me in Saleembhai's flat. That will solve all your problems. Hang me, haaang me.

Rajkunwar ignored him.

But now Hari Babu was in a state.

I deserve to be punished, I deserve to be hanged.

Tears were dripping down his cheeks.

Rajkunwar got up, slowly, and, just as slowly, he slapped Hari Babu on the cheek.

Shut up, he said.

But Hari Babu did not shut up. Yes, yes, hit me, he cried, hit me, hit me.

And Rajkunwar did, methodically, as if he was used to slapping people. The scene – Hari Babu begging to be hit, Rajkunwar obliging – continued for more than three or four minutes, until Saleem forced the two apart.

As Saleem wiped up after him – Hari Babu had returned to the sofa and curled up to sleep – he suddenly noticed the stillness of the night. It was almost dawn. It was just before the birds would wake up. But between the fireworks of midnight and the birdsongs of dawn there was this thin strip, this gauze of silence that filled

Saleem's heart with so much joy and so much sorrow that he knelt on the bathroom floor, rag in hand, and felt tears in his eyes. He did not know that he was crying for all that had been and all that could never be.

'I keep talking of nights and dawns and shadows and dreams, young man. Perhaps Hari's idiomatic turn of phrase rubbed off on me. He hardly ever said "film" without attaching "dream" to it. A "dream-film", the "dream of films", "dream shot". And his films too teemed with dream sequences. They were done to death in later years, of course, but he must have been among the first Bombay directors to use such episodes as a regular commentary on the action and motivation of characters. Still, for all that, no one really knew what he dreamt of. I remember one of the very few story sessions of Aakhri Raat *that was also attended by Bhuvaneshwari. Hari had been suggesting yet another dream sequence, a cinematic cliché with petals and roses signifying love, which was – as we had come to expect – opposed and scoffed at by Rajkunwar. Hari Bhai, he said, your dream sequences do not resemble any dream that I have ever had. Hari had responded with some idiomatic cliché. Later, I recall, Bhuvaneshwari said to me, as if apologizing for Hari, he is so lost in films he cannot speak any other language; he wasn't always like this. She was the first person to realize that Hari's films had filled with standard formulas just as his speech had come to be cluttered with idioms and sayings. It was almost as if he was afraid of letting himself go and sought the crutch of other people's*

perceptions. And she was right: there was a time when Hari must have been different – not every man abandons all for a dream – but somewhere along the line he had done something that made him distrustful of his own self, even his own dreams.'

Time the flying machine. How it.

She remembers the day they arrived in Dallam, surprised by the rockiness of the terrain. Raheeman Cha had been there, and the Sarpanch with his entire family, swooning.

We are honoured, we are honoured, we are honoured that mai-baap have finally come to stay. This house has missed its masters. This village has missed its masters.

The Sarpanch had been full of fine words those days. Fine words and shifty looks. His eyes taking in all around and about him. He leaned on his bamboo staff, a pockmarked man in his fifties, powerfully built, bald, he leaned on his lathi when not speaking to Rajkunwar and observed. Even then she could sense his disapproval. And this disapproval would have meant the death of the studio before it had produced a single film, had it not been for Seth Dharamchand, and of course, obliquely, for that eccentric old saint, the Mahatma, the Sant of Sabarmati. For Seth Dharamchand, whom Rajkunwar met through the Raja of Manpur, ruler of a principality adjoining Anjangarh (who was in Bombay those days chasing a well-known actress), had sent his goons to convince the Sarpanch to cooperate – which he had ever since, albeit reluctantly. Even so had their first film not been a retelling of the return from exile of Lord Ram and had it not been released in the same week that the Mahatma was released from prison by the British, and had the rumour not gone around that this was not a coincidence, the film might have flopped, for it was, otherwise, a largely unremarkable film, shot on loaned equipment using Orthochromatic filmstock rather than the Kodak Panchromatic film which was being preferred by the better studios. And had that not been the case, they would have been left with nothing but this building, inherited from the deceased 'Bombaywalli mausi', that Bade Thakur had made over to them, or at least to his younger brother, once Chotte Thakur, now Rajkunwar.

The building had been neglected for the past ten years or so, ever since Rajkunwar's widowed mausi died. But the uneven plotted fields attached to the house were immaculately green. Thriving crops covered the small stones and dark earth of the fields. They had been cultivated by the Sarpanch and his family. They stretched out to the road on one side and the village on the other, wavy with the green stalks and ripening white heads of wheat, one of the few expanses of fertile soil in a region that was mostly rocky and uneven.

She had learned to respect the Sarpanch, and distrust him, knowing that here again she had found an implacable enemy. It was as if all these guardians of places and tradition – not the owners, but their right hands and managers, the pundits, babus, munshis, sarpanches – saw through her thin disguise, recognized her unbelongingness despite the dresses, manners and names she assumed.

All of them had assumed names here. For Bhuvaneshwari, it had been just another name, moving on from the Durga she had become when she ran off with Harihar the Bioscope-wallah, who had now assumed the respectability of Director Hari Babu. Even Rajkunwar had remoulded his name, so to say, in his preference for Rajkunwar over Chotte Thakur. Not the small owner of some jagir-landlordship in the far-away village of Anjangarh, but 'prince' and 'heir apparent' no less.

But heir to what? Rajkunwar of what?

Perhaps the Sarpanch's suspicion and hostility had nothing to do with Bhuvaneshwari. Perhaps it had to do with the way the house was restored and gradually turned into a studio, the fields taken away from him and turned into sets, lawns and a miniature zoo, and, following the success of the earliest films, a new wing added to house a small private theatre. They even had an elephant once. And horses, dogs, parrots, monkeys, deer.

That was what she liked most about the studio. The

animals, not really the people. Not the studio hands with lewd voices, the stars and directors and producers full of themselves and their own dreams, not even the villagers sucked into other people's dreams, which they could ill afford. No, she had preferred the animals. Do animals dream? She had walked out with old Raheeman Cha, who had taken overall control of the menagerie. He had been the old guard of the mansion. She had walked through the stables and to the fenced-in areas and the cages, watching the animals and birds doing ordinary things. Eating, grazing, jumping, sleeping, trumpeting, chattering, defecating, licking. If they dreamt, they kept their dreams to themselves.

The animals, however, had disappeared one by one over the past four years. After the first flop. And people had been telling them how the old family studios were becoming a thing of the past. Bombay Talkies, Prabhat Film Company, Imperial Films Company, Ranjit Movietone, Minerva Movietone, all those long-established film businesses were either dead or dying. But Hari and Rajkunwar had been unwilling to listen at least at first. Their initial success had made them stubborn. And their dreams were built around a studio like this, not a technical box in the city. But then the elephant had died. And they had sold the horses (except of course the old mare, who had vanished) and dogs to recuperate some losses, cut down expenses. The monkeys and the birds had stayed until the night they found all the birds poisoned and the wire cages of the monkeys cut open. And that was when the trouble really started. And the letters. They had gotten used to the cryptic threats and insults of those letters, which had come first in the mail and then, over the last month or so, rolled up and tied to stones, tossed at the main door at night. Always at night.

She wonders whether they would have poisoned the monkeys too if monkeys had not been holy.

Who are these people? Or are they only shadows? Shadows that had lost their bodies in the struggle to build a house, maintain a family, get a job; shadows of the hate or ambition of other unseen bodies? She wonders too whether the Sarpanch is behind it all. Raheeman Cha – who they'd inherited with the mansion, their guard and (while they still had them) keeper of the animals – refuses to countenance the possibility of local villagers being involved. No one from the village will raise a hand against this house, he says in his ancient rasping voice, no one would throw a stone at this house. Look at my white hairs, look, and he pulls out his beard as if it were a piece of fabric being displayed to a customer. Ya Allah, he sighs, I have known the birth of every man and woman in this village. These are passing hooligans. Nothing but passing hooligans. No villager would throw a stone at me.

And he rubs the spot on his hip where a stone struck him the other evening when he left the house to urinate. Raheeman Cha still uses the fields. Toilets are alien to him. But now he only goes out during the daytime, carrying his old one-barrelled shotgun. Its barrel is spotted with rust, wiped repetitively with oil but incapable of being erased.

But the passing hooligans have been coming back night after night now. If she wasn't more scared at the thought of leaving than staying, she would leave. And she might have left some years ago, if she had not fallen so much in love with this pile of bricks and stones, this house, this home. She might have left some months ago even, if she had not come to fear what happened to people and their shadows. Perhaps she would even have left some weeks ago, if Saleem Lahori had not walked in one evening cradling two children, Kabir and the girl, whom she calls Rosy because she does not want to impose either a Muslim or a Hindu name on the child's stricken anonymity.

But the others have left. All except. Except.

Except those who stay because they have nowhere to go: Raheeman Cha, with his white beard and his one-barrelled gun, and the two village youths, Ramji and Kishen. (Why are they here? Do they need their salaries that badly? Is it because they are afraid to go back to the village or is it due to the fascination with machines and films that she has noticed in their eyes?) And then there are those who stay behind because. Because. Hari Babu, Rajkunwar and that strange man, that beautiful ageing, ageless man, Saleem Lahori. That man whose eyes follow her everywhere and make her feel young, younger than she has ever felt.

And her of course. She has stayed. Has she stayed because of her fear of the relentless partition of shadows and bodies all over the land outside her safe haven, this studio; her reluctance to take Kabir and Rosy into the vast enemy territories of Muslims and Hindus, or to leave them stranded like Manto's lunatic in the barbed no-man's-land in between? Or is it because – as Raheeman Cha put it to her, as he sat there, rocking on his haunches – this house keeps its mistresses. Has she become the next mausi? The ghost of someone else's authority and inheritance? And the word Raheeman Cha had used: Maalkini. It had made her start.

(There had been a Maalkini somewhere else. She associates keeping with Maalkinis, but perhaps those who keep are also kept, those who possess are also possessed.)

If time is a flying machine, it carries no passengers.

Evening is falling. The stones begin to fall with the evening. They will come. Through the chinks in the shutter, she sees small bats describing swift, teetering circles against the dimming sky. There is the roar of time in her mind. It sounds like a plane taking off. It sounds like the sea at Chowpatty. It sounds like distant thunder and lightning flaring against the rising rocks of the Deccan to the south. It sounds like men shouting.

She puts four spoonfuls of tea into the boiling milk, diluted with water. They will be out of milk if the maids do not come again tomorrow. They are village girls and might have been prevented from coming by the men who besiege the place each evening. Or they might have sold the milk, as has happened in the past, more profitably to a passing buyer. Raheeman Cha has offered to go to the village and fetch milk, but they have ordered him to stay indoors: if those stones have a target, it must be him. Him and Saleem. And, of course, her – if they had known. If anyone but Hari had known the Muslim name her mother had given her.

It has worried all of them, this burden of words, the way names can be death. But Rajkunwar and Hari had to get the film canned and edited. It was their comeback film, the first film directed by both of them together, the result of all their dreams and differences, a film based on a story-idea by Hari. And now they had done so, completed the film and sent everything back to Bombay in charge of the assistant director Chatterji and writer Joshilla. Each with a letter from Rajkunwar to a couple of people in authority, friends of his, asking for a police party to be sent to the studio, for the Khopoli police station has ignored all his requests in spite of frequent phone calls in the days before the telephone line – for which too, like the electric connection, Rajkunwar and Hari had paid much – was cut. The studio bus has driven them out, leaving behind a faint puff of smoke and dust suspended like hope as it crunched away from the studio driveway and onto the Poona–Bombay road.

One spoon per person, her mother used to say. Not that her mother ever brewed tea. She would stand there and instruct. One spoon per person. Wait until it starts to boil. Stir, stir, stir.

Have you thought how much a film theatre resembles a tunnel? he had asked her the other night, when they were sitting in the small viewing theatre, watching the reels of *Aakhri Raat*. Most of the actors and actresses had left a long time back. Kabir and Rosy were finally sleeping deeply enough for her to be able to extricate her arm and leave them breathing softly under the blankets. Most of the studio hands had been sleeping too, and would leave altogether the following day. All the junior technicians and the remaining boys, clapperboy lightboy dabbaboy thisboy thatboy, and music director Tripathy, assistant director Chatterji, editor D'Souza, co-writer Joshilla. They had worked overtime for days, cutting, processing, canning, in spite of the occasional stones that landed on the haweli at night. (And the shouting: Muslims and Muslim-lovers, go to Pakistan! On and on for the past four or five nights, like a stuck record, Muslims and Muslim-lovers, go to Pakistan! And then the insulting sexual innuendoes: Send your women to us; we will broaden the tight little holes of your bibis; send your bibis to us, we will open their minds. And back again to the stuck refrain: Muslims and Muslim ass-lickers, go to Pakistan!)

They had run the reels once already. The electric generator – the theatre was on the side of the stables where the generator was installed; they thought it was just a power cut and it was only later they realized that some one had cut the wires to the studio – was making so much noise that they could hardly hear the dialogues.

No one had noticed her walk into the room. No one but Saleem, for he had this knack of noticing her all the time. Not staring, just noticing, making her feel like she was the centre of his attention.

Did he make all women feel like that? Was that why he had such a reputation?

He stood up and came to her. He sat down, gently, in the seat next to her. He explained to her the parts that she had missed. And then he made that remark: Have you thought how much a film theatre resembles a tunnel?

When I first saw a film what struck me was the darkness of the theatre. A dark theatre? Strange, isn't it? Who can see in a dark theatre? Impossible. But here we have a theatre darker than any other, a theatre as dark as a tunnel. And at the end of that tunnel, a screen, light.

Saying that, he lays his right hand over her left hand, as if by mistake. His hand hesitates, fluttering like a bird. (She always associates him with birds: the pigeon he had drawn out of his pocket like a magician; the birds of his expressive hands making a point or quoting a line; the visible fluttering heartbeats of Kabir and Rosy as he had carried them in; the caged birds he used to feed every morning before – he was the one who discovered them, poisoned. And later that day he had dug holes for each individual bird and buried them. It had taken him the whole morning.)

She lets her hand stay where it is. And his hand stays too. They sit like that for the remaining hour of the film, the story of young lovers; they sit there, no longer young, both in their forties in a time and a land where tens of millions never reach that age, but turned for the moment into young lovers in a cinema. They sit there, hand in hand in the dark, watching the light at the end of the tunnel.

Who told you about this, Batin Sahib? I remember asking. Batin had picked up his glass to take a sip. My question stopped his hand. He put the glass back on the table without touching it to his lips. He looked at me, as if seeing me for the first time, or perhaps not seeing me at all.

She has pegged herself to her role in the studio and her respectability, for otherwise there is no one to give her commands. She knows that she can leave Hari with no more than a word being exchanged, for they have not even slept face to face for years. She could abandon Rajkunwar with no preamble longer than a sentence. She also knows that love has come into her life. It sounds like a cliché. It is a cliché. Except she is no longer young. He is not young. To fall in love in old age: it is a possibility she had never considered. And this is no childhood love come back. There is nothing of the child left in both of them. Perhaps there never has been; perhaps that is also what they share. And yet, surely, youth, if not childhood, must be part of love. But it is old age that will be part of their love, tied like a bottle to the tail of a dog. Old age which, she had always heard, begins at forty.

There is no one to slam the door on her. And yet she does not leave. She does not even regret the past, for the past makes sense to her. It is the past that has led her to this present. This love is a present of the past. She cannot disown the ways – limited, disabled, deficient, whatever they might be called by others – the ways in which she had been attached to Hari and to Rajkunwar, to Harihar and Chotte Thakur. Above all, she cannot forget the way in which she lost her son, lost him as much to her own dreams of safety and home as to Hari's dreams of films, Rajkunwar's nightmares of the nautch. She knows that she has been complicit in that transaction. She has handled the pieces of silver too, if only in ignorance. And now she waits, surrounded by the possibility of hate – and accompanied by the beautiful absurdity of love in old age – she waits . . .

Outside the studio compound, the youth with the MK21 US Army binoculars around his neck is uncertain of his identity. He has been with these country bumpkins too long. He needs to return to his own kind in order to feel that he is more than a disembodied shadow flitting from one elaborate set to another. He misses other sevaks like himself. He misses their determination to serve and to follow. He needs to hear the voices of other sevaks, of the Pramukh, their vociferous chanting of slogans, the explicitly sexual language with which they describe the violence they have inflicted, or will inflict on those motherfucking Muslim bastards.

The sevaks in his shakha: they are all men, mostly young, mostly bachelors. A couple are from Pakistan and have dreadful stories to narrate about what happened to Hindus there. Others are from different parts of India: those from the North have their stories of what they have done to Muslims. Only a few of them were actually born in Poona. They might have nothing in common but this concentrated anger they direct at the enemy. Not just any enemy: the Muslim, the Mussulman. Their hate fuses them into one; it reduces their differences. It reminds him of his days as a boy, running the trash-strewn back alleys with other boys, bickering and fighting and swearing, all of them so many groups or individuals – until a stray dog crossed their path. How that unfortunate dog would unite them, how the tortures – stone, stick, can – they devised for that accidental victim would make them one.

When he thinks of this, he almost doubts himself – and that is when he most needs to join his friends, the other sevaks, in a drill in the maidan or a raucous invective against the Mussulman and his protectors: Nehru and the man that even some of the sevaks call the Mahatma, the man even the Hindu Mahasabha had listened to during the riots of 1947, the Sant of Sabarmati. This fragile unity they achieve depends so much on certain rituals of hatred, on myths of violence, on the language of rape – and the only way he can avoid facing this fact (for he is by no means an unreflexive man) is by convincing himself (and others) that he and his organization are always on the defensive, that they only act in defence. They are never the aggressors, for everyone knows how lustful and aggressive the Mussulman is.

And that is why this tiring wait outside a slowly emptying studio building in the middle of nowhere, this constant lurking in the shadows of the night threatening an enemy that has shown no sign of hostility, confuses the Sardar, this young man from Poona with a pair of dented binoculars hanging down his neck. He wishes someone would send more men like him to these fields, for that would enable him to finish his business here and return to his family; it would enable him to retain a grip on his own identity. Meanwhile, he wonders why his organization has not bothered to get this over with. After all, that, he recalls, had been the original plan. That is what the Pramukh and Guruji had promised.

'Al-Baruni writes, my young scholar, that "shadow" is a covering from the sun, and because of the contiguity of shadow and light, how the one cannot be without the other, the Arabs call the shadow which is limned by sunlight a follower.'

They were now sitting in the drawing room, behind an intricately carved wooden partition. The husband had poured himself and the scholar some Scotch. The lady doctor had been brought a glass of cola by the servant, but had yet to take a single sip from it. She resumed her recollection once again.

A strange mood had fallen on my parents, settled on them as visibly as a shawl. It was as if they had moved into another element, were breathing a different air.

That evening, after we returned from school, Papa shut himself up in the guest room for an hour and then he called me, Manik and Mummy into the room. He had moved some of the boxes that were usually stored there. One – I had been once slapped for prying into it – was empty, and its previous contents were now lying on the guest bed, covered with an old sheet.

He kept us waiting for a few moments. Then he whipped off the cover with a flourish. It is a Panorama Box, he proclaimed.

Time had left messy fingerprints on the box. All the reflecting surfaces, or whatever it is they used in such contraptions, were layered with dust and the joints and nails were rusted. Even the stills to be inserted had faded and yellowed, so we needed to use all our imagination to fill in the gaps, in order to translate the blurred images into a woman threshing grain, which is what Papa said it was.

He was disappointed, I think, despite his brave words: It is very old, you know, very very old. My father and Chotte Thakur Uncle made it in the Anjangarh house, when was it, in 1929 or 1930. It is a marvel it still works.

He never ran it again. The 'panorama baksa' basically lay there on that bed until we had the next guest, when it was moved to the storeroom (where it might still be lying around behind the old furniture and mouldy carpets). However, uncovering the box had released some of Papa's earliest memories and, for the first time, he told us – in bits and pieces, occasionally – of his years with his own (biological) father and mother, touring the land with their travelling cinema and music troupe, and about his (real) father's friendship, going back to their college days, with Chotte Thakur Uncle, the younger brother of Dada. But as you can see, I still have trouble thinking of them as anything other than Papa's biological father and mother, for of course when I say grandfather I think of Dada and when I say grandmother I think of Dadi. Not Badi Ma, as Papa referred to her until the moment of his death; for me she was simply Dadi. He had two mothers to remember, but I knew only one grandmother.

Reel VI

Rasa Furious

In later years he would remember this as the last
dream, a strangely prescient nightmare, that he had in
Dallam, a place he associates with dreams not only
because there his unnatural daytime sleep had been
broken by strange visions and imaginings but also
because his days outside the studio in Dallam came to
seem to him, in later years, as only half-real. In fact, it
could *not* have been the last dream he dreamt in Dallam, for he was to sleep one more day in the abandoned
shed outside the studio grounds. But it is a dream that
would return to him year after year, mixed up with
what he saw the next night at the Studio and what he
heard on the radio the morning after that, so that in
old age he would not know what was real and what
was not, and as an old man he would repeatedly escape
the custody of his children and grandchildren to turn
himself in at the local police station for having murdered Mahatma Gandhi with a sword. With a sword!

The policemen would always laugh at that and escort him back to his family.

So this was the last (or not the last) dream or nightmare he had tossing on his charpoy in Dallam, under the green shade of a tree:

He is looking through his pair of binoculars it is dark he is stroking its metal slightly with a finger as he often does it is dark he sees suddenly how how can he see in the dark he sees a door open in the building of the studio the hated studio he knows that this is his opportunity this is what he has been waiting for this is it and he takes up his lathi he takes up a burning torch he runs with a shout a cry Jai Bajrangbali with a warlike cry Har Har Mahadeo he runs for the door he senses others running with him they are screaming there is a thudding of feet like hooves he is screaming the door is there it is dark he bursts through the door torch blazing mouth open wide in a scream he does not hear because behind the door there is silence silence silence there is a gutted house he is standing in the middle of rubble smouldering furniture blackened bricks metal plates that had melted in the heat fluttering scraps of charred paper warped plastic he is alone it is dark and then he senses a movement in the dark he knows it is a Muslim a sneaking cowardly Muslim a Pakistani a Mughal a Mullah the son of Babar the son of a pig a Muslim a Mussulman he strikes him with his sword he is holding a sword suddenly he thrusts forward with the sword he feels the jolt of metal in flesh he feels the resistance of life to death the man falls his lathi falls it is dark it is dark but now he can see the man it is an old man frail and half-naked he knows the man it is the Mahatma it is no Muslim it is the Mahatma it is the Sant of Sabarmati

That is when he woke up under the green shade of the tree where he had dragged his charpoy to sleep and realized it was growing dark and cold, and he was drenched in sweat.

The Dream Machine

As night deepens and his stone-casting followers arrive in desultory groups of two and three, muffled in chaddars and patched woollens, some chewing paan or zarda – one of them bearing the calendar photo of an actress wearing a strapless dress, which they all ogle and then consign to a small bonfire kindled from the boarsi that they keep burning through the night – the man with the binoculars thinks about the meeting he attended on the day he left Poona for this place. He had already packed and said farewell to his family, for he had been informed by the Pramukh that he would be sent away for a few months 'on duty'. He was one of the three sevaks 'hand-picked' from his organization's shakhas in Poona. It was a great honour.

He can recall the meeting as if it was a film, so alive he had felt at the honour of his selection. It was December, a few days before Christmas, which he knew as Bada Din, and the fires of the Partition were still simmering in some corners of India and Pakistan. The sunlight fell from the window in such a way as to cover the bare wooden table like a white table cloth.

He and two other hand-picked sevaks stood near the door, both carrying bags and bundles like him (though he doubted that either of them had binoculars in their bags), both about his age, both dressed in regulation white shirts and khaki half-pants despite the chill, and carrying their compulsory bamboo lathi. The seven men sitting around the table wore warmer clothes. Three were dressed in Western trousers, shirts and woollen sweaters, while one wore a safari suit and the other dhoti and kurtah. He recognized only the seventh man in the group, dressed in the uniform of his organization, but wearing long pants and a half-sweater. This man was the Pramukh of all the Poona shakhas. He was the one who had observed and selected the sevaks standing there. All the others were at best names he had heard, some – like the man in dhoti – not even from Poona. He had heard of the man though – everyone called him Guruji, which was as much in recognition of his senior position in the organization as of his vast erudition.

It was Guruji who did most of the talking. He was a striking elderly man, with snow-white hair, and immaculately drawn caste marks on his forehead. What he said rang with authority and conviction. The three young men who had been chosen for the assignments by the Pramukh were thrilled by the intensity of his conviction, the furiousness of his determination 'to weed Muslims and communists out of the studios from which they make films to pollute the minds of young Hindu men and women.'

How would the young men have reacted had they seen beyond the hooded eyes of Guruji to the many causes of his fury? Would they have been shocked, disgusted, disappointed, fascinated? For there *was* something fascinating about this man who dressed in Indian clothes right down to the wooden slippers he wore on his feet, but who had attended universities in England and Germany, this man who was committed to the removal of Muslims from India but who knew more about their literature and languages than most Muslim scholars and – what was more – spoke highly of the Muslim contribution to India's art, music, architecture, cuisine? A man who had made a fortune and was the organization's strongest link to the financial sector of Bombay, but who lived simply, even ascetically. A man who quoted Sanskrit shlokas at random, but also ate meat (everything, it was rumoured, except beef). A man who was absolutely truthful in his business dealings but who lied to people about matters of history or politics without hesitation. A man who hated Mahatma Gandhi, whom he only referred to as the Shant of Shabarmati or even, in moments of exceptional anger, the Cunt of Sabarmati, but who remained adamantly opposed to any bid to assassinate the man.

If the young sevaks being despatched to different studios to foment trouble and force them to fire Muslim employees had known all this about the man, they might have read his furious harangue differently. They might have doubted the long list of studios that the man brandished, for most of the names were there just for show. They might even have realized that some of the studios were under the protection of the man's business accomplices, or owned by his partners. But above all they might have suspected that the man was furious not only at Muslims but also people like them.

For it was Guruji's burden to have to deal with people like them, with followers (and colleagues) who did not understand his dreams. Had they done so, would they have discussed – or even joked about – assassinating the Shant of Shabarmati? What foolishness. At that moment, when history was finally shaping India into the sort of nation he had seen in Europe, lands in which the persecution of Moors, heretics, witches, ethnic minorities, Gypsies, Jews had joined people into one national-ity, at that very moment there were people in his organization who would do the one thing that might divert the burgeoning anger of Hindus from its target: Muslims. To assassinate the Shant of Shabarmati, who had always set himself up as the perfect sacrificial victim, would be to reprieve the Muslims. And if the Muslims were reprieved, how could a united Hindu India come into being?

Modern nations, Guruji knew, were not built on ideals, traditions, not even science and technology. They were built on great gushes of blood, on massacres that left no shadow, or faint manageable ones. And that is what he dreamt for his country; that it would, one day, remember the Muslims of India, sacrificed on the altar of the Indian nation. He knew that is what the European nations did to their minorities over centuries; that is what they were doing to the Jews now. Once the Muslims – and he almost wept for them, for he was a man sensitive to music, art, culture – once the Muslims become the sacrifice that this nation needed, they would become a faint shadow in the past. Who fears shadows? Do lies cast a shadow? Have the massacres that made the European nations left more than the slightest shadow? What can a shadow do? Once the body of the nation has come into being, it will cast its own shadows. And he hoped he would be there to limn those shadows with the sunlight of, no, not lies, of words.

Yes, that was his dream. But these men, young and old, these men driven by ignorant lusts and petty vengeance, they talked of assassinating the Shant of Shabarmati, little realizing it would divert Hindus from the real sacrifice, that the bloody Mahatma had turned himself into a scapegoat for the Muslims. To assassinate him would be to do what he wanted; it would save the Muslims, pacifying the Hindus and rendering them a people lacking the iron and blood to make a modern nation.

Haranguing the young men that day in December, Guruji was worried about the rumours he had heard of a group within the organization planning to murder the Mahatma. It was just a rumour, but he had heard enough rumours to be able to tell. He had floated a few himself. He knew when rumours needed to be taken seriously.

If necessary, he told himself, furious at the stupidity of his followers and fellow-leaders, if necessary, I will stage such a conflagration that everyone in my organization will have to lie low for years, long enough for the Shant of Shabarmati to die in bed, long enough for the anger against Muslims to fructify in the minds of all Hindus, long enough for the great Hindu nation to be born in a torrent of necessary violence.

What would the young sevaks have thought if they had known this?

Later, glancing through the notes I took that night, I was surprised by how sceptical my questions and rejoinders had grown with the hours. Some of it must have been due to the confusion I was plunged in when Batin did not turn out to be my idea of a paan-chewing Urdu writer. I was in any case suspicious of this secular Muslim who had moved to Pakistan. (Secular Muslims in India can be among those most sceptical of Pakistan, for they are the people who never believed in the idea of an Islamic nation but have been made to pay the price for its creation over and over again.) I realize that these were factors that must have influenced my response to him that night. But perhaps there was another factor to add to the equation: an academic's insistence on facts. However much I might have admired writers like Batin, I was an academic; for me, errors, lies, even vague conjectures were to be avoided, and perhaps I was disturbed by the realization, dawning on me around that time, that in order to believe in Batin's stories I would have to differentiate between lies and lies, errors and errors. That is why my notes record this exchange at that point in Batin's narrative:

Q: Isn't a lot of it just conjecture, Batin Sahib?

Batin: What do you mean, young man?

Q: I mean, how can you suggest that in the organiz-ation that was involved, directly or indirectly, in assassi-nating Gandhiji, there were people – or one man, anyway – who actually tried to save him by creating trouble elsewhere? How could you know?

Batin (frowning): I am not a name-dropper, young man. I could say that I spoke to people, that there were rumours: you will recall that I went back to India once in *the 1970s, though – to be honest – that was more for my wife's sake. She wanted to check on a close relative there. But I do not want to mention names. And you would not believe me anyway, for all of it will be hearsay to you. But, young man, there are lies and there are lies. Some make life possible; some draw death closer. But death comes on its own, finally; it always does – what has to be attained and preserved is always life.*

For days after that slapping scene on New Year's Eve, Rajkunwar and Hari Babu did not meet each other's eyes. The incident haunted Saleem. Its suddenness, the monotony of its violence, the apparent ease with which it was dismissed, almost as if it had never taken place – all this hinted at stories Saleem, and perhaps even Bhuvaneshwari, were only partly aware of.

'It is strange how much we are always able to overlook, young man, if we want to believe in something. I remember the day Hari, who had been negotiating, came in with the news that he'd secured funding. Seth Dharamchand ki Jai, Joshilla shouted. Long Live Dharamchand! All of us – even Saleem Lahori, who had experienced the Seth as a millhand and knew what the man was capable of – even he joined in the celebrations. The only person who stayed away – pleading a headache – was Rajkunwar. It ought to have made us think. But it didn't. We wanted to believe in the future. We didn't ask what Hari had

pledged to get money from a sahookar of Seth Dharamchand's sort, a new breed of backers who had upped the financial stakes in films by ploughing in black money accumulated in the war years. We didn't guess that Rajkunwar knew, and that the slapping session had been, in a frustrated confused manner, his last attempt to prevent Hari from striking that particular bargain.

But, young man, looking back I can understand why Hari did what he did. For him the film was the only way he could justify what he had done in the past, write a note of apology. Or perhaps not apology, for that was the difference between Hari and Lahori, finally, if I may allow myself to say so. The day came when Lahori realized that he had, in a way, let down people he had loved and who had loved him: his parents, whose different – Hindu and Muslim – funerals he had attended secretly for fear of advertising his own background, and surely he had let down Satish Mama. He had been too busy to stop, to ask, to intervene. He had been too greedy for life to realize that it cannot be lived in isolation and that both action and inaction cast shadows. And when this realization came to Lahori, he decided – perhaps without becoming conscious of it until later – not to let it happen again. What happened to him, for better or for worse, was a consequence of that realization.

Hari, on the other hand, tried to explain away the past by weaving it into a film in which he could view events through a soft focus. And hence, young man, he had to make that film. But what he did not realize until too late was that we cannot justify the past by repeating it even in soft focus, and that *redemption is ultimately a personal effort, a private one, not a public show.*

But perhaps none of us realized this then. And if some of us had breathed a sigh of relief on learning that financial backing was in place, and if we had hoped this would mean less bickering and arguing between Rajkunwar and Hari and their cronies, we were soon to be disappointed. Somehow, Seth Dharamchand's backing spoiled the relationship between Rajkunwar and Hari Babu even further. There was a reason for this, of course, and we were to discover it soon enough.'

The mahurat of *Aakhri Raat* was a subdued affair. In keeping with tradition at Rajkunwar Studio, a small puja was performed in a small room outside the main building and attended primarily by regular members of the studio. The room normally housed various religious icons and props – statues of all the major Hindu gods and goddesses but also of Jesus and portraits of Kabir, Mirabai, Sai Baba, Guru Nanak, paintings of the Kaaba and Muslim dargahs, even a star of David and other possible backdrops to religious scenes in the films shot there – all of which were piled in a corner temporarily. A token scene was shot. Later a few still photos were taken of the hero and the heroine, and some of the supporting actors. Sweetmeats and snacks were distributed. Then the studio bus took the few people – including the hero, heroine and Saleem Lahori – who had

come from Bombay back to the city and everyone waited
for the first real day of shooting.

Between that day – the day of mahurat – and the
first day of shooting, the relationship between Rajkunwar and Hari deteriorated so much that Bhuvaneshwari
actually called close friends, such as Saleem and Joshilla,
to come and mediate.

This cannot last. They will tear each other apart.
They will destroy this place.

These were the first things Bhuvaneshwari said
when she saw them.

We have spoken to them, she added. All of us. Even
Raheeman Cha. But they can hardly sit together without
getting into an argument, calling each other all kinds
of names, disagreeing about small immaterial things.
Especially Rajkunwar: he keeps alluding to Hari as a
traitor for no reason at all. That traitor, that turn-coat,
that seller-of-his-mother: always something in that vein.
How will they make this film together if they are
fighting even before the shooting has started?

After two evenings of discussions, when they finally
got to the heart of the matter, the answer was – it
transpired – that they had no choice: they had to make
the film together no matter what because Hari had,
without consulting Rajkunwar (and despite the fact that
the deeds were in the latter's name), obtained Seth
Dharamchand's financial backing by standing the studio

building as 'surety'. If the film was not released by a certain date, Seth Dharamchand would become the owner of the building.

Dr Surender pointed out that, legally, Hari's agreement with Seth Dharamchand was worthless as the building did not belong to him. If necessary, Rajkunwar would need to point this out to the Seth, but the matter might never come to that. All they needed to do was to get the film made and released on time.

Hari and Rajkunwar pulled themselves together. In a few days, after Saleem and his friends left, the two partners went back to disagreeing and shouting over the making of *Aakhri Raat*, but they always stopped short of derailing the film.

'You see, young man, Hari did not feel he had an option, which is perhaps the greatest crime we can commit. There is as much hubris in considering oneself without options as there is in thinking that all options are the same or equally available. But I guess none of us – not just Hari – realized it at that time. Hari felt he had to make this film. He was as driven to it as he had been, or so he must have felt, when he met Chotte Thakur in Anjangarh and agreed to a different bargain with Badi Maalkini. So, young man, in order to redeem the past, he repeated it: bartering away something that did not belong to him.'

★

While Hari and Rajkunwar bickered and battled over the making of *Aakhri Raat*, Bhuvaneshwari was left more alone than ever – and she realized that this new space came as a relief to her. She still had the bunch of keys with which she ran the studio, took care of the kitchen, organized the small garden, supervised the diminishing zoo. It was a busy life, as it had always been. Had she been less busy, she might have brooded more over her separation from Ashok. But things and events had interfered, as they always do, interposing their substantial surfaces, their granular or smooth presences, filling her world, so that the years had passed by with the occasional letter, first from Anjangarh, then from Phansa, and once or twice from Patna, and a faint expectation of visits. Badi Maalkini sent her a photo of Ashok every year, which she framed and kept on tables next to her bed. She looked at the photos, comparing them to the only one she had of Ashok from the time before Anjangarh. It depicted a rather thin boy, perhaps even mildly undernourished, in faded shorts and a slightly torn shirt, scowling into the lens of the camera. The later photos, sent by Badi Maalkini, showed a healthier, happier boy, dressed in expensive clothes, once seated in a Victoria, once leaning out of an Austin.

There was a progression of photos, the last one depicting Ashok as a medical student at the Prince of

Wales Medical College in Patna. The photos reassured her. They made her feel that the sacrifice had been worth it, that when in the future Ashok would visit her – and she had little doubt even then that he would one day – she would be able to claim him without having to lie or pretend. Surely what had happened to him would justify her absence, the lack of a past she could have passed on to him?

For some reason neither Hari nor Rajkunwar had ever wanted to talk of Ashok. This had been, at least to begin with, more surprising in Hari who had, she still remembered, loved and known the child. If she had known Hari less, she would have accused him of callousness, of forgetting, of letting his dream carry him away. But she knew that Hari had cared for the boy, had always considered him his own son. She excused Hari by assuming that the man found it too painful to talk of Ashok.

But there was another reason. As always the past hid more than the present could reveal. She would discover that reason just days before the past and the present ended in a shower of diamonds and gems.

How do you know? How can you know? I almost shouted to Batin in that room in Copenhagen. I think I would have put it just as bluntly to him, if Batin had not, at that moment, stood up to fetch some more water and ice cubes. But the question kept ringing through my mind and a part of me responded sullenly to his narrative, not quite believing it, somehow not wanting fiction from a man who was, ironically enough, a writer of fiction.

Having become the film-maker he had only, hesitantly, dreamt of becoming once, Hari remained the methodical, studious man he had always been. He was more a student of cinema now than he had been as Harihar. He had a library full of books on cinema. He regularly went to lectures in Bombay, sought out foreign cameramen and directors for long discussions in English. In this he was both like and unlike Rajkunwar, for Rajkunwar had confined himself to his interests too, films and dancing. He had cast himself as the dance director, and occupied himself with directing young men and women, getting them to rehearse their steps. Like Hari, Rajkunwar was focused, engrossed in what he did. But while Hari had delved deeper into his field, Rajkunwar had stayed where he was. It was as if he did not want any more.

Bhuvaneshwari had started noticing this difference between the two, as well as the relentless bickering that they indulged in over the smallest of issues. The bickering, it sometimes seemed to her, had the stuck-record note of a marriage gone wrong, a love affair grown stale.

The conflict between the two men ran far deeper that Hari's rash deal with Seth Dharamchand; it had started soon after they had moved from Anjangarh. Their initial success had smoothed over their differences, but recent failure had intensified them.

Bhuvaneshwari, with the space now to ask the question, wondered where their differences originated. She no longer fooled herself into believing that their bickering was due to sexual rivalry: she knew it had to do more with what they sought in life, what they had gained and lost in the process of realizing their dreams, perhaps even in the very closeness of the dreams they had shared or still shared.

Like many other women from her sort of background, Bhuvaneshwari tended to underestimate her own significance. She never once imagined that she had played a part in the realization of their dreams – and she had no idea that Ashok had been the cornerstone on which they had reared the edifice of their studio, the sacrifice that had assured their future.

To have lived for decades with two men, to have played wife and mother, whore and protector, mistress and manager to them, to have run their studio, advised them in their work, to have shared the same roof with them and not to have realized the secret, that they had kept from her. And then to have the secret revealed to her in such a manner, as part of a flaming row between

Hari and Rajkunwar over some minor cinematic matter, to be given that secret in public as if it was of no consequence. Just the words they had spoken. So self-centred, so blind to their effect on her.

The words reverberate in her mind, though it is now a few days since she heard them.

You motherfucker, Hari had shouted at Rajkunwar, you rich motherfucker, you buyer of souls.

That is rich coming from you, Hari Babu, Rajkunwar had retorted with cold anger, you who sold your son to gain a studio.

And who brought me the paper to sign? Hari had launched himself at Rajkunwar, only to be held back by Lahori and others.

They had still been struggling and shouting when, almost simultaneously, they saw her standing by the doorway, turned to a photograph by the words.

She remembered sunlight falling on Ashok's thin legs as he scampered after their bullock cart, imitating birdcalls or picking up round pebbles for his sling, the dust on his legs glistening like silver.

Her mouth filled with the saliva of disgust at the thought of that word, silver, silver as in money, as in the silver screen. She spat onto the floor, breaking one of the first rules of etiquette she had taught herself on becoming Bhuvaneshwari. But there was more saliva in her mouth and more disgust, and she spat again and again. She ran into the bathroom and rinsed her mouth with water, spitting into the small marble basin.

'Now the secret – they had not given away Ashok for his own good but sold him for their dreams – that Rajkunwar and Hari had kept from Bhuvaneshwari for two decades became another lie to fight over, another advantage to be won or denied. Each blamed the other, accused the other of being greedy or thoughtless or devious – and, for the time being, neither considered the horror and pain with which Bhuvaneshwari greeted their revelation. For she got the full facts for the first time. She was shown the document Hari Babu – as Harihar, the father of Ashok – had signed on their behalf, giving Ashok away to Bade Thakur and Maalkini of Anjangarh, in return for 'an equal share' in the film company to be set up by Rajkunwar. I do not know who, in the end, showed her that document, Hari or Rajkunwar, but it brought the betrayal home to her in a way she could not – perhaps ever – forgive, with its legalese and official attorney's stamp.'

Hari, she recalled, had a theory about dramatic structure. He had picked it up from some visiting British photographer or assistant director whose lecture he had attended in Bombay a few years ago. She had heard him repeat it to Batin and every other writer who had worked with him. Remember the stock phrases, he would say.

Remember the stock phrases and you can never go wrong.

And then he would list them, counting them off by folding one finger at a time, as one would do when making a point to children: Once upon a time, there lived a, who, but, so it happened one day that, as a result of which, but meanwhile, so that unknown to, until the time came that, when suddenly to the surprise of, so it turned out that, and for ever after.

She goes through the list again. She fills in the gaps. She knows she is on the verge of hysteria. She knows that her mind needs to focus on something, and this is the only thing she can find. Hari's stock phrases. But the phrases fill up with the event that has overtaken her . . .

> Once upon a time, in a village called Anjangarh, a small boy, a five- or six-year-old boy, comes to a cave-castle filled with riches. His parents bring him to that castle on a bullock cart. They are drawn to the castle by rumours of its wealth. Perhaps. But he, the boy, loves the feel of the stone, its coolness, its solid safety.

> There lived an old woman in the castle

> Who had lost her son.

> But the child who entered the castle bore the name of the lost son.

So it happened one day that the woman came to the father of the child and offered to fulfil all his wishes if he let her keep the child forever. To this the father agreed, but he did not have the courage to tell the mother. Instead he spoke about how good it would be for the child to have a home, and an education, and a renowned family name, the name of the Thakurs.

As a result of which the parents left the child in the castle and went away to where the father could fulfil all his dreams. The mother tried to stay in touch with the son, followed him through the years, dictated letters to him, letters sent to Anjangarh (and, later, elsewhere, to Phansa and then · Patna), sometimes received replies that had to be read out to her. She thought of the time when he would be returned to her as a successful young man, a doctor, a man as engaged in facts as his father was by fiction. She believed the past could be reclaimed.

But meanwhile the son had made the castle his home.

So that unknown to the mother he had no real desire to be reunited with his parents, or if he desired the reunion it was a desire mixed with so much pain and disappointment and betrayal and change that he failed again and again to retrieve it from dream to daylight.

Until the time came that the father inadvertently, during a minor argument, revealed to the mother . . .

But she cannot fill in all the other stock phrases. The story ends here; it's a script Hari would have scrapped.

This is a strange thought coming at that moment. Have Hari's dreams taken over her realities to such an extent? But no, she knows that she has been living out her own dream here: this might have been a studio to Hari, but it has been a house to her. She knows that. The keys she carries in a metal ring tucked into her petticoat attest to that. And that is why she says nothing to Hari and Rajkunwar about what has happened. Nothing, except that she has no plans to leave the studio with the departing artistes, that she will stay on with Hari and Rajkunwar (and Kabir and Rosy), that she will keep faith with her own dream.

'I can see it in your face, my young scholar. I can see the doubt: am I making it all up or did she tell me?'

There was a time soon after they had moved into the studio building when Durga had seen Ashok walking through the buildings. The same height, the same gait, the same clean but threadbare clothes. She'd run after him, reached out to pick him up, only to find another face, some boy brought in by one of the villagers who worked at the studio, a different boy every time.

She had experienced such a jolt of emptiness then

that she'd the feeling, the physical feeling, of falling, and she had clutched at a wall to keep herself steady.

It had happened more than once.

Then she had become accustomed to Ashok's absence, thrown herself into Hari's dreams, Rajkunwar's interests, the management of an expanding studio, convinced herself that she was making a house Ashok could return to with pride. But that time had never come. And she had become used to that too. Until Saleem Lahori had walked in with the two abandoned children, and she had begun to faintly realize the extent of her own deprivation.

When she thinks of this now, she thinks of Kabir and Rosy and of Saleem Lahori's presence, the slight pressure of his fingers on her hands.

'I can still see her, young man, this woman in her early forties. I can still feel her presence within those broad old walls of the studio, limned with newness that was wearing off again, the paint and pictures and posters; the pleats of her sari, the fall of her hair, the rise of her high forehead. I see her sitting there in the emptying studio, thinking of a son who is nothing more than a shadow, his very body exchanged for the materiality of the building she inhabits, her home. Kabir and Rosy are playing around her. They call her mother now. She is distracted by them, as you are too, young man, I can see it from the way you raise your eyebrows every time I mention these two children.

You wonder who they are, and how they entered the studio building and this story.

Perhaps I will tell you about them, Kabir and Rosy, the two children lurking in the corners of my narrative. But right now, I can only see them playing around her knees, as she sits there, Bhuvaneshwari, Durga, lost in thoughts, rethinking her past, present and future. She had known for sometime that if she left that building, that studio, with her two foundlings, she would not be able to make a home for them anywhere in what had, by then, become India and Pakistan. But equally, with the stamped and signed deed of betrayal fluttering in her face, how could she expect the bricks of this building to keep out those howling for blood outside, now that its walls had been hollowed from inside by betrayal and falsehood?'

The night has been quieter than usual. The film has been rewound, the cans packed away for transportation the next morning. The distributor, who bought it on a profit-only basis – a coup, Rajkunwar announced – is waiting for it. Uncertain of its future, the studio sleeps.

It feels as if the building is sleeping too. Its windows and doors have shut their eyelids; it breathes softly. No one walks the corridors of this building at four in the morning. It is still dark. No stones have been thrown for the past two hours at least.

Do houses have dreams? If they do, what might this

house be dreaming of? Would it be dreaming of the hands that raised it, made it of stone and brick, mud and chalk and cement, wood and iron? Or would it be dreaming of the hands that have made dreams inside its rooms?

The various rooms breathe softly: Rajkunwar in his cluttered room on the walls of which hang a selection of riding whips and in one of whose corners there stands a Berliner gramophone, manufactured by the Victor Talking Machine Company, perhaps one of the first featuring Francis Barraud's painting of *His Master's Voice*, and beside it a couple of newer machines; Hari and Bhuvaneshwari lying back to back, as they have for the past twenty years or so, the photo of a seven-year-old boy framed on their wall, sitting in the lap of a woman next to a large silver vessel; Kabir and Rosy sleeping in a bed that has been pulled up next to Bhuvaneshwari's bed; the various other rooms, some crowded – with studio hands lying side by side, tossing and turning and snoring lightly – others reserved for a special occupant or two, and the viewing theatre, in which Saleem still lies in exactly the posture in which he had held Bhuvaneshwari's hands. He has not gone back to the room he shares with Ashiq Painter. He has fallen asleep in the empty viewing theatre, in this dark room where the finished products of so many dreams flicker to life on a screen. But he does not seem to be dreaming. Saleem

Lahori who has been known to walk about at night because he could not sleep, Saleem Lahori whose incoherent dreams have been plagued by scenes – silent stills – from his early films and the noise of the kothas, Saleem Lahori is sleeping more soundly than he has for years, his consciousness purged of dreams for the moment, his eyelids restful, as if he does not have to desire anything anymore.

But this is a house of desires, and dreams stalk its rooms like ghosts.

Rajkunwar wakes up twice with the cry, Ma, ma, stop him, stop him. And he cowers in bed, as if being whipped, thrashed with slippers.

Hari's eyelids pulse. He is unused to dreaming at night, but something is happening under the surface of his sleep. It often does these days. He is dreaming of a bullock cart trundling up a dirt track to a mansion, a glittering mansion. He is driving the cart. He feels a shapeless dread well up in his heart. He looks back and there is a boy running after the cart. At first he is skipping and singing; then he starts running to catch the cart. Hari wants to slow down for the boy but he is afraid the mansion will disappear. For some reason he has to get there. He drives the bullock on. The boy is crying now, stumbling and crying, picking himself up and running again after the cart. His knees are bleeding.

Harihar can see the tears on the boy's face. But he cannot stop. He cannot stop.

'No house, not even a studio, young man, has a monopoly on dreams, and of course millions would have been dreaming all over India and all over Pakistan that night. Think of how the nights teem with dreams, all those shadows of desires stalking the land, mind to mind, to fade or fall the next day on the screen of sunshine, to be pursued or forgotten. And what was the Mahatma dreaming that night, for – as I have said, young man – I believe that the story of Rajkunwar Studio returns in subtle ways to the story of India and Pakistan. What would the Mahatma, the Sant of Sabarmati, have been dreaming in the house of a rich admirer in Delhi, clad in loincloth, sleeping alone or next to his nieces? For there was a time when the Mahatma had a strange ability: he could make other people dream his dreams. Not force them to, for he was a gentle man and a man who had realized, more than others, that violence is not simply an act; it is an infection like the plague, and self-perpetuating. It can never be answered by violence, for that is the way it spreads.'

No, violence is not simply an act. Rajkunwar knows that too, and better than most. That is why he has anticipated violence in most cases and tried to pre-empt it. He has also inflicted violence on those weaker than him because he realizes it keeps at bay those stronger than him. But he was given no chance to pre-empt anything in the Seth's office one hot afternoon in 1947.

He had gone to Seth Dharamchand because the deadline for the release of *Aakhri Raat* was looming and Rajkunwar wanted to tell the Seth, once and for all, that his deal with Hari was not worth the paper it had been typed on.

How do you like his prick, asked Seth Dharamchand, laughing and solicitous. The man appeared to laugh at the slightest excuse, as if he was so full of goodwill towards his fellow beings that it had to bubble over as boisterous mirth. Rajkunwar could see tiny bubbles at the corners of his mouth, which the Seth wiped with the back of a fat, hairless hand.

He has a big prick, doesn't he? the Seth continued in the colloquial Bombay Hindi that he had switched to as suddenly – and around the same time – as the bald man had pulled out a chaaku.

The man holding the chaaku in the vicinity of Rajkunwar's rectum – its sharp point pressing hard enough to hurt but probably not, or so Rajkunwar hoped, cut into cloth or flesh – the man adjusted his position and grunted. He was a huge man and he was sitting squarely on Rajkunwar's back. It was his weight that prevented Rajkunwar from answering what he took to be a rhetorical question. But the Seth saw Rajkunwar's silence in a different light.

Perhaps he doesn't feel your prick yet, Shetty. You know, our prince here is used to pricks in the back, they say.

Shetty pressed harder with the curved knife and Rajkunwar felt the steel nick his skin.

He has a big prick, doesn't he, the Seth repeated.

Rajkunwar grunted a yes.

And you are wondering how it got there?

That was exactly what Rajkunwar had been wondering, for, just two minutes back, he'd been seated in one of the plushy chairs in the Seth's office, discussing the 'mortgage' that Hari Babu had taken out on the Studio and telling the Seth that Hari had no right to do what he'd done since the building, legally speaking, belonged to him, Rajkunwar. The Seth had remained uncompromising and Rajkunwar had suggested, without really thinking about it, that perhaps they should resolve the matter in court. It was at this point that the man who had been sitting at the back of the room – a close business acquaintance, the Seth had said by way of introduction – and whose name now turned out to be Shetty, had grabbed Rajkunwar's chair from behind and toppled him out of it. Then, even before Rajkunwar knew what was happening, he was on the floor, the bald man sitting on his back, pressing a knife first against his neck and then, turning around, against his rectum.

The Seth was still jovial, laughing as if it was all a big joke.

We know, Prince, continued the Seth – somehow he had always called him 'Prince' rather than 'Rajkunwar', translating the name into English – We know, Prince, that you are not averse to big pricks. Not averse at all.

After he had recovered from a high-pitched peal of laughter that had tears rolling down from his eyes, the Seth continued in more sombre tones: You see, we know more about our friends than they know about themselves. We believe in keeping ourselves ready to help our friends, don't we, Shetty?

Shetty pressed harder with the knife in reply.

Now, Prince, I am sure Shetty won't mind obliging you with his prick, if you ask him politely. If you do not use words like court and judge, heavy English words that, you should know, Prince, none of my business partners uses, no, not even the Parsees. You see, my Prince, there are pricks and there are pricks. Just as there are mortgages and mortgages, legal deeds and legal deeds. You may want his prick, but you do not want that prick. We are interested in the legal deed Hari Babu has signed, not in your legal deed. You see, don't you?

Pricks and pricks, deeds and deeds, mortgages and mortgages. You see, Prince?

And the Seth laughed so much that he started choking.

When he recovered, he waved a podgy hand at Shetty. What are you doing, Shetty? Don't you see Prince is suffocating? He is not used to our rough sense of humour. There, help him up, help him up, and tell Helen to hurry up with the tea.

But when Rajkunwar had been literally picked up and deposited back in his chair, he saw that for the first time – and fleetingly – Seth Dharamchand was not laughing.

It is this – a story he has told no one but Hari and Saleem Lahori (he could not say it to Hari alone for fear of losing his temper and causing serious injury to his partner) – that explains Rajkunwar's refusal to vacate the studio even now, in spite of the nightly barrage of stones and curses from the men lurking outside. He does not believe they are communal Hindus angry at the fact that the studio employs – employed, in actual fact – so many Muslims. He believes they are a handful of the Seth's goons, and they want the studio. But Rajkunwar does not believe they will go further than intimidation – the Seth cannot risk getting directly embroiled in criminal matters, and how will he manage to wriggle out of it if his hoodlums are implicated? Unknown to Hari, Rajk-unwar has instructed his lawyer in Bombay to have Hari's agreement with the Seth declared fraudulent and void, and he is certain that these shadows haunting the outskirts of the building will melt away in the light of the court proceedings.

He is convinced that all he has to do is wait until the film is released, and pay back the Seth with the profits, or, if it comes to that, sell off part of the lands and more of the studio equipment. As it is, he has decided to close the studio anyway: his must be one of the last family-studios that are still running. Most of the others have already closed down, rendered redundant by develop-ments in the film world, with the rise of technical labs and outdoor shooting, the money ploughed into the industry by new backers like Seth Dharamchand.

But deep down there is a stubborn hope in Rajkun-war's heart – and this he shares with Hari and always has even in their most heated arguments, for both are true gamblers in the world of films. He hopes that he holds the winning hand. He hopes *Aakhri Raat* will be a hit.

'Sometimes dreams do come true, young man, and it may not make a difference anyway. I will describe a scene for you. Imagine it.

The man is singing. He is dressed in a startlingly white silk shirt with beads, buttons and medallions, and narrow-bottomed, broad-hipped trousers. His boots are pointed and two-tone. You cannot tell their colour. It is a black-and-white film, one of the last to be made before colour, first used in 1937, became the norm in the 1950s. He is twirling a walking stick. Halfway through a line about the arrow of love, the man flourishes the cane and thrusts it into one of the bushes behind him. The bushes look artificial; the forest scenery at the back is obviously part of a studio backdrop.

The man, the hero, has eyes only for the heroine. Even when the heroine takes up his lines and sings them, he continues to stare at her.

(They are young, so young. What can they know of love?)
He stands stiffly.

The woman stands stiffly too. She is wearing an embroidered silk sari, her hair done up into one of those elaborate hairdos of the time. She is sitting on a fallen tree trunk. She hardly ever looks at him. Most of the time, she looks at the floor. Their voices rise and fade.

You may recall the scene, young man. Perhaps not many people from your generation would, but you are a scholar of films from that period. Surely, you must recall it, the second last song of Aakhri Raat. *Even other men and women from your generation might recall the tune, though the actors are now almost forgotten. They never made it big, in spite of the success of the film itself. But at the time, the scene was widely copied:*

the dress of the man, the hairdo of the woman, the twirling of the cane and the placing of the heroine on a fallen tree trunk. The thrusting gesture to illustrate the arrow of love striking home. Aah! Some film critics even claim that it inspired Shammi Kapoor in his Yahoo-type film songs later on.

It bent the trend, young man. It became the style for a while.'

The scholar is in the lady doctor's car: he sits in the back seat. The lady doctor and her husband, who is driving, sit in front. They are driving him back to his hotel.

The night has emptied the provincial town of Phansa of whatever glitter had been bestowed on it by sunlight during the day. The bodies of animals, people (there are some sleeping on the pavements) and even buildings have shrunk as the shadows have grown, filling up the town with their insistence on what is not seen. The shadows and the night have made the spaces in the town seem more claustrophobic.

The scholar is familiar with such provincial towns; he grew up in a town like this one. But now, after many years abroad, a feeling returns to him: it was part of what had driven him away. He is shaken by the bleakness of it all, the paucity of possibilities. The shops aspire to affluence by claiming names from other places, other times: Glorious Emporium, says a sign in rusted tin over steel shutters that are not more than a yard wide; Imperial Tailors claims a shack; Raja Medicines, Taj Mahal Dhabba, Golden Properties . . . When he had been young and struggling to escape, such signboards had, at times, sent him into a panic of anxiety. He knew the world was bigger, broader, solider, and he did not want to end up as its shadow. For that is what such signboards, such places had come to seem to him: shadows of places more real, more solid. Then, struggling to make a career in universities in Europe, he had forgotten the panic. Now it comes back to him, but along with it comes the voice of the lady doctor; she is still recounting the changes that had taken place in her parents' life after Ashok, her father, unveiled the panorama box.

You see, she says, raising her voice over the sound of the engine and half-turning her head. You see, he kept insisting on the respectability of his biological parents, especially his mother. I guess there must have been rumours about them when he was younger, though I never heard anything at all about any of them. By the time I was growing up, they had been forgotten, and only people like Ramesh Uncle, dedicated film buffs, even associated the films made in the Rajkunwar Studio with Papa's biological parents. But for Papa, their respectability was important. He insisted on it.

A pity, says the lady doctor's husband, laughing.

A place like this could do with a bit of scandal and colour.

It could, couldn't it? But think of Papa, with his princely Anjangarh upbringing – and he had a daughter to marry off.

Wouldn't have made a difference to me.

And to your mother? I am sure she would have had a thing or two to say.

My mother, god bless her, has a thing or two to say about everything.

Somehow this light banter relieves the scholar of his growing panic. The car's headlights sweep a mound of rubbish and dilapidated shacks by the roadside. But they do not make the scholar feel as constrained and desperate to get away as he would have otherwise. Perhaps the lady doctor and her husband were proof of the possibilities of even such a place. Whatever it was, the scholar does not experience the place as solely oppressive anymore.

The lady doctor continues, you know, that was our Rajkunwar Studio year. Later other things happened and the studio cropped up only once in a while. By a strange coincidence, that year also brought us a visitor who had known Papa's biological parents. I think he had worked at Rajkunwar Studio as a scriptwriter or something. I don't recall his name, but I do recall him, a tall, distinguished-looking man, who patted me and Manik on the head and gave us expensive toys – which my mother thought rather excessive. He also took some photos of us, family photos you know, promising to send them to us. Come to think of it, I don't know if he ever did.

Reel VII

Rasa Odious

Hé Ram

Was that the elusive phrase of his dreams, he wondered in later years, the phrase with which he could
have saved himself? Not Har Har Mahadeo, not Jai
Bajrangbali, not even Jai Shri Ram, but Hé Ram? Hé
Ram? Such a weak invocation, so ambivalent, an expression that flew circled and dipped, like homing pigeons,
and did not slash at the world outside with steel talons
and iron beak. What was it: an expression of repulsion
or a gasp of surprise or a last appeal to God? Hé Ram:
just that? Just that? No, it cannot be.

The Ride on Grapeshot

I didn't manage to go to Dallam until the day before I
was to catch my flight back to Berlin. After meeting the
lady doctor in Phansa, Ashok's daughter, I went back, via
my hometown Gaya, to Bombay and, a day before I was
supposed to leave for Berlin, I finally decided to go to
Dallam after all. I decided impulsively, for I had been told
that the studio was nothing but charred bricks, now owned
by Dharamchand and Sons, and even most of the original
villagers had been dispersed by encroaching urbanity. It
was true: I could not trace Ramji or Kishen, and only one
member of the Sarpanch's family was still there. But in
retrospect I am happy I hired a taxi to go to the scene. It
did not provide me with much new information, any hard
facts. But in a way it rounded out my narrative, though
of course no narrative can come a full circle and be closed
for good. Still, it enabled me to tell the story of Lahori and
Durga and Chotte Thakur and Ashok and so many
others, all those persons who had made a life out of their
different dreams, their various nightmares, all those individuals who had manufactured illusions for a land in the

years when that land had known, more than ever before or ever since, the terrible glory of dreams. But how can you manufacture dreams? How can you discipline the imagination? How can you partition freedom? I asked myself these questions on the way back to Bombay from Dallam, as the taxi jolted through the dusk, and the scenery unfolded in jerky, broken images.

Seth Dharamchand laughed into the silver receiver of the tiny telephone. His hairless hand covered most of the receiver; his belly shook with mirth; his eyes rolled. He was being watched by his secretary, Helen. She had a noncommittal look on her face. It was a look she had patented.

She was sitting on the chair that Rajkunwar had occupied a few weeks ago. The air-coolers were not on.

They were on the fifth floor of the Dharamchand and Sons head office in the heart of Girgaum, not very far from Majestic Cinema. Even the noise of the passing trams and the morning traffic did not reach them here. Helen was proud of the room, with its tasteful decor and burnished wood: the Seth let her decorate it as she wished. She sat there, hands poised on a pad, pen in hand, wearing the face of a poker player.

The Seth laughed and slapped his thighs. Paan juice splurted from his mouth and stained the glass top of the large table, dotted some of the files. She reached out unobtrusively and wiped the stains with scented tissue paper, imported.

Can't you turn the damn music down, the Seth was saying. I can hardly hear you. What is it you are playing anyway?

Indian classical? *Indian* classical? Who listens to that junk? Yes, do turn it down, my good friend. Now what is it you said?

Yes, yes, yes, the Seth said, still laughing. Yes, you have my permission, my friend. You have my permission. As I said, it is a rule in my business dealings: friends do not take matters to court; people who take matters to court are not friends. It's a simple rule. Yes, and very effective, that's true, that's true. But, my friend, it is effective only because I do not permit any exceptions. A rule is only effective if there are no exceptions to it.

No, don't worry, I have the papers in hand. Mortgage and all. Ask the men to do what they want. Clear the place. But no one from Bombay, mind you. No one from Bombay: I don't want a single finger pointing in my direction. Apart from that, no condition whatever. Do what you wish. Frighten the Pakistani bastards. I want that litigating half-and-half prince and his pimp out of there. Torch the place, if necessary. Yes, yes, today, my friend, today if you want to.

There was a short dry reply from the person at the

other end. Seth Dharamchand laughed again, even louder, shaking helplessly with mirth. I like it, yes, I like it, he said. Credit in the heavens and credit in the bank. Yes, I like it by God.

He put the tiny silver receiver down and beckoned to Helen. He crooked his little finger at her, twice. His hand was podgy like a baby's. She walked over to his side of the table and bent slightly, her back to him, wearing her poker face. He slapped her on the buttocks, boisterously, and laughed again, his belly heaving like jelly.

A vendor has pushed his trolley into the park. The trolley is of wood; it has heavy wheels with rubber tyres on them; on one side is hand-painted the legend 'Juici Van'. He pushes it by two handles sticking out of one end. On the trolley sits a heavy metal machine. It has serrated teeth and an arrangement of rollers and wheels. He inserts a bunch of sugarcane sticks, gripped tightly, into the teeth of the rollers and turns a handle. A frothy juice trickles and then pours into a metal jug. He folds the sticks (now papery and brittle) and mashes them through the serrated teeth of the metal rollers again. He pours the juice into glasses and adds a pinch of spices. They look like glasses of sunshine turned ordinary, of trapped dirty sunlight. The vendor moves on, doing a brisk trade in glasses of ordinary sunshine.

Two men are sitting on the bench. One of them has snow-white hair. He is dressed in a spotless white kurtah, a plain grey vest, and dhoti, wooden sandals and long woollen socks. He has a silk shawl draped around his neck, falling down one side. He looks prosperous and cultured, and clean shaven, immaculately barbered, clean, tidy, compact. He is old, probably sixty-five. There are cleanly, carefully drawn caste marks on his forehead.

The other man is younger. He cannot be more than twenty. He has not shaved, stubble covers his cadaverous jaw and he sports a thin moustache. He is dressed in a thick striped jersey and trousers. He smokes a bidi, until he sees the older man waving away the smoke. Then he tosses the bidi into the flower bed behind him.

The older man sits at leisure, his arms stretched along the back of the bench. The younger man occupies one edge of the bench, slightly huddled, tense.

There are sparrows in the bush behind them. A chocolate wrapper has stuck in the bend of one of the bench legs. It flutters in the strong breeze, which is cool at this time in the afternoon but will soon turn chilly.

The older man takes out a piece of folded paper from his kurtah pocket. He removes a blunt fountain pen clipped next to one of the buttons of his kurtah. He unscrews the pen slowly. All his actions are slow, unhurried, considered. He smooths out the paper on the space between them. The younger man cranes to see.

The old man is about to say something when an ayah walks past, pushing a pram in which a baby sits like a Victorian doll, frocked with frills, sucking violently on a pink pacifier. The old man looks up and smiles at the dark ayah and the fair baby. He waits until they are almost out of sight round a corner. Then he turns back to the paper. The young man is looking on impatiently. Perhaps he is cold.

The paper contains a long list of names and addresses. The elderly man puts an X next to one of the addresses. He skips two and puts another X next to an address. He continues down the list marking four out of a total of more than a dozen. These, he says, these are the studios that are still soft on the enemy. He says 'dushman', enemy, with unexpected vehemence, a slight touch of the theatrical.

The young man accepts the paper, folds it carefully and stuffs it into the back pocket of his trousers. I just have to give the word, Guruji; we have people in most of these places, he says with eager pride. The man speaks the mixed dialect of the streets of Bombay.

Take just one, the weakest, the most isolated, Guruji says, smiling benignly, but his voice has a hard edge to it. Set an example. Take the one in Dallam.

Just one? The young man appears displeased.

One at a time, one at a time . . . But go to Poona, get men from Poona. Ask the Poona pramukh, what's his name? He knows; he will help you.

Why Poona? We have good men here . . .

Poona. I do not want any of my boys directly involved. No one from here except you: I gave Dharamchand my word. No one from Bombay.

They are interrupted by loud music blaring from a nearby radio. The young man gets up with a muttered curse and looks around. But Guruji raises an arm to signal restraint. Raagni Pahari, Guruji says, nodding approvingly. Khan Sahib Ashiq Ali Khan of Patiala. He closes his eyes and nods his head in time to the tune.

The younger man looks surprised, almost pained. Then he says Jai Shri Ram, somewhat abruptly, and he turns and walks away. The old man smiles, his eyes still closed, his white-haired head swaying to the intimate raag sung by a dushman. He sometimes despairs at people like the younger man who has just left him, at their blind anger, their inability to think with anything other than their fists or penises.

If only they did think, of course, he wouldn't be in this predicament, worrying about that band, previously members of a sister-organization, who have pledged to get the old man, the Shant of Shabarmati. He doesn't know what their precise plans are. But he has heard rumours, reliable rumours. They are out to get the old man, the so-called Mahatma, and soon.

He would be the last one to shed tears over the Mahatma. He still remembers reading with bitterness how the bastard was walking all over India saving Muslims while Hindus were being butchered in Pakistan.

And yet, the Mahatma cannot be killed; why didn't these young men realize that? Not because he doesn't deserve to die but because he has to be killed by a Muslim. That will let loose the kind of ritualized violence against Muslims that the nation needs, the kind of sacrificial violence that will heal the differences among the Hindus, wield their many desires into a common desire for Muslim blood. It would be like the old horse sacrifices of the Vedas. But, he shudders at the thought, if a Hindu were to kill him, the Mahatma himself would become the sacrificial victim he has always wanted to be, the canny bastard, uniting Hindus and Muslims, secularists and traditionalists, liberalists and socialists, setting the Hindu cause and the Hindu nation back by decades.

He hopes that the action he has sanctioned against Rajkunwar Studio will frighten those young men into dropping the plan to murder the Mahatma. Let the bastard go to Pakistan; let a Muslim murder him. He sighs. It is all so simple. If only people thought rationally.

★

The old front-mounted engine of the single-deck bus was groaning with strain as they negotiated the incline. Most of the hills had been left behind; this was one of the last steep sections of the road. There were bushes turning brown, as if burnt in a sudden fire.

The sides and roof of the Leyland Titan bus were plastered with tattered posters of Rajkunwar Studio films, all fourteen or fifteen of them, and the legend 'Rajkunwar Studio: Where dreams come alive' lettered in cursive silver. The silver was greying along the edges; the paint had peeled in many places; the left headlight was cracked – but the bus still communicated an infectious sense of optimism. And all his memories of previous rides in the bus were full of fun and laughter. Ribaldry and vulgarity too, but still. Conversations about women, crude at times, flirting, food being shared, gossip exchanged, games of antrakshri between actors and musicians or men and women (the songs following one another in an endless sequence, the last alphabet of the last song becoming the first alphabet of the next one), and suddenly they'd be crossing the common chawls that marked the borders of the dream-city, Bombay. Time would fly.

But not this time. No one was singing. People were talking, but they had huddled into separate groups: the cold of the January day was not sharp enough to make people huddle like that; perhaps it was fear or uncertainty or suspicion. Gernail Singh, the other studio guard, sat next to the driver, a shotgun that was the exact twin of the one Raheeman Cha carried, clasped between his knees.

Saleem had found himself sitting with Joshilla and Ashiq Painter. It was only when Ashiq raised the subject of Pakistan that Saleem realized he was, perhaps for the first time in his life, part of a group that was solely Muslim.

Ashiq would have objected to this in the past. Communist, he would have said, flashing a card. I carry a party card. It says Communist here, not Muslim.

But Ashiq appeared to have lost that card in just one year of Independence. He didn't flash it any longer. He spoke of Pakistan more and more often.

And what about the others, Saleem wondered. He could guess what had happened to Bala in his lonely hotel room. He knew what had happened to Avik Sen: he had dropped out of their circle the day he snapped, entirely out of the blue, but yaar whatever you say, whatever Ashiq Bhai says, no matter how many communist cards he carries, you saala Muslims are going to cut India into bits. (This was before Independence, and the worst riots had not yet started. But it was when the Partition had become an open secret, when they were still trying to live with, each in his own way, the aftermath of a train that had arrived without Bala. He remembers the date. And after that Avik Sen moved about in a new circle of friends, all of whom happened to be Hindus.)

And Doctor? Where was he? Had he really, as it was said, taken sanyaas, put on girwa, smeared ashes on himself and disappeared into some ashram, his mind unable to take what was happening to his Bombay, the place of his abandoned dreams?

So was this all that was left of their original circle? Ashiq Painter, Joshilla and Saleem himself, in the bus. And back at the studio, Rajkunwar, Hari Babu and Bhuvaneshwari, with the two children who had clung to him when he was leaving and would not have let him go if she had not been there. All protected by the gun (probably never fired) carried by ancient Raheeman Cha or, perhaps, by the trust in the basic decency of the villagers – trust that was shared, in different ways, by both Raheeman Cha and Rajkunwar.

Why had Hari stayed behind? Hari, the old man, the husband, who had so little belief in any thing or person. Did he, after all, love her in his own way? Or was it the studio he could not leave?

Was that all that remained: the three of them, all Muslim, in the bus going away, and the three of them, all Hindu, in the studio under nightly siege?

And even Ashiq Painter was talking, in hushed tones,

of leaving. Leaving for 'there'. Muslims in India seldom said 'Pakistan' in public, not after Partition.

Some had remained where and what they were. But so few, oh, so few. He often recalls the letter from Nitin Kumar that he had received just before he left for Rajkunwar Studio to finish the last bit of shooting. That was about four weeks ago. Ashiq Painter and Joshilla had already been at the studio, along with the core crew, and Saleem had pleaded a few days extra in Bombay to wind up a business matter. Though few people had believed his plea: Like Ashiq, they were convinced that he had gone off to Umrao Bibi's kotha for a few days.

Nitin's letter had been written in painstaking Urdu, which in itself was a touching gesture. Its grammar was all wrong. It lapsed into Bangla tenses and gender at times. Its spelling was faulty. It had made him laugh, not in derision, but with happiness. It was less a letter than a note. It said, Dada, remember I am here. Do not leave. Do not leave, Dada, no matter what they say, what they shout. It will pass. This madness will pass. This is as much your home as it is mine. We all remember you; come and stay with us, that is what my wife asks me to tell you. Do not leave.

It was such a misplaced and vulnerable letter. Saleem knew Nitin was as limited as the rest of them, that he did what he could, and if his concern was misplaced, it was nevertheless justified by its sincerity and vulnerability. He had come to fear not people who showed misplaced concern about the plight of their Muslim friends but people who commented on how Bombay had stayed 'mostly' normal in 1947 – for these often were people who would not have borne the brunt of any kind of abnormality anyway and who would have been, Saleem feared, as willing to excuse genocide as they were to overlook the few clashes that had taken place in and around Bombay, the weeks of tension when Muslims had disappeared from trams and trains, the anonymous threats to Muslims and their employers, and the gradual drifting away of many of their Muslim colleagues.

Saleem had laughed with tears in his eyes when he had perused the letter the first time, though he had never thought of leaving. Nitin's concern was misplaced. But of course Saleem had a Muslim name and he had recently sold his flat (finally unwilling to live with a reminder of his failure towards his parents, a flat bought from sale of his mother's jewellery): even Nitin could come to only one conclusion by putting those two facts together. Muslims had been leaving Bombay. Only the other day, he had been told that Manto had left, leaving his beloved city to join his family in Lahore. Manto, he had felt like crying out, what will you do there? But he knew Manto knew; he knew Manto had chosen the easier death – not the death of all he had known and believed in, not the death of friends whose faces disappeared or were turned to an icy mask, but his own death. The death of just one person. One witness. One writer.

'You know what was distinctive about Bombay films before your generation started talking of Bollywood? No, no, not all that academic theory, young man; what was distinctive about them was the use, the subtle and extensive use they made of flashbacks and dream sequences. It was as if even the most frivolous narrative knew that it was poised between changes, between past crimes and future possibilities, between past possibilities and future crimes. And almost all the flashbacks and dream sequences had a smoky quality, making vision uncertain but not impossible, making the world a play of shadow and solidity.'

There is no smoke and the road is getting crowded. He can feel the bus breathe a sign of relief. What has been happening at Dallam is not happening elsewhere. Even Khopoli, which they left some time back, had been crowded and normal.

But Ashiq Painter is whispering.

I am leaving the day after tomorrow, Saleem Bhai. Josh, I am leaving. I am telling you. I have everything arranged. There is a ship leaving for Karachi. I know the captain. I know others who are leaving. It's not expensive. Take my advice and pack what you have, leave. Get out while you can. There is no future for us here. Nothing but stones and screams in the night. Nothing for us.

His voice dips even lower, becomes almost inaudible, when he says 'us'.

You, Saleem Lahori jokes, are you saying this, Mr Party Card Holder?

Dammit, yaar, you can hold a party card there too.

But can you make films there? Can you paint there?

There are people making films there. C'mon, they are not all fucking mullahs. And what about here? Do you think Nehru will do anything for the industry? He considers it below his phoren-educated dignity to bother with such cheap mass nautanki. And the Mahatma considers films evil and decadent. He wrote so. It is not modern enough for one and it is too modern for the other.

No, Painter, we will continue, we will continue as we always have, says Joshilla.

You can continue if you wish; I am getting out while I can.

But not as a communist, Painter, you are getting out as a Muslim.

Better a living Muslim than a dead communist, yaar.

And he laughs, bitterly. Joshilla looks tense, as if he cannot speak the words he is thinking. Saleem looks out at the scene outside the window and he is struck by how ordinary it all is. He tries to imagine Karachi, and he can only see Bombay. He tries to imagine Lahore, and can only call up memories of Delhi. He wonders whether Painter is fleeing to a land that he too cannot imagine, the terrain of someone else's dreams.

'I don't see why you have to sound so scathing about Ashiq Painter, Batin Sahib,' I had interjected at this point in the narrative. 'After all, it was not as if you stayed on in India.'

Sometimes the smallest phrase, a tone, an insinuation can be heavier to bear than the burden of clearer, more direct accusation or blame. I had been sullen and sceptical a number of times that night. Batin had mostly responded with a kind of wry humour. But now, finally he exploded. This was the only time during our long night together that I realized how fragile our sense of the past is, how much of the mural of time was hidden and would always remain so in spite of the fragments that we may restore. What made Batin grab my hand and shout at me? His eyes frightened me, for a few seconds they were tunnels that took us from the fourth-floor flat off a side street near Copenhagen Zoo to a place desolate and smouldering. I remember him shout: I don't have to take that from you, young man. What do you know of me? And have you never known fear or doubt? Have you never changed your name to a Hindu-sounding one when taking out a rail reservation? Tell me you didn't during the Bhagalpur riots. Go on, tell me to my face! Have you never made your Muslim identity clear by some gesture or word when passing a Muslim Mohalla in the aftermath of a riot? Tell me you haven't? Tell me to my face.

But then he controlled himself. The moment passed and he was back to addressing me in his slightly old-fashioned manner, saying to me those enigmatic words that I have already recounted and to which I have returned again and again in the process of writing this book: 'No, young man, I did not choose to leave . . .'

After a pause during which we restored our nerves with whisky, he added: Don't you see this, young man? Don't you see how everything that we had done or failed to do in the studio was not different, not so very different from what they had done or failed to do in the land? Don't you see? I think she, Bhuvaneshwari, saw it better than the rest of us. She was not interested in politics and did not really know what was happening and why. But she was good with people. She could see it happening to people. Not to ideals and parties and maps, but to ordinary people. For, finally, the Partition would have been impossible if it had taken place only in Parliaments and on paper; what made it possible was that it took place in the hearts of ordinary people. I have often thought of what she said to Joshilla and me when we left the studio. She spoke *so low I was not certain I heard her correctly, and for some time I told myself that she could not have said what I thought I heard her say. But this is what I heard: May you keep body and shadow together, both of you; may you keep body and shadow together.*

Well, perhaps we did, in different ways perhaps we did: Joshilla by remaining in Bombay and I by doing what I had to do . . .'

Saleem Lahori has made up his mind.

The gaily painted Rajkunwar Studio bus crosses the strand of sea and the huge peepul tree that marks for him the end of everything that is not Bombay. Now there will be buildings and billboards, chawls with drying clothes fluttering from dark and dingy balconies, the streets lined with small shops bearing boards, 'Vaishali Stores' and 'Janata Hardwares'. There will be bags holding red chillies outside shops, vegetables and fruits along the roadside, carts selling fruit juice or coconuts. And finally the glittering necklace of Marine Drive on the bare bosom of the beach, and all the names that have passed into folklore: Cuffe Parade, Apollo Reclamation, Churchgate, Colaba Causeway, Oval Maidan, the Gateway of India, the Kala Ghoda statue of King Edward. There will be chimney stacks and factory buildings with soot-blackened walls. There will be tram lines serrating the roads, and Victorian and Gothic facades, art-deco film theatres, incomplete constructions with the shacks of labourers nesting in erupted earth. There will be trees too, peepul and heddi and amha and naral and palas, but they will be dwarfed by Bombay's urbanity, made immaterial.

He gets up and grabs his suitcase. He goes into the driver's cabin and shouts something into the driver's ears. The bus slows down and stops. He disembarks.

Ashiq Painter says something. Saleem Lahori simply waves in response.

He steps off the bus and watches it roar into Bombay. The sign facing him diminishes, its silver legend diminishes. 'Rajkunwar Studio: Making dreams come alive.'

It has worried him for a long time, the different ways in which the people he had known had made sense of life: there was no rule to it, but there was always an effort involved, a certain commitment to the expanse of life. He finally has an idea of how he can make sense of life.

There is dust around him for a few seconds. He coughs, but feels younger than his years. He knows that he has to go back. He picks up his suitcase and starts walking towards the small taxi stand he had noticed a minute or so previously. He is headed for Rajkunwar Studio.

He cannot forget the way Kabir and Rosy had clung

to him; cannot forget the mute look, guarded and expectant, on Bhuvaneshwari's face. It was, in some ways, the look on Satish Mama's face on that day in the mill. Above all, he cannot forget what he has finally come to recognize as love, though it is foreign to the languages of film and literature: the light in his parents' eyes whenever they were together. He knows that this is his last chance to claim something like that illuminescence.

How they had let go of hands, each betrayal a tiny link in a chain of tragedies. All of them. And it was in letting go of the other that they lost their own selves. This is what he has finally come to realize. And standing there, a tall and tattered man dressed in the remnants of past dreams, he knows that there can be no redemption of the past, that there is no redemption whatsoever unless it involves a firm clasping of the hand extended to you in the present.

But I was still dissatisfied with Batin's account. I felt he could – should – have told me more. I said to him, there is so much you have not told me. Surely you have more to tell?

Batin turned and looked at me in the bleak light coming in from the window. 'You know, young man,' he said, 'what Saleem Lahori would have said to that? He would have quoted you a line from his father's incomplete translation of al-Biruni's book on shadows. (He loved quoting from obscure books, and that was his favourite, perhaps because no one else had heard of it. A scientific book on shadows by a medieval writer from those regions?) So in answer to your, if I may say so, young man, rather impertinent question, Lahori would have quoted a line from al-Biruni: "There is nothing so troublesome as an attempt to exhaust everything in the world."'

Then he added, softly, almost as if speaking to himself, 'But I am not Saleem. I am a tired old man...' He paused and looked at me, his eyes disconcerting in their focus, and spoke with greater force. 'Yet, young man, if you have listened to my account, surely you will be able to fill in the blanks. If you have listened.'

Those were the last words I heard from the lips of Rizwan Hussain 'Batin'.

Bhuvaneshwari sees Saleem Lahori first from her bed-room window, her gaze drawn to the last rays of the sun glinting off the taxi. She sees him getting out. A lonely figure, tall and stiffly upright, wearing his trademark long coat, getting out of a taxi near the gate of the studio, next to the fallen signpost. She knows who it is. She is surprised, because he has returned, and relieved, because his return indicates normality of sorts.

She sees him drag his suitcase to the building. She sees Raheeman Cha and Hari and Rajkunwar rush out to greet him. She can tell they are glad to see him, and that they, too, are relieved by the normality his return suggests: the shadows lurking around the studio each night are an anomaly; the cut electricity lines and the dead phone are accidents. Soon the requested police party will roll up in a van, the area will be cleared of the troublemakers, the sarpanch warned or arrested, the connections restored. In the morning the studio bus will reappear (for the driver had refused to drive back at night, perhaps less from fear and more to spend a night with his family in Bombay); and with the bus will come the other studio guard, Gernail Singh, and the becalming knowledge that the cans of *Aakhri Raat*, filmed with both hope and acrimony, have reached the distributor.

She hears Kabir shout in joy and the pitter-patter of the two children's feet as they scramble down the stairs. She rushes to catch Rosy, who has just started running at a risky tilt and tends to negotiate stairs with unnecessary bravado.

There is a moment between day and night that can be seen only in the villages and fields of India. The villagers have a word for it: godhuli. It is not simply 'dusk'. It is the moment when cattle return to the villages, shrouding them in a thin film of dust. It is the moment of cowdust. It is a narrower strip of time between dusk and night, so narrow that it disappears in the cities, is diminished to nothing by the lights and traffic, the buildings and people. It is the time when the mist in the trees is cattledust; the fog shrouding the small headlights of a jeep jolting over the narrow rural track is cowdust.

Because the grey Ford GPW jeep came from the direction of Dallam village, the youth with the binoculars and his companions, who had gathered for their nightly vigil, thought for a few seconds of panic that the police had finally decided to intervene. Only the ghostly headlights were visible to begin with: even the model of the jeep, the spare wheel and jerrycan on the back panel, the inverted-U cross member supporting the radiator, would become clear only once it stopped.

Some of the men rose from around the charcoal boarsi where they were warming their hands, wrapped their chaddars around their shoulders and melted away into the growing dark, in the direction of the slate-roofed village of Dallam on one side or into the shadows of the hills behind the studio. The man with the binoculars stood his ground – he had the education and experience to realize they had not broken any laws by congregating there – and so did four or five of the more dedicated followers. But they looked nervous. The studio still exuded an air of authority, and the police, they knew, sided with authority. Sardar, one of them said to the man with the binoculars, sardar, what do we do now?

The youth with the binoculars did not have an answer. The jeep drew nearer and just when it appeared as if it would run them down, the vehicle screeched and skidded to a stop, throwing up a cloud of dust and disgorging its load of nine or ten men, all carrying some weapon. A voice the man with the binoculars recognized as that of one of the sevaks from his group in Poona cut through the shroud of dust: It looks like we will have to help you after all, you lazy tapori.

After the newcomers are seated around the boarsi, relegating the five villagers who have remained to the colder fringes, the man with the binoculars is reassured by the fact that all but one of the faces are known to him. They had been part of the drill groups that his organization ran in Poona. The one new face: a man in his early twenties with a pencil moustache, a stubble covering his jaw.

He is the only one of the group who speaks a Bombay dialect. They call him Pramukh.

It is this man who sets out the plan. He does not ask for suggestions. It is obvious that he, not the Sardar with the binoculars, is in charge now. To begin with, he interrogates the Sardar. His interrogation is thorough, not only taking in what the young man with the binoculars has done over the past few nights but also the layout of the studio building and the stories surrounding it or emanating from it – the departed bus, the few people (perhaps six, perhaps ten) left in the building, the music played once in a while from within that, says the young man, probably indicates a film being shot, the guard with the gun, the mythical mosque in which Hindu statues have been interred, the haunted stables.

Having obtained the information he needs, the pramukh ignores the young man with the binoculars. The five villagers on the outskirts notice this, and two of them disappear from the scene. When the men pile into the jeep once more, having warmed themselves by the boarsi for a couple of hours, only three villagers join them. They hang on to the rods and sides of the jeep as the vehicle traces its route back past the village of Dallam and on to the Bombay–Poona road. From there it turns towards Rajkunwar Studio and, horn blaring, descends the dust track leading to the fallen signboard that marks the entrance to the studio compound.

Bhuvaneshwari is putting Kabir and Rosy to bed when she hears the jeep's horn. Its headlights describe a sweeping arc, flashing across the windows of the room, as it negotiates the curve leading to the studio's driveway. Shadows of palm bushes are thrown on the screen of the white-washed building.

She is not surprised. She has expected the letter that Rajkunwar had sent with Joshilla to result in a police party. (She is only surprised that it has taken the party so long to arrive.) Now it has arrived at last, things can go back to normal, at least for Rajkunwar and Hari and this house of their dreams. She does not know about herself, except that she wants to be with Kabir and Rosy, and with Saleem Lahori. It has taken her almost a lifetime to realize that her sacrifice in Anjangarh was unnecessary: houses do not make a home.

She might have gotten up to look out of the window at the approaching jeep, but Rosy is holding her thumb in a tight little grip. This is how she has fallen asleep every night since the day Saleem brought the two children to the studio.

Raheeman Cha hears the jeep well before Bhuvaneshwari sees its headlights throw shadows on the walls of her room. Raheeman Cha is old and walks with an effort, sometimes leaning on his shotgun for support. But there is nothing wrong with his ears. He can hear the traffic on the Bombay–Poona road. He can hear a vehicle turning into the gravel of the path laid out to the fallen signboard at the gate of the studio.

Raheeman Cha is the guard. He gropes for his gun – he had been in bed – and goes to the front door. Ramji and Kishen are already there. There is hope and apprehension on their faces. Raheeman Cha unbolts the door and steps out. The jeep has just come to a stop.

The headlights illuminating the veranda prevent Raheeman Cha from seeing into the jeep: he assumes the men are policemen carrying lathis.

It is good you are here, says Raheeman Cha, walking towards them.

Even when the Pramukh's shrill shout reaches him – Saala, Mussulman hai! – Raheeman Cha does not understand. By the time he does, three or four men have already surrounded him, wielding weapons, lathis, spears, swords. He is on the stairs going down to the driveway. Two of them dart behind him. So intent are the young men on Raheeman Cha that they do not notice the open door behind him, with Ramji and Kishen standing at the doorway.

Raheeman Cha knows he is surrounded. Slowly he raises his gun and points it generally in the direction of the men. You have no right to be here, he says. Go away, he says, as if addressing a bunch of village boys stealing from some guava or mango tree in the compound. Go away.

As the men move towards him, taunting and raising their sharp weapons, Raheeman Cha fires and one of the men curses and stumbles, clutching his thigh. Then, calmly, as if he had all the time in the world, Raheeman Cha bends down to load his gun. For a second the men stop. Then there is a roar of outrage and they run at him, snatching his gun from him, knocking him down the stairs. After that there is only a jumble of limbs, a flash of weapons, screams and curses. So intent are the men on their victim that they do not notice Ramji and Kishen step back into the studio building and pull the heavy studio door shut behind them.

Inside, the studio is awake and, apart from Bhuvaneshwari and her children, huddled behind the now bolted door. Everyone is silent, listening to the sounds outside, perhaps struggling with the desire to help Raheeman Cha versus the prudence that assures them of the futility of such bravado. Eventually, the screams and curses die down. It is too late to do anything. There is the sound of someone being dragged away. The person who is being dragged away is surely not still conscious. And perhaps not alive. For some reason the men drag him into the fields and gardens.

It was from this patch that the police later recovered Raheeman Cha's mutilated body.

The jeep has turned the curve into the portico and its headlights no longer throw shadows onto the shutters and walls of the room in which Bhuvaneshwari lies, waiting for Kabir and Rosy to fall fast asleep. There is only a small lantern burning in one corner of the room; the children are frightened of the dark. A moth has flown into the room and now it circles the lantern; its shadow expands and grows. The moth is a small fluttering leaf, its forewings hooked, yellow brown with silvery markings, just a small dry leaf blowing in the wind; and then it is a dark growing monster on the walls.

There are voices from downstairs, from the veranda. Then there is a shot.

Rosy wakes up, whimpering, clinging to Bhuvaneshwari. Kabir is awake too. His face is pale and bloodless even in the weak yellow light of the lantern. He is asking for Saleem. Where is Ba, he asks. Where is Ba?

This is what the children have called Saleem from the day he brought them to the studio. It is a word that could be a corruption of Abba or Papa, or some other expression even. They do not know why they call Saleem Ba.

But that is what they were calling him when he walked in, carrying both, one on each arm. It had been monsoon, late in the evening. But it was not raining outside. There were clouds, dark and inky, and the wind sagged, heavy with moisture, like wet clothes on a line. To the south, where the rocks of the Deccan rose higher, lightning fizzed and flickered against the highland. The ground was wet with the last downpour, frogs hopping on the veranda, most of the studio hands sitting out, gossiping or playing cards, guzzling tea. It was too late in the day and not the kind of weather in which one could shoot.

Saleem had arrived in a white van belonging to

Aakrosh, a radical theatrical company in Bombay for which some of his friends worked or wrote. Bhuvaneshwari knew that Saleem and his friends were doing volunteer work in riot-hit areas of Bombay and neighbouring towns, distributing clothes and food and performing small skits to promote communal harmony. The van had driven away after dropping off Saleem. And the two children.

Saleem had walked in, his kurtah muddy, the children – though some attempt had been made to wash them – caked with filth. They clung to him and when Bhuvaneshwari tried to take them in order to give them a proper bath, the boy set up a wail and stretched his arms towards Saleem shrieking that word: Ba.

Saleem was the one who had to take them to the bathroom and stand by while the women washed them. Later he had sat there and fed them with his hands. It had taken Bhuvaneshwari about a week before she could put them to bed or feed them without him being present.

Bhuvaneshwari did not even need to ask the story of the children. She could imagine it. (Such stories were not uncommon in those days, when there were accounts of entire trains and buses going to Pakistan or arriving in India filled only with blood, limbs, corpses and three or four scared children.) But later that evening, over cups of tea, and speaking in a low whisper that could not be overheard by the children, who had by then

recovered enough to play with some stage props, Saleem
had told Bhuvaneshwari, Rajkunwar and Hari how he
had found the children.

The children had been recovered from a burnt-out
section of a town. It had been a mixed area – containing
both Hindu and Muslim houses – before the riot. After,
it was a mass of blackened ruins. The minibus had
paused there on its way to another part of the town.
Saleem had gone into the empty husks of the burned
houses to pee. At first, he thought the movement in a
dark corner was that of some animal, a dog or some rats.
Birds, perhaps. Then he had noticed an arm. He had
approached the corner and found two children, dirty,
cowering in the shadows, their eyes large with fear.
They looked emaciated and ill. There was nothing to do
but to pick them up and turn them over to the authorities. That is what Saleem had done – except, instead
of turning them over at a thana, he had brought them to
Bhuvaneshwari at the studio. At the end of the week,
when Saleem had to return to Bombay for work, neither
he nor Bhuvaneshwari mentioned the possibility of the
children going anywhere else.

In a building that was slowly emptying of people and
animals, the children had come to stay, to fill a space in
the lives of Bhuvaneshwari and – surprising everyone –
Saleem.

★

Bhuvaneshwari lets the moth tap against the glass of the lantern flame. She picks up Rosy and Kabir, wraps them in a thick blanket, and carries them down the stairs to where the men stand clustered behind the main door. It is strangely silent, both inside and out.

Saleem's attire is extraordinary. He is wearing loose pantaloons and over them a long kurtah that she recognizes as one of the courtier costumes from a film about Anarkali. He has tied the kurtah down with a cummerbund, a woman's cummerbund of the sort that courtesans wear in films. Bhuvaneshwari can see that each item of his clothing – his night dress – has been taken from the studio's wardrobe. Saleem, always attentive to her presence, catches her eye and says, no clean clothes left. It is an inappropriate domestic remark but it partly dissipates the tension in her mind. He takes Kabir from her. Kabir clings to him, desperately, just as he had the day Saleem first brought them here, but Rosy (and Bhuvaneshwari feels a surge of pride at this) stays with her.

There is a crash outside as something large and heavy – perhaps a flower pot – is thrown at the door. All of them are startled; the children start crying again. Then the shouting resumes, the swearing and taunting: Muslims and Muslim-lovers go to Pakistan.

★

Ramji clears his throat. He speaks with his eyes cast down. If you allow us, he says to Rajkunwar and Bhuvaneshwari, turning slightly in their direction, if you allow us, huzoor, we would like to go.

Go? retorts Rajkunwar. Go where?

Leave, he means, huzoor. Go back to the village, explains Kishen. The two are almost like twins; they complete each other's sentences.

Rajkunwar laughs. Why? he says. Are you afraid of these paid goons of the Seth or the Sarpanch? They are all bark, no bite. And how do you think you will leave, anyway? You don't intend to walk out of the front door, do you? Or the back, for that matter?

The shouting has been organized. Now there are two groups. The group by the front door raises a slogan and that's then taken up by a smaller group at the back. Torches have been lit outside and their glow sometimes rushes past the chinks of windows, creating a fleeting impression in Bhuvaneshwari's mind of a shuttered train compartment rushing past an illuminated city station.

The window in the light room upstairs, huzoor, Ramji replies. It does not have bars and it is very easy to climb from that window onto a branch of the heddi tree. They won't be watching it.

Rajkunwar pauses. He knows that once on the ground it would not be difficult to slip away undetected – the terrain is so uneven and the studio compound full of bushes and trees and buildings and structures of all sorts. You go, then, he says to the two villagers.

Ramji and Kishen turn to leave. Then they pause. If we may be allowed, huzoor . . . They hesitate.

Yes, says Bhuvaneshwari.

Perhaps it is best for all of us to leave . . .

Rajkunwar explodes. What, he says, you want me to run from these monkeys? Leave behind my own studio . . .

He looks at Hari, who shrugs.

We are Hindus. Why should we go? But perhaps Saleembhai ought to consider . . . says Hari.

But Kabir clings to Saleem, refusing to let him go. Bhuvaneshwari looks at Saleem and knows he won't leave the place without her or the children. Ramji and Kishen wrap their chaddars firmly around their shoulders and start walking up the broad marble stairs.

Rajkunwar looks around as if canvassing for support. Joshilla must have delivered my letter by now, he says. Joshilla can be trusted to do it. We simply have to wait a few hours.

Hari backs him. Once again the two partners are united, though Saleem urges them to follow Ramji and Kishen's advice.

Bhuvaneshwari is the only one who has not said anything. She can see that both Hari and Rajkunwar have invested too heavily in the building and what it symbolizes to be able to leave it. They cannot let go of the past – or the past as they imagine it, and both do imagine it differently (and in that, perhaps, they are not unlike the Hindus and Muslims thirsting for each other's blood across India and Pakistan). At this moment, she resolves that she will take Kabir and Rosy away from this place; she will, if possible, take them away from their past of violence and retribution that will surely, otherwise, always shadow them.

Rajkunwar was right: Joshilla, as all his friends knew, was a man to be trusted with responsibilities, errands, secrets.

Joshilla *had* spent the whole evening outside the office of the policeman, a common friend, to whom Rajkunwar had addressed his letter. But every time Joshilla reminded the policemen outside the office, urged upon them the urgency of his errand, one of them would disappear into the cool, dark, curtained corridor that led to the office and come back, sometimes after a long time, with the same message: Sahib is busy. He has asked you to wait.

It was during this wait – for it was midnight before the officer finally saw Joshilla and assured him, with bad grace, that he would despatch a police party to Dallam 'in the morning' – that Joshilla made up his mind never to leave Bombay or India. What happened the next day simply strengthened his resolve. He would not make it easy for people who thought that by shouting or by not listening, people like him could be made to disappear.

There is a hint of smoke around the studio building. Some of the men have collected sets, props and garden furniture and set them alight on the lawn. Then, slowly, methodically, three or four of them go about pulling up the rose bushes, the bela flowers, the harashringar plant and adding them to the flames.

There is a moment of indecision. Even the shouting has ceased. The Pramukh is huddled with two of his best men, talking. The Sardar is roaming with his villagers, breaking into the rooms, some locked, around the main building. He is looking for the mosque he has been told about.

The Pramukh takes out his pistol and fires at the building. It brings most of his men to him; they come running, carrying flaming torches, enthused once again. When the shouting resumes, the slogan has changed. It is now: Come out or die there; come out or die there.

There is also the sound of hammering. Barbed wire is being nailed across each of the ground-floor doors and windows.

How did the fire begin? Was it started by the hood-lums? Did a stone send an overlooked candle or lantern crashing into the curtains? Nothing is certain. Later Ramji and Kishen told the police that they had escaped by putting a ladder out of a window and onto a branch of the heddi tree. From there it was simple to clamber down. No, they said, there was no fire then. It did not start until much later.

What is also uncertain is why the hoodlums ran away so soon, not waiting to see the results of their handiwork. The manner in which they left suggests panic, for villagers from Dallam saw them, silhouetted against the fire, suddenly run to their jeep and roar off. The police did not arrive until next morning, and the villagers were keeping their distance, so there was no obvious reason for such a hurried getaway.

The youth with the binoculars is worried. He had not imagined the fire would give out so much heat, so that even in the adjoining sheds – which have not caught fire yet – he is afraid of his binoculars being damaged.

He has kept away from the main building, not wanting perhaps to witness another death. It is the second time that night – the first was when the Pramukh was hacking away at the body of the bearded guard – that he has felt a twinge of doubt, a pang of regret.

Instead, he is searching for the mosque he has pledged to destroy, venting his dull anger on the outbuildings by demolishing what he can with a pickaxe. The three villagers are with him. Perhaps they too were shaken by the grotesque extremity of the Pramukh's anger, his dismemberment of Raheeman Cha.

The villager next to him says, This is it. This is the mosque. It is true.

They have spoken about it. It is a rumour he has used to incense the villagers, this rumour about Hindu gods being polluted in a mosque.

For some reason this shed is locked. They force the lock open and find themselves in a small, paved place, with a regular display of statues of Hindu gods. Lakshman, Sita and Ram, Shiva, Ganapati. It looks like a warehouse of gods and the thought crosses the youth's mind that perhaps it is just a room used to store statues for sets and shoots. Then the villager next to him points at one of the walls, lit up by the glow of the fire outside. On the wall, next to a cross and a picture of the Sai Baba, is a large framed picture of a square black building. It is surrounded by people wearing white. It is like the black lingam the youth had dreamt of a few days ago. The villager pointing at it says, See, what did we say, Sardar, see, they have a picture of Kaaba here. It is a mosque.

The youth has heard the word 'Kaaba'. He knows it is the most sacred of holy sites for Muslims. He had never thought it would look like that. He feels his head throbbing. Why had he dreamt of the Kaaba? What was the difference between the Kaaba and the Lingam? Is it only a matter of size and a few angles?

Smoke has entered the shed now; its roof is burning. Come away, come away, the villager shouts, running out.

The youth stands there, his head hammering. A million hooves are beating through his mind. Then he turns and runs in blind panic. The villagers are already outside. They are surprised when they see him and try to stop him but he tears past them towards the jeep, shouting, Leave me alone, leave me alone, screaming something about horses, clutching his head, screaming something about the Kaaba and the Lingam, horses, hooves in his head. He looks in the direction of the shed behind which lie the stables.

The villagers are confused at first and then they remember the stories they had told one another around the boarsi. Comprehension dawns on their faces. And with it, terror. They begin to run too, shouting about the ghost of a dwarf on a horse of fire.

So this is what I imagined at first, in line with what the police records suggested. I imagined completing the cinematic clues, the stock phrases Hari so loved: . . . when suddenly to the surprise of, so it turned out that, and for ever after.

When suddenly to the surprise of the youth with the pair of binoculars and facial birthmarks a horse of fire comes out of the burning studio. It is ridden by a dwarf. The youth shouts and throws himself aside. Then the horse is gone. And with it leave the vandalizers, piling into the jeep, shocked not by the prospect of flesh burning, trapped in barbed wire, but by the sight of the spectral, fiery horse and its deformed rider.

So it turned out that the studio burnt with not a single witness,

And for ever after there was silence.

But that was not true. There is never only silence. Newsprint survives, so do memories and films. So do people, sometimes. The silence is not absolute.

Back in his hotel, the scholar wondered about the great discrepancies between what Ashok had told his daughter, the lady doctor, and what Ashok's parents and the Chotte Thakur had told Batin, the writer – and what both, in turn, had told the scholar. Over the next few days, he would trace his way back to Berlin, and just a day before flying back to Berlin, he would hire a taxi to Dallam. And there he would find little other than what has already been revealed to him: a village now encroached upon by urbanity, a building still in ruins, the shadow of impassive rocks behind it. He would find very few memories of the studio and its inhabitants, but many memories – sometimes grossly embroidered – of the fire that had engulfed the studio, feeding greedily on the wooden beams and the panelling, the cardboard scenery and the costumes, the furniture and the film reels, and finally of course on flesh. And he would for a moment wonder at how long the news of death carries and how soon the signs of life disappear. But then he would check himself, or he would be checked by the recollection of his silence at the house of the lady doctor in Phansa, and he would begin to understand that silence. It had been respect for life that made him keep quiet about the discrepancies in her story. For the story she had told the scholar was part of the life she had learned to live: it connected her to the dead. He understood, if vaguely, that life cannot be remembered as memory, for that will make it seem like death; life always survived as life. It was tenacious. It learned to crawl under the barbed wires of hate; it even managed to escape the loving embrace of still photos. How else would it be alive?

And so when the scholar tried to envision the last hours of Rajkunwar Studio from the softened, misty viewpoint of that late hour in a hotel in Phansa, when he imagined the studio in its last moments before the fatal fire, he wanted to see a tableau-vivant titled 'Forgiveness' or 'Acceptance' or 'Understanding' or 'Heroism' or, even, 'Sacrifice'.

But this vision failed the scholar too, for he knew in the pith of his bones that each of those four adults – Rajkunwar, Hari, Bhuvaneshwari and Saleem – so strange and so normal, must have wanted to live, wanted desperately to live, to be alive, but were in the end also, for the first time, perhaps not wholly unprepared to die. He knew that they would shriek for air, claw the flames, they would try their best to survive, for they were still learning to live with the past, each in his own incomplete way. And he wanted to believe that they would survive, and the two children would escape the fire. He suspected that this tableau-vivant was something he had erected in the last few hours of charmed domesticity at the lady doctor's house, and that it was just as close or far from the truth of what actually happened in those unreported last moments of the studio as the police report, the villagers' gossip, Ashok's conjectures, the news reports, the shadows that trailed the man with the binoculars or Hari's completed dramatic structure.

Those last hours of the fire were never reported from the inside. And even what was witnessed from the outside has faded, like the few splinters of glass that the scholar saw in the fields around the studio, filmed with earth, dust, moss, rain, refuse over the years.

One thing is certain, for it was mentioned in all the eyewitness accounts in various news reports. When the fire reached its height, when the glow from the conflagration lit up Dallam, the adjoining villages and the cold rocks, when embers shot up into the dark sky like insects moving through lamplight, when almost all villagers in the vicinity were awake and a few even running to the studio, there was a gigantic explosion, diamonds and opals and pearls erupting into the air and falling in a shower as far away as Dallam. The glass roof had exploded from the heat and the gases of the fire. For years, the neighbouring fields and the thatched roofs of huts in Dallam would glisten with gems of glass on sunny days, and sometimes the soles of bare feet running or working the fields would bleed drops of red.

I had not noticed anger in Batin's voice when he mentioned the studio fire. Sadness and hesitation, some reluctance to speak about it, but not anger. Actually, checking my notes, I realize he mentioned it quite early on in our conversation:

'When I went back to India in the 1970s, my first and last visit after leaving the country, I looked up the police reports. Do you know what they said, young man? That the fire was an accident. It was not premeditated, but was – at worst – vandalism. They also said there was no evidence to indicate anyone had been murdered, and a charge was finally registered against "unknown persons, currently absconding", under the category of "culpable

homicide". They found (and I can recall it almost verbatim) "Bone pieces, including 80 per cent of a skeleton
entangled in barbed wire, recovered from the site. Forensic
evidence suggests that the bone pieces belong to at least
two individuals."

'The only thing they found unusual were the lengths
of barbed wire around what was left of the studio building.
But they hardly commented on the body of Raheeman
Cha, retrieved from the fields, unburnt and intact except
for his penis and hands, which had been hacked off, either
before or after he was stabbed and beaten to death. I know
the police had a more important crime to attend to that
morning, but, young man, that – historic – crime took
place in Delhi and even without that excuse I wonder
whether they would have tried to clear up the Dallam case
anyway. As it was, though, what happened in Delhi that
very morning must have been part of the reason that
everyone – papers, politicians, policemen – forgot about
the Dallam case so soon.'

Perhaps it was this comment, which lingered in my
mind, that ultimately persuaded me to visit Dallam to
prove there was one person at least who'd not forgotten. I
asked the taxi driver not to take the new six-lane highway
between Bombay and Poona, but instead to take the old
road, now used mainly by carts and trucks and cattle.

A newly constructed police thana marked the turning
– still narrow but fully tarred at least – leading to Dallam.

The irony did not escape me: all those stories of the thana inspector (not this but the Khopoli thana, a few kilometres away) ignoring requests from Rajkunwar to post a couple of policemen at the studio. Dallam was different from how I had imagined it. Bombay was simultaneously knocking on its doors and also partly unreal here.

It was the fields where, I knew, I would find the charred remains of the studio. After speaking to a few elderly villagers, some of whom recalled how Ramji and Kishen had been interrogated by the police and almost charged with starting the fire, I left the taxi and its driver in the village and walked along the edge of a field to where the blackened bricks of the studio were still visible. I knew all about what had happened to the place after the fire: how the land had been claimed by Seth Dharam-chand, with a rather dubious mortgage paper. The case had not been contested by the Anjangarh family, who were too far away, too affluent and too busy coping with the tragedy that had befallen them. The Seth had sold off the arable land in chunks, but the building had remained. It would have been costly, even as a ruin, to clear and land prices hadn't, in the past, been high enough to justify the expense. But I was sure it would be sold soon, for the region was now teeming with holiday cottages for the affluent in Bombay, and surely the owners would sell it to a constructor. It was simply a matter of time.

I struck the tall yellow-green grass along the aari with

a switch. The fields on both sides were filled with small yellow flowers, as if sprayed on green leaves and stems, their smell overpowering and familiar. For a while the ruins of the studio were partly obscured by a large kadamba tree – heddi is what it would probably be called in these parts – with its heart-shaped leaves, its associations with Krishna and his flute, its trunk full of hollows in which the rainwater would collect during the monsoon. I recalled servants drinking the rainwater, claiming that rainwater collected in the hollows of the kadamba tree assumed the taste of honey. I looked into the hollows of this tree, but they were dry and empty except for some flower petals lying in them. The tree was not flowering, it only blooms when the skies are overcast and the thunder of the monsoon sends birds scurrying for cover, so I imagined the petals to have been put there by some village urchin.

I stepped around the tree and suddenly the ruins were there again.

The entire upper floor had collapsed, and so had the roof of the ground floor. There was no sign of the outbuildings, the stables, the animal cages, the sets and scenery. They must have burnt with a vengeance, as had the film material lying in the studio; a villager had told me, not without a note of pride, that the conflagration had been visible from villages more than ten kilometres away. Film is inflammable, he had added for my benefit.

All that was left were the walls, sometimes the full height still, but more often crumbling to three feet or less. Creepers had covered some of the walls and a peepul tree had taken root on one side, pushing the bricks apart. Many bricks had also been removed by human hands: they would have gone into some of the new houses that had sprung up since 1948. Nothing was wasted, except that which could not be used because it was broken and disfigured, or too big and difficult to dismantle. And the barbed wire; it lay in tangles in the undergrowth, rusted the colour of blood. (But surely, the wire had value; what had prevented the villagers from removing it?)

The bricks, stones and plaster were black in parts, despite being washed by rain and beaten by the strong sunlight, even the glass pieces embedded in the rubble, singed and blackened. As I approached, there was a series of claps, like shots at a distance. A flock of doves fluttered out from the holes in the walls, their wings flapping. They – and other small birds – were obviously nesting in the ruins.

Nothing remained now but for me to go back to Berlin. I did not even know whether I had a story. I did not know whether I could tell it. It was not just that there were so many gaps in the narrative. The problem was time and space. Everything had happened elsewhere, in a different era. How could I enter those spaces? Did I dare to be

*possessed by the spectres of that time? Even my one
connection to the studio – as a scholar of Bombay films –
was tenuous, for I had grown up in the times of Bollywood. (Bollywood, I recall Batin saying in Copenhagen,
Bollywood, young man? We never called it that. No, it is
your generation that needs a Bollywood. We only knew
Bombay. Yes, Bombay, and Calcutta and . . . and yes, we
saw films from Hombay, Hondon and Herlin. And Hos-
cow and Haris too. Some of us did, anyway. And Batin
had laughed uproariously at his weak joke, spluttering,
whisky spilling on to his pot belly.)*

*I was startled from my recollection by a sound behind
me. I turned and caught sight of a young couple standing under the kadamba tree. They were putting flower
petals into one of the trunk's hollows, the woman holding
the man's hand, timidly. They hadn't seen me; as I
approached they sprang apart: they were, I thought, lovers
who did not want to be seen together. Or they could also
have been a newly married couple, too shy to hold hands
in front of a stranger.*

*The woman appeared frightened, spooked. And I think
she at least would have run, had I not spoken to them.*

What are you doing? I addressed the man.

It is an offering.

To the tree?

*Yes, to the tree and to the prait that inhabits the ruins,
he replied. The woman giggled and whispered something*

to the man. He nodded and added, *young people come to ask for boons here.*

Young married couples? I asked.

Young people, he repeated with a grin. The woman giggled into her sari corner again, having apparently forgotten her initial fright.

I sat down. There is nothing new about praying to trees and spirits inhabiting them, not in the villages anyway. The sun had almost sunk. It was the hour of godhuli, when the cattle are driven back to the village, when dust hangs in the air like a thin gauze curtain dividing day from night.

The woman whispered to the man. He turned to me: *She is saying that perhaps you should return now. It will be dark soon.*

His statement sounded like a tentative suggestion, but I had the feeling he knew something I didn't.

Why, I asked, *is it dangerous here?*

No, he replied, *no . . .*

Then the woman broke in: *But she is said to come out after godhuli.*

Who?

The prait we have asked for a boon, the man explained. *It's believed that the spirits of two lovers inhabit these ruins and the tree. It's said they come out after the hour of godhuli, the man from the direction of* the highway and the woman from the depths of the tree, and enter the ruins for the night.

People have heard them singing from the ruins, singing love songs. That is why young people come here with offerings. They listen to lovers, said the young man.

And are the praits dangerous as well as musical? I asked, not without a slight curling of my lips, a faint indication of my urban superiority and disbelief.

The man shook his head, either in response or in disgust, and started to walk away. But the woman spoke to me in a slightly irritated tone, But, Babu, they are friends, don't you see? You have to let them lie in peace.

She was too shy to say lovers, but that's what she meant by friends. And her last sentence disturbed me. I had heard it before, perhaps more than once and in different contexts. I could not recall when, but the words were there in my notes somewhere. Suddenly, in the diminishing light, the shadows that accumulated in and around the ruins seemed much more than the sum of its parts.

I looked up and the heart-shaped leaves of the kadamba were shivering in the dusk, making a sound that was eerily like the sound of a flute. The ruin had opened up in the dusk, become bigger, more shadowy, more different from other buildings. Bats were flitting in the darkening sky. The relative lack of sounds had sunk *further into a secret indescribable mood. For a moment it seemed that the sky and the earth, the tree and the birds and the charred bricks and stones had all come together to withhold a secret, or to whisper just beyond the range of my hearing.*

A large leaf fluttered down from the topmost branches of the kadamba tree and was received by the crowded earth without the least trace of rancour. The flock of doves clapped a retreat to the broken walls of the ruin and were swallowed up by its holes and shadows to such an extent that I could not discern the slightest feather, the faintest motion. Tiny birds flitted dark against a darkening sky, which was now unimaginable without the quicksilver motion of their silent, sickle-like shapes. I knew I was not needed here. If there were stories to be recounted here, they were beyond the range of my human tongue. I followed the couple back to the village.

On the highway, careening round the hairpin bends of a mountain road, the rocky Deccan with its dark stones and rich brown earth opening up before it, the dawn touching the high grounds, there is a grey jeep full of exultant young men. All but one of them are shouting or singing. They have recovered from the shock (that only some of them had felt) of the old guard's murder and from the panic in which they fled the fire. But there is something forced about their jollity. The only one of them who is quiet has a pair of binoculars slung around his neck. The spare mountain trees pass by his eyes with the haziness of a dream: He is going home; He is with friends, with other sevaks like him; They have achieved their goal. It is a bleak landscape. Only crows have flown over them for miles. And a few small brown monkeys jabbered angrily at their passage from boulders by the road. If they were not so enthused over their success, so charged with adrenalin, they would have considered it an augury.

The young man's reverie is shattered when one of them who has been fiddling with the large black knob of the 'transistor radio' manages to catch a station. The reception is poor, full of static, often lost in the roar of the jeep and the wind rushing past their ears. Listen, listen to the news, says the young man with the radio, turning up the volume, listen to the effects of what we have done. (Some of them cheer at this.)

A huge tragedy, comes the voice from the radio. It is lost in static. It merges with the sound of the straining engine. Then the voice is back. There are words about loss, national loss, darkness, the sun going out, and similar metaphors – all interrupted by waves of static – which the young men take as describing what they have achieved. They are about to cheer again when suddenly, like clouds lifting from the sun, the static clears and they hear clearly the sentences: The father of the nation is no more. At 5.05, while going to his morning prayer meeting at Birla House in Delhi, Mahatma Gandhi was shot to death . . .

The static surges back. For some reason not one of the young men cheers, though only moments ago they had been joking about the best ways to kill the Mahatma. The young man with the binoculars hears his own voice haranguing the villagers of Dallam: the Sant of Sabarmati, the Shant of Shabarmati, the Shaant . . . In his mind, the young man cannot help repeating that word with a long 'aa' – the sound of shaant echoing its meaning, 'peace', 'quiet' – and now the word that runs like static through his mind, in which there is a bleakness and a great rushing wind corresponding to the scenery around him, is this: Shaant, Shaant, the Shaant of Shaabarmati . . .

In an immaculately clean flat in Bombay, a man dressed in starched white dhoti and banyan, with carefully drawn caste marks on his forehead and a visible caste thread which he has just grasped, jerks up from the lotus position in which he performs his puja. Guruji. He performs the puja for half an hour every morning, with the radio on behind him. He hears the words on the news and he stands up, the puja tray crashing to the ground, its offerings of flowers, coloured powder, rice, coconut and fruit spilling around him.

Guruji's face is inscrutable as ever. Only his lips move. Too late, he says, too late. He can imagine Seth Dharamchand laughing. He has never liked the Seth. It is sad he has to work with people like the Seth. Too late, he mutters again, going down on his knees to pick up the scattered offerings.

What a waste, he adds.

I dream of my night in Batin's flat. The dream comes to me as I try to tie up the loose ends of Batin's narrative, and the narratives I found, as I knot them together. The dream is based on those words of his, when he had momentarily lost control and grabbed my hand: 'No, young man, I did not choose to leave, I never chose to leave ... Pay more attention; look in the shadows; listen to the spaces in my story ...'

This scene is changed subtly in sleep, so that when I wake up I am not sure I recall what he said exactly as he said it. Is what he says in my dream one of the many sentences I didn't jot down in my Moleskine notebook, because I did not, at the time, consider it significant enough?

But I hear him saying it in my sleep, I hear his voice in my head, saying words he might or might not have spoken that evening in Copenhagen: 'Listen to the spaces in my story, young man. Why do you suppose that they could not have escaped a building like that, a building

*with so many doors and windows, with a tree next to it
that one could reach from the upper floor and climb down?
After all, Ramji and Kishen escaped, didn't they? They
climbed down the kadamba tree and ran to the village
unseen. Why do you suppose Bhuvaneshwari and Saleem,
Kabir and Rosy could not have escaped and taken on other
identities? Those were disturbed times, times when people
disappeared in more ways than one. How can you be
certain they did not escape to live on somewhere else? And
if they did, would that have been wrong of them, having
discovered that the past cannot be reclaimed but it can be
redeemed – if only in the present?'*

*So vivid is this dream that, when I awake, I am
almost certain that it had really happened that night in
Copenhagen, that it happened and was not recorded by
me, was forgotten for years for some subtle reason. It is
only now, as I wrap up the loose ends of his stories, that I
have dreamt it up once again. For what are dreams but
the shadows of our waking hours falling on the wall of
sleep?*

*I also recall something that I cannot verify, for I have
not been able to trace Mrs Batin or her adopted children, I
recall – or did I dream this too? – that as I left their flat
and Mrs Batin saw me to the door, she walked with a
slight, almost imperceptible limp.*

★

There was smoke in the air. Clouds had accumulated in the steep sky, banked like wool or textiles in the store-room of mills. Ash fell sometimes in gusts like powdery snow.

Most villagers were at the studio, watching the policemen in action, poking into the smouldering ruins, looting when and what they could, although the needy, the really poor, had torn themselves away from the last spectacle created at Rajkunwar Studio, and returned to their domestic chores, their petty businesses, their des-iccated plots of land around Dallam.

The sun was sweeping shadows of clouds – or bundles of ash caught in the wind – across the uneven landscape, dragging patches of darkness from west to east, for the wind had changed now and was blowing from the west. Birds, disturbed by the smell and the ashes, were out in considerable numbers, doves, spar-rows, mynahs, pigeons, crows screaming their messages from one side of the village to another.

The two bullocks turning the heavy wooden beam of a thresher were not disturbed by the events, unlike the birds. No, they were used to fire and ashes, the inevit-able proof of man's presence, and they turned the beam slowly, pausing for a second or two to chew the cud or grab, when the farmer's boy was not watching them, a mouthful of discarded husks. Would they have bridled at the sight of two shadows, each carrying a live bundle, moving past the village fields, from tree to tree, shadow to shadow, not really hiding but not exposing themselves to sight either? Would they have stopped in their slow circular movements around a wooden post, husk and dust from their hooves suspended in the air, a flock of sparrows fluttering around their legs?

The tree casts its shadows on the wall of the house with no barbed wires. Perhaps the wires will return, some small gesture, the inhumanity of a lie or a truth, some real or imagined fear threading the eyes of those bare, rusted rods at the top of the wall with barbed wire. But at the moment, and for many years, the house has not been defined by barbed wire.

They are all asleep there, so soundly that the solitary dripping tap can be heard even out on the veranda where the scholar had sat listening to the lady doctor. They are all asleep: the lady doctor, her husband, the child, the mother, and the servants. Even the unseen parrot in a cage somewhere in the house. They are used to the night and its shadows. For them there is nothing shabby about the place they inhabit, neither in the light of day nor the shadows of night.

That, surely, feels the scholar, is an achievement, for he has just recently, while being driven back to the hotel, felt the dread which can only be felt, not described, the dread of shabbiness in a soul that had glimpsed – whether it be through intuition, travel or texts – the extent and hard glory of the world. Now, in his hotel room, he feels more assured, he dreads this shabbiness less, for he has come to perceive its absence in the lives of the lady doctor and her family. He knows that it is a momentary reprieve for him. He cannot stay here, or in places like this. The dread will return to drive him away to places where there are other kinds of loss and danger to distract him from his dread of shabbiness.

The scholar is unable to sleep. He paces around his bare hotel room, with its drawn curtains of rough dusty cloth that can hardly keep out the light of the street lamps. He expects a power cut, but the lights keep burning. The Tortoise mosquito coil in a corner fills the room with a pungent fragrance, dribbling concentric circles of ash on the floor, driving mosquitoes away. He finally switches on the reading lamp on the bare table, somewhat surprised to find it functioning, and takes out a new Moleskine diary from his bag. That is his sole indulgence, he likes to imagine: he carries along at least a couple of Moleskine diaries. He opens the notebook to its first page, crisp, creamy and thick.

"We say that being illuminated is a quality possessed by a non-transparent body when it is confronted by a luminary, together with a transparent medium between them. So that transparent thing will permit the passage of all of the light through it, but it will be the portrayer of the colours and shapes facing it."

(Al-Biruni, 973–1048)